UNKNOWN WARRIOR

H. ATKIN

© Copyright 2003 Hilary Atkin

The right of Hilary Atkin to be identified as the author of this work has been asserted in accordance with the Copyright, Designs and Patents Act 1988.

All rights reserved. No reproduction, copy or transmission of this publication may be made without written permission. No paragraph of this publication may be reproduced, copied or transmitted save with the written permission or in accordance with the provisions of the Copyright Act 1956 (as amended). Any person who does any unauthorised act in relation to this publication may be liable to criminal prosecution and civil claims for damage.

Cromwell Publishers 405 Kings Road London SW10 0BB
An imprint of First century Ltd.

Website: www.CromwellPublishers.co.uk

E mail: Info@CromwellPublishers.co.uk

ISBN 1-903930-21-9

From St. Nicholas Church, Hockerton: Burial Record;

1643 May 20th, John the souldger

THE BEGINNING

She was not there. For the woman who sat at her dining room table was not called Elisabeth, neither was she a descendent. Tracings of estate maps, the Tithe Commutation map and copies of Victorian Ordinance Survey maps, sheets of closely written note paper and photocopies littered the surface. She gazed out of the small window: the light was fading. She always sat in this low ceilinged room with its great black beam which cut across from fire place to the opposite wall in preference to any other room. Here she felt comfortable. Here was a feeling of calm and acceptance of life that was almost tangible. The windows now were double glazed plastic with small panes to simulate the original. But which original she wondered as this part of the cottage was marked on the earliest estate map of Hockerton and it had obviously been her before that was drawn. She had been trying to piece together the history of the village with snippets from the library, the archives, census returns and newspaper reports.

A knock at the low door startled her out of her reverie. It was Penny, one of the churchwardens, holding a bulging carrier bag.

"The parish records," she announced, coming in and plonking the bag on the table. "Let me know when you've finished with them."

After a few pleasantries and an exchange of village news Penny left. Taking out the mass of papers the woman found letters, bills and the printed sheets of the registers of births, marriages and deaths going back to the sixteenth century. She spent an interesting hour combing through these before pausing for coffee. As she sipped from her steaming mug she flipped through the registers for the Civil War period. Little information had been found and all she knew was that Parliamentary troops had been stationed in the village and had demanded supplies from the neighbouring village of Upton. This had been recorded by the Upton churchwarden. There was nothing surprising in either the births or the marriages but in the burials there was a surprising entry. May 20th John the souldger. No surname, no information on which side he had fought. If he had been one of Parliament's men in the village there would have been more..... a mystery then, an historical conundrum, who was John the souldger?

CHAPTER ONE

Afterwards Cicely Plowright always wished she had never penned that letter to her brother, David. But she did. That year of 1914 had so far been an uneventful one for her and Cicely, often restless, had badgered her quiet, stay-at-home husband George to go up to London in the gloriously fire-red summer days to see a show or two, call in on a couple of old friends...that was how she and Elizabeth met up again. They had been at boarding school together light years before. Cicely, robust, sporty and popular never really a friend of the quiet, studious Elizabeth, but they could take tea together and exchange news about friends they had both known thought Cicely after their chance meeting in the park. However, Elizabeth seemed unwilling to go along with this suggestion and said that they could walk through the park together as it was on her way home. So that was what they did. Cicely thought that under her smart costume Elizabeth's body seemed bony and frail and her wide brimmed, fashionable hat did not quite hide the shadows under her wide grey eyes nor the thinness and pallor of her cheeks.

As they ambled along slowly in the warm sunshine, Cicely asked tentatively if Elizabeth was quite well? No, not really quite well, came the curt reply. In fact she had been quite ill and was still recovering. Cicely advised her to get out of London and breathe in some good country air, wondering why Elizabeth did not go home to her parents in the Cotswolds. She didn't have to ask, the unvoiced question was answered for her by Elizabeth remarking flatly that her people had cut her off and did Cicely know a cottage that she could rent.

Cicely did. But George refused. The cottage in question was earmarked for a new estate worker and her friend would have to look elsewhere. Cicely, determined to find a cottage for her wrote to her brother, David, a farmer in Nottinghamshire. Could he help? Did he have a cottage to rent out?

David Enleigh's farmhouse and scattering of barns were of pinkish brick with steep pantile roofs dating back to the 1600s. They stood at the end of a long track that led down from the main Newark road in the small village of Hockerton. Below the house was a deeply entrenched stream called in these parts a dumble, shaded on either side by bushes and small trees, which flowed eastwards to join another similar stream at the far side of the village below a gently rising hill called Wheatgrass Hill. To the north of the few houses which made up the settlement there was another ridge of rising ground and also a rise to the south so that only westwards did the road wind along the level until it finally dropped down the steep hill to the neighbouring village of Kirklington.

David's wife, Anne, picked up the post from the tiled hall floor and took it into the kitchen. Recognising her sister-in-law's handwriting she opened Cicely's letter first. The summer day was warm and still, birds flew in and out of a tree silhouetted green against a painted azure sky. Swallows probably Anne thought feeding on the hosts of flying insects in the hazy air. Sunshine poured through the window, warming the tiled floor, dust motes danced between her and the huge oak dresser that lined the opposite wall. The whole dearly familiar room with its workman like table and chairs, stone sink, great, black range and multi-hued rag rugs was bathed in its light. Anne sighed with contentment and turned to read the letter in her hand. There was news of Cicely's theatre visits and gallery viewings in London; snippets of family events and enquiries after her own health. She leaned back in the chair and surveyed her gently swelling body. She felt marvellous and contented. She wondered whom the baby would look like? Like her, tall, statuesque and blond or like David, dark-haired, brown-skinned and wiry, or maybe neither. She had reached Cicely's description of her meeting with her school friend Elizabeth. Poor soul, thought Anne, who had a kind and loving nature. Turned off by her family, unmarried and in poor health. Not a person to be envied even if Elizabeth's father did have a title and she herself was an honourable. Anne daydreamed how she would take this poor creature under her wing. To begin with she realised on a more down to earth note there was an empty cottage. The one at the end of the farm lane. Cicely's friend Elizabeth could rent that. She planned happily how she would get a couple of farm labourers' wives to give it a clean up as she sliced ham, buttered bread and got out a jar of pickles. She was just pouring out some of her own home made lemonade when her husband's voice could be heard at the door. Good, she thought, putting the big, earthenware jug on the table, now I can get everything organised.

Against his better judgement, because he knew nothing of this woman, and suspected that this could be another one of his sister's sudden whims, he listened to his wife's plan. Cicely had been prone to these good ideas since she had been a small girl and although they were initiated by her the consequences were usually shouldered by other kind-hearted and unsuspecting persons. This time it will be Anne and me David surmised accurately. He didn't want to disappoint Anne as she had obviously been planning this since the letter had arrived and the cottage had been empty for nearly a year now since Sam, the old cow man, had died last November and it would be better cleaned, aired and lived in, so he agreed.

After their meal David departed and Anne sat down at her small desk in the sitting room to compose a reply to Cicely and a note to Elizabeth assuring her of a warm welcome. The letter addressed and stamped, Anne put her every day hat on top of her blond curls, skewered it firmly with a hat pin and letter in hand went to catch the four o'clock collection.

Hockerton was a small village of only sixty-six souls on this late summer day in 1914. It lay about seven miles west of the small market town of Newark on what had once been a main toll road with gates still manned by handy villagers until about twenty-five years ago. At the top of the farm drive were a pair of cottages on the opposite side of the road and it was the right-hand side one of these which was empty. Anne crossed the road and went through the front gate. She peered through the small, many-paned window. The sitting room was empty, dusty but certainly not damp. She moved past the low front door and looked through an even smaller window into the living room. Again no major problems. Satisfied that she could quickly clean the cottage up Anne made her way along the side of the road the afternoon sun casting her long shadow before her. There were no more dwellings on her left, just fields guarded by a high hedge until she passed the empty barns and ivy-clad ruins of Sparrowthorn farm. On the right across the road were two more minute dwellings and then a larger one which had once been a farmhouse.

She reached the corner. The travelling smith was shoeing a large, black horse at the inn, which had originally been a smithy in front in the days when the village had had twice as many inhabitants as it had now. From across the road which rose gently northwards from here she could see a line of washing hanging stiffly in the still air in the high garden of the first cottage on the bank opposite. She could hear faintly the chanting of children's voices; far too few these days, coming from the school room which was the end of the village on this side.

She went to a small post box let into the wall and dropped her letter in. While she was here she would go across the road and check the state of the flowers in the church; it was her week to provide them. There was another cottage on the right side of the church lane and the vicarage on the left. The lane fell gently to two more cottages at the bottom near the dumble and the church stood on a knoll to the left. Glad that the large, dragging oak gate was open Anne climbed the stone steps to the churchyard.

Elizabeth sat numbly in the leather armchair in the London flat wondering if Cicely had meant her promise or whether she had already forgotten their encounter. Even though dusk was falling Elizabeth made no move to light any lamps. It was still too early to draw the curtains, someone might notice and think it odd that an empty flat's curtains moved. She had borrowed the flat from a friend of her brother's. She didn't want anyone to know she was here; not her friends, who had a convalescent home lined up for her, not her acquaintances who lived in London and certainly not the police. She had to get out of London. Quickly and anonymously.

In the end it had been quite easy Elizabeth reflected, leaning back against the headrest and closing her eyes. The clickety-clack and rolling motion of the train lulled her tired body and racing mind. Getting Cicely to arrange the collection of her furniture from her own flat using a suburban firm of hauliers had been surprisingly successful.

Cicely had fallen for the romantic notion that her friend was fleeing from a too-ardent and unwanted suitor. She had arranged for the furniture to be collected and stored under a fictitious name and in a week another firm would deliver it to Hockerton, no one except Cicely knowing who the real owner was. Cicely thought it was huge fun and Elizabeth was sure that she would keep the secret. She would make sure of that once she had taken possession of the cottage by informing Cicely that it was the police not a suitor she was evading. Well-brought-up Cicely would never tell then in case her snooty friends found out and ostracised her.

Elizabeth thought that she had not fully realised in the heady days when she had first joined the women's suffrage movement that she personally would find such intransigent opposition from her family and friends. She had known that the number of people who wanted women to have the vote was a tiny minority and that the rest of the adult population were opposed to it in varying degrees. Politicians of all parties felt that if women could vote it would have a detrimental affect on their party's power in the county. Well-known women even opposed women's suffrage believing that women would be corrupted by politics to the extent that they would be unchivalrously treated by men, would not marry and that women had smaller brains, were more emotional and were incapable of sound reasoning. Elizabeth thought that while she was perhaps at times more emotional she was certainly not less intelligent. Her father had allowed her to attend school but had refused to let her go on to university yet he had had no such qualms about allowing her brother John to go. Although she loved her younger brother dearly and she knew her feelings were returned Elizabeth knew that she was the cleverer by far and in this John agreed with her and had even campaigned with her against her father but to no avail.

Elizabeth was determined then to continue her education herself as well as she was able. She read widely, she cultivated the friendships of like-minded women within her circle so that it was inevitable that she would pay her shilling and sign a declaration of loyal adherence to the movement's policy to join the W. S. P. U. when it moved its headquarters to Clement's Inn in the Strand. Her family had an apartment in town and it was easy for the now grown-up and past-marrying-aged Elizabeth to use it to meet friends. It was from this time that she learned to keep her own counsel and to engage in white lies to cover up her real inclinations and aspirations. Soon she was taking part in deputations to Parliament and rallies and processions at the Royal Albert Hall and in Hyde Park.

In 1908 Elizabeth, like other suffragettes, began to arrange her wardrobe so that she was wearing the movement's colours of purple, white and green. After she had been arrested at a peaceful demonstration and roughly handled by the police Elizabeth became more militant and joined the campaign of window-smashing. In prison she wondered if she would be able to withstand the harsh regime meted out to the suffragettes, but she did and she suffered and endured. She had never thought that when she was imprisoned that her father would bar his door to her and forbid her mother and brother to have any contact with her. She should have seen it coming for she had always known that he thought that women should remain at home subservient to the dominant male. Ill from the force-feeding and refused even the use of the family apartment in London Elizabeth wondered in desperation where to turn. Then John, her dear brother, John had found her a flat of a friend who had gone abroad. Elizabeth wondered how she would have managed without him. He had hidden her, given her money but most of all he had shown her that he still cared in a largely uncaring and hostile world. And now she would be safely hidden in the countryside like a little mouse and she would not emerge from her hole until there was no danger of being rearrested. Elizabeth knew that both mentally and physically she could endure no more; the women's suffrage movement would have to fight its battles without her.

Opening her eyes Elizabeth saw that the light was fading over the flat, monotonous landscape rushing past the train window. A dull, sepia land dotted with here and there with a cluster of houses, pierced by a church spire. The train sped north, Elizabeth slept.

Elizabeth stood on the dimly-lit platform blinking owlishly around, her bags piled at her feet. Other passengers who had alighted from the train were now scurrying away into the gloom. The train had pulled out yet no one emerged from the door of the waiting room and there was no sign of anyone coming through from the road. Cicely's brother, David, who she presumed would come fairly soon was a person only dimly remembered from school days as a small, tousle-haired boy in short trousers with grubby knees. After a few minutes Elizabeth realised that apart from the porter desultorily moving some parcels she was alone. She would go to the station master's office and see if any message had been left for her. As she made her way across the platform she read the news hoarding propped up against the now shuttered paper stall. War news, huh thought Elizabeth, it's a pity what they say isn't the truth. A few weeks ago, just after the troops had fought their first engagement Elizabeth had read with pride of the army's great victory at the little town of Mons and how they were now regrouping, until she looked at an atlas and discovered that regrouping actually meant that they were now many miles further west and that in fact it was the Germans who were advancing. Since then she had read the reports and followed the track of the army on a large scale map of France and Belgium that she had purchased for just this purpose and formed her own conclusions as to whether each report of fighting constituted a victory or not. She wanted to know what was happening over there for soon, much too soon, her dear, younger brother would be finished the training he had to do here and would be en route for France. Just as she reached the door of the station master's office a tall figure in a long overcoat and muffler, hat pulled down obscuring his face bounded on to the platform, glanced around wildly and then heaved a sigh of relief when he saw her standing there.

"Miss Bateman, Miss Elizabeth Bateman? David Enleigh." He stuck out a large workmanlike hand, grasped her thin gloved one and pumped it up and down. "Sorry to be so late, I've got the cart outside."

Picking up a bag in each hand and somehow thrusting one under his arm he strode away with a long loping stride back the way he had come with Elizabeth trying to keep up with him. Outside stood a small, rather spindly governess cart and a pony. Surely, thought Elizabeth he's not expecting to get the bags and us two into that and hoped that the journey was not a long one. But he was and he did. When Elizabeth was settled with a rug over her knees against the now damp and chilly night air David clicked his tongue and the pony sped off at a surprising pace.

Elizabeth took in little of the town; pools of light from the gas lamps and uncurtained windows gave only glimpses of brick walls and cobblestones. There were few people about and soon they seemed to be crossing a river and were out into the countryside. The land here was flat and featureless, they crossed another bridge and sped through a small village and then on into the darkness again. How dark it is Elizabeth thought, an inky velvet sky studded with stars, a small crescent moon peeping in and out of the trees which now lined each side of the road, then the shapes seeming to crouch as trees changed to hedges, but no light, no habitation, only the dim ribbon of road winding before them. I shall wake up soon thought Elizabeth and find it is only a dream for the whole journey had that dreamlike quality, the silent man beside her, the rushing cart, the menacing darkness all around.......

David Enleigh was no conversationalist. In fact he had not spoken since they had left Newark station. It was as if she were a parcel, safely collected and stowed aboard that he could now forget about. The trap began to gain pace as if the pony smelled home, a warm stable and a net of hay. They were going downhill and now Elizabeth could see the odd pinprick of light at ground level.

"Hockerton." remarked David tersely.

It didn't seem very big. Elizabeth glimpsed an odd building or two before they turned off the road and went down a farm track. The cart bounced over the hard rutted ground. I shall be black and blue in the morning thought Elizabeth ruefully. They pulled up in front of what was obviously the farmhouse. The door stood open, lamplight spilled out on to the flagstone yard in front of the door. Elizabeth, with David's gallant but still silent arm to help her got down stiffly, cold despite the rug, and stood tiredly as David once more collected her bags. She felt so weary, she ached with tiredness, a wave of weakness flowed through her as she followed David into a flagstoned hall with a large copper pot of bright leaves and flowers dominating an old scarred chest of drawers. David dropped her bags unceremoniously on the floor and strode on, calling as he went,

"Anne, Anne, I've got her!"

Makes me sound like a runaway animal. And Elizabeth thought that was really quite a good description of herself. She followed him into a large farmhouse kitchen. Bright red gingham curtains were drawn across the windows, the room was warm and golden with lamplight. A tall, blond, obviously pregnant goddess stood on the rag rug which covered most of the stone floor with her arms outstretched. She enveloped Elizabeth in a warm hug.

"I'm Anne" she smiled, releasing Elizabeth, "Take your coat off, and sit down, supper's ready."

She indicated the large table in the centre of the room, set with cutlery and glasses. She crossed to the big, black range and stooped down to take something from the oven.

"I hope you like game pie?"

Although she asked for the smallest portions Elizabeth found that she could not finish her plateful nor manage any of the blackberry fool which followed. She explained rather guiltily as Anne scraped her leftovers into a bin outside that she had not got her appetite back yet after her recent illness. It would not do to say that her throat was still so painful that she could barely swallow as that might invite awkward questions. Anne secretly thought that she had never seen anyone as thin and grey-faced as Elizabeth Bateman. Her clothes hung on her, her skin had an unhealthy pallor and her eyes were undershadowed with dark rings.

"You must also be very tired after your long journey," she sympathised. "I'll take you to your room; David will bring your bags. I've put a hot water bottle in your bed and I'll bring up some hot water so that you can pop into bed straightaway if you wish."

As she followed Anne up the wide shallow stairs and along a rather narrower corridor Elisabeth thought that the word bed must be the most wonderful word in the English language.

Some time later Elizabeth lay beneath the warm, scented sheets, there was a fire burning in the grate and the flickering light from the bedside candle made a pool of light around her, the fire cast a warm glow across the room. Anne had brought her a cup of milky, sweet cocoa that she had sipped gratefully, savouring every drop. I hope the cottage is as lovely and peaceful she thought snuffing out the candle and snuggling down under the bed clothes. She lay for some time deliciously warm, sleepy and content watching the flickering fire. She heard an owl cry and the soughing of the wind in the trees outside the window. Safe she thought and slept.

Velvet darkness lay over the village; only pinpricks of light escaping from chinks between closed curtains mirrored the jewel stars above. Sparrow Cottage slept, dim and empty. The moon's white beam saw only bare floors and walls, nothing, not even a mouse scurried across the interior.

Next door in Thorn Cottage the soft, yellow light of an oil lamp illuminated the old, creased face and sparse white hair of Samuel Turner as he sat in his chair by the dying fire. At nearly ninety Samuel slept little, a preparation he thought wryly for his final sleep. Samuel's lips moved slightly as he read the story of Jesus and the children. He stopped and looked into the fire. He loved to hear the village children playing on their grassy patch next to the school room at the other end of the village. He enjoyed a daily walk to lean over the wall and watch them at play. He envied them really; not their youth; his childhood had been a good one with loving, if strict parents. There had been the beauty of the countryside around, trees to climb, rivers to paddle and swim in, birds' eggs to collect, blow and arrange in the wooden box that his father had made for him. No, he envied them their chance to learn. To read and write with ease. Samuel had never been to school, the dame school in Southwell had been beyond the means of an agricultural labourer's son. When he had been in his sixties he had had rheumatic fever and had been confined to bed. Being a bachelor he had no friendly wife's chatter to amuse him so he had borrowed a bible from the vicar and slowly and painstakingly taught himself to read. It was now his greatest enjoyment to sit of an evening and read a portion of his own 'good book' and picture the scene as he sat contentedly in his padded, wooden, high-backed chair. He closed his book, carefully marking his place with a piece of paper and placed it on the table beside him. Time for bed. He poked the dying embers and put up the guard, making his way slowly into the adjoining room where he now slept. Soon he thought he would have a neighbour again. In a few minutes he was in bed and Thorn Cottage was also silent.

CHAPTER TWO

Elizabeth awoke with the sun on her face and wondered where she was. Panic rose like bile in her throat until she remembered her journey of yesterday. Anne was standing at the sink peeling potatoes when she reached the kitchen. Realising it was very late for breakfast by country standards she hesitated at the kitchen door until Anne turned and smiled, enquiring if she could manage porridge and toast for breakfast?

As she ate Anne explained that the cottage had been scrubbed down from top to bottom but that it needed a spot of decorating. Two of the village women had scraped off the old wallpaper downstairs and were giving the walls a coat of white paint. They would go along directly Elizabeth had finished eating she added putting the potatoes in a saucepan of cold water and drying her hands.

They walked up the farm track together, the sun shone hotly above them and the trees on either side showered deliciously green dappled shade along the way. It was obvious that someone was at work for the cottage windows and front door were all wide open. They hesitated in the doorway. A stout woman, her grey hair escaping from the bun at the nape of her neck wiped her face with the end of her apron and bade them come in. The ceiling between the low wooden beams had been freshly painted white. The woman whom Anne addressed as Mrs Weaver assured them that this room would be finished today. She pushed open a door to the right of the front door, revealing the other front room, and waved a brawny arm.

"Sitting room's done." Elizabeth looked into the small rectangular room similarly painted white.

"And Mary's done all the front bedroom above, she's off home at the minute to fetch the blacking and the brushes." Mrs Weaver pointed to a rather rusty grate in the sitting room with picture tiles running down each side. "She'll do this one while I finish the painting and then we'll both tackle the one in here." She indicated a small, black range in the living room. "You'll be needing this one for heating the water and cooking," she explained. Elizabeth noticed that at the side of this range was an oven door and a small hot plate door above that, both set with plain, dark green tiles.

Two more rooms led from this one. The one on the left to a small cubby-hole of a room with a stone sink and a minute, high window that let in very little light. There was a tin bath hanging from another one of the large, black hooks that Elizabeth had noticed randomly adorned the walls of the other two rooms but the sink boasted both a pump and a tap. The right-hand door led up a narrow dog-leg staircase to a small landing with a step running at right-angles. There were two rooms at the front; one up the step with a high ceiling, which had also been freshly painted, and a second facing the top of the stairs with a low ceiling whose crooked beams barely skimmed Elizabeth's head. This room was untouched. A faded cream wall paper with equally insipid pink roses almost stuck to the walls. Although the room did not smell nor feel damp the paper had in places come away and now hung in sad strips. The ceiling sloped down to within shoulder height at either side and the window was small and very close to the floor. There was just room for a bed, chair, set of drawers and a single wardrobe thought Elizabeth and despite the fact that they obviously did not think she would want to use the room she had decided that it would be here she would sleep. Another room lay at the back. Going down the stairs and outside Mrs Weaver showed her that beneath it lay a brick-floored wash room with a brick copper and another stone sink and a store room next door. This end of the cottage with its five rooms Anne explained was much newer and had been added on in the 1850s. When Elizabeth enquired when the living room with its upper floor had been built Anne had to confess that no one really knew but that it was very old indeed.

Outside was another small building filled with logs and a small pile of coal. The garden rose in a three-foot step with a brick wall and four blue brick steps. They went up and along a path which led to an earth closet where the path stopped. Beyond this and up the rise there was an orchard of gnarled old apple, pear and plum trees and finally a tall hawthorn hedge red with berries. A dyke ran down the eastern side making an oval pond, overgrown with water lilies about halfway down before it disappeared underground. A tall hedge and lower down a high wall ran down to the road. The whole garden was badly overgrown with tall nettles and other weeds which Elizabeth could not identify. Attached on the western side was a cottage just a mirror image of this one except it had an air of being cared for and lived in; the windows shining and the garden tended lovingly. Though this cottage was small and primitive after what she had always been used to Elizabeth loved it on sight. She had the strange feeling of having come home; especially in the two low ceiling rooms, for in them she found a feeling of peace and if not exactly happiness then one of supreme contentment. She turned and smiled at Anne.

"It's lovely, I can't wait until my furniture arrives so that I can move in."

"Lovely blouse she had on," remarked Mrs Weaver to Mrs Peters who had just started to black lead the range. "Silk I shouldn't wonder, real silk not that shiny cheap stuff, with real handmade lace on the collar and cuffs."

"What colour was it?" asked Mary Peters, rubbing hard with her brush.

"Pink, a lovely deep pink, not that it made her look any better though."

"What do you mean?" Mary rested back on her heels for a minute.

"Looked real poorly she did, but a real lady. Thanked me ever so kindly she did for showing her around and was real happy with the way we'd cleaned the place up. Said she couldn't wait to move in."

"So she should be, it's been hard work in this heat," Mary resumed her rubbing.

"There, that's done." Amy Weaver put down her brush and surveyed with pride the gleaming walls. "Shall I give you a hand when I've washed up or shall I fetch us a cold drink?"

"Cold drink," Mary replied decidedly, "Is she coming here to rest then?"

"Yes, Mrs Enleigh says that she's been ill, very ill and she had to leave London on doctor's orders. Looks bad, she really do. She'll need to pick up a good deal before she goes back to all that smoke and noise they do have in London."

"Why, have you been there then Amy?"

"No fear, not me," Amy said, "You wouldn't get me going down there you wouldn't, not with all them riots and such like going on and that."

"Do you mean the women who want to get us the vote, smashing windows?"

"That's it," nodded Amy "Why they can't find enough to do in their own house without making a mess everywhere for other folk to clean up I don't know?" She bustled off, indignant for all the mess she couldn't control in the capital city. Amy's greatest love in life was cleaning up and getting everything shining.

Mary made no reply but as she continued her brushing she thought that she ought to be able to decide who should make the laws just as men did. She was just as clever as most men, cleverer than some. Her husband for instance, pretending that he liked to hear her voice when he really wanted her to read the newspaper because he could only manage the easy words. But she wondered if she would be brave enough to do the things that those women were doing and perhaps be arrested and sent to Holloway Jail.

A few days later all was ready when Elizabeth's furniture arrived. Mary Peters had promised to come along and help and her husband would be on hand to help move the pieces into place. When the carrier's cart arrived Elizabeth was not there so Mary took charge asking the men to unload the rugs and carpets first. When Elizabeth came Mary noticed that she was out of breathe as if she had been running. Elizabeth instructed the men where to take each carpet and Mary unrolled them, making them fit as best she could.

"Are you sure?" She queried when Elizabeth asked for the bedroom carpet to be put in the small, unpainted room. Receiving an affirmative reply the carpet was unrolled and the bedroom furniture carried up.

Soon all the larger pieces were in place and the tea chests had been put just inside the front door for unpacking. Mary suggested that Elizabeth should sit down while she unpacked these and put things where Elizabeth indicated. Soon books and ornaments were in place and pictures had been hung. There was only a large trunk of personal items which had been carried upstairs to unpack and the crockery in the chest in the small back room.

Mary made Elizabeth a pot of tea and said that she would finish the unpacking. She took out all the crockery from the straw-filled crate, washed and dried it and stacked it on the dresser in the living room. Elizabeth, she noticed, had finished her tea and had fallen asleep by the fire. Mary covered her with a shawl and went upstairs to unpack the trunk. She hung skirts, coats, dresses and jackets in the wardrobe and filled the chest of drawers with underwear, stockings and blouses. At the bottom of the trunk was a small leather case which she presumed held jewellery so she lifted it out to put it on top of the chest of drawers.

Elizabeth heard the squeak of the trolley coming nearer and nearer, down the corridor, stopping at the door, footsteps, voices at the door now, a key turning in the lock...

"No," she screamed, "No, not again!"

She awoke with a start. Had she screamed in reality or only in her dream? The kettle sang on the trivet and the fire coals glowed warmly. She could smell something delicious and meaty cooking; rabbit, Elizabeth loved rabbit. Was there a pie in the oven or was she dreaming again? Her eyes closed again and this time she slept without dreaming.

Mary bent down to pick up the items which had fallen from beneath the case when she had picked it up from the trunk. Two newspaper cuttings, a letter, a couple of photographs and something small but heavy wrapped in tissue paper. One newspaper cutting showed a funeral, a horse-drawn hearse preceded by rows of women four abreast all wearing white dresses and hats, with black armbands and carrying wreathes. In their midst was a purple, silk banner bearing the words 'Fight on and God will give the Victory.' The woman holding the banner on the near side and looking grave and sad but much healthier was none other than the woman asleep downstairs. The other cutting was an account snipped from 'The Daily Mirror' of June 5th reporting the protest of Emily Wilding Davison who had stepped in front of the King's horse, Anmer. The photographs showed a young man posing proudly in a captain's uniform and the other showed the woman downstairs in the centre of two others dressed in what was reported to be replica prison uniform; dark dress, white apron and cap with contrasting arrows on them and wearing prison number badges. Very curious now she unwrapped the tissue paper to find an oval, silver brooch with enamel rings of green, white and purple, with the fastener missing. Amazed but not really so surprised that the woman downstairs was a suffragette, Mary hastily rewrapped the brooch and put it and the letters, photographs and cuttings under the leather case.

It was late in the afternoon when Elizabeth finally awoke. The fire had been banked up and still gave out some heat and someone had covered her with a shawl. Elizabeth rose and stretched. Taking the poker from the green-tiled hearth she lifted the coals and flames licked up, she pushed the trivet and kettle over them. On the table under a cloth was a plate of cold meat and salad, a jug of lemonade and one of Anne's freshly baked loaves. There was a note from Mary Peters saying that butter, cheese and milk were in the scullery on the cold slab. As Elizabeth sat down to eat she wondered where the rich, meaty smell had come from earlier. Stacking the dishes in the stone sink in the scullery after only managing part of her meal and returning what remained of the milk to the slab Elizabeth went out into the garden. The sun was setting over the fields to her left. She walked up the brick path and stood in the orchard, enjoying the quiet, sweet-smelling peace all around her. She picked an apple from a low branch and was just biting into it after rubbing it to a rosy red on her skirt when she heard the clopping of horses' hooves along the road and the jingle of harness. She could hear the low tones of men talking but could not distinguish any words. Although from here she looked down a slope to the road she could not see any of the horsemen as they passed by and their voices had now faded into the still air. Elizabeth made her way slowly back munching her apple. She would write to her brother and give him this address and then go straight to bed.

Lighting the oil lamp she took pen, paper and ink to the table under the front window.

'Dear John,' she wrote,' I have found a haven of peace and quiet here. Do not worry about me any more, nor about my health for I am sure that I shall soon recover now. Do come and see me if you can find time before you go off to France.' Oh no Elizabeth thought that sounds as if he is going on a holiday not going to war. She looked at what she had written but decided not to change it. That was how her brother and the other men thought of this war. A great adventure, a holiday, all over by Christmas. She would do as well to copy their optimism even if she did not feel any of it. 'If you can't come' she continued 'then don't forget to write often.' She underlined the last word. She knew that he would write and pour out to her all the things he would be unable to write to their parents just as he had done when he had been sent away to school. Not really the same now though thought Elizabeth ruefully, their parents would never want to hear from her, they didn't want anything to do with a wilful woman who had just come out of prison and had not even served her full term and could be hauled back off the streets if she appeared fit and well enough to go back to finish her sentence. She signed herself 'your loving sister,' sealed the note in an envelope, addressed and stamped it ready to go in the post tomorrow.

In bed in the little room above Elizabeth stared at the wavy beams above her head, each one a quarter of a tree trunk. It was quite dark now and moonlight shone palely through the window where she had decided not to close the curtains. Just as she was drifting off to sleep she heard the horsemen again passing beneath the window... and later, much later the sound of weeping in the room beneath her. Was it she who cried or another? And if another why and for whom?

CHAPTER THREE

Elizabeth woke refreshed. She lay for a while warm, comfortable, cocooned in bedclothes and reluctant to emerge. The little room faced south so the sun had not yet reached the window. There was a small, black fire grate in this room and an alcove on one side of it, in which her chest of drawers had been placed. The room was an L-shape and lay partly above the living room and partly above the scullery. It was very quiet outside, no sound of horsemen this morning. Elizabeth decided that she would post the letter to her brother after breakfast and ask the carter who kept the public house how she could get to a doctor's for there wasn't one here and her throat was so painful now that taking any food was an exquisite agony.

It came as quite a shock that she would have to clean out the ashes and get a fire going before she could even have a hot drink. She decided that a small piece of bread and butter and a glass of milk would do for now. Putting on her jacket and hat she looked around for a key to unlock the door. Then she remembered that she had not locked it last night. This thought sent a shiver down her spine as she thought of who could have walked in while she was asleep. There was no key anywhere, search as she might she found nothing. She would go and ask Anne later. She walked slowly down to the post box. There was no one about anywhere. Crossing the road she made her way up the steps and into the churchyard. There were two ancient and massive yews and the gravestones stood drunkenly, leaning this way and that, choked with grass and weeds. The porch door hung open on broken hinges and once inside Elizabeth was amazed to find straw on the floor and a strange smell; the smell of horses. How dreadful she thought that this tiny, but beautiful Norman church should be so badly treated. She left hurriedly and decided to go up the lane opposite. When she had reached the top, she stopped to get her breath and look down on the three cottages at the side of the road below her. Nothing stirred. No smoke rose from any of the chimneys. Looking around she saw she had reached a rounded, walled enclosure; a pinfold; and on her left was a narrow lane. She took it. Fields, unbroken by hedges stretched on either side and in front. They were strangely striped with strips of what looked like crops or the remains of them and intervening grassy banks. In the distance were a number of figures bending over as if harvesting and a cart harnessed to a cow with large horns stood docilely nearby. The path went on downhill, splitting in two, the left fork curving down into a long dip. Elizabeth took this, which descended into a damp; and even after all the sunshine recently; marshy hollow. She stopped and rested again in the shade of the trees when at last she came to the point where the path met the road.

About twenty minutes later she had reached the farmhouse and was sitting in Anne's kitchen. Anne was searching through the dresser drawers for the missing key.

"You won't really need it though," she commented over her shoulder, "no one ever locks anything up around here. There's no need. Nothing will be taken and there's always someone about to watch what any strangers in the village might be doing. Not that there is ever many of those."

Well, the whole place was more like a grave than a village this morning and I'm a stranger and no one was watching what I was doing thought Elizabeth with a touch of rebellion.

"Ah, here it is," Anne brandished the missing item and then handed it to Elizabeth. She took it; it was almost six inches long with a piece of string and a wooden tag attached to it. Elizabeth examined the tag. "Strange name, Sparrow Cottage. "

"The next door one is called Thorn Cottage. They stand on a piece of land which was once part of a big field called Sparrowthorn Field." Anne explained. The ruined house further down was the farmhouse."
Elizabeth said nothing for she hadn't seen any ruin, but she had noticed a farmhouse with a rectangle of barns around it.

Anne continued, "Now the three big fields are enclosed with hedges. They are called something like five acres or well furrows but everyone knows the old names. The two cottages on this side are called Well Cottage and South Cottage as this side the field was called Southwell Field, and yes, before you ask, Well Cottage does have a well."

Elizabeth nearly said that the fields that she had walked past this morning had not been hedged but Anne did not give her chance.

"I'm going into Southwell tomorrow if you would like to come. Didn't you say that you needed to see a doctor about your sore throat?"

Elizabeth had had to tell Anne this as she had found it very difficult to swallow the food that Anne had provided. She agreed that she had said so and that yes she would like to go with Anne the following morning. She rose to leave.

"Anne?" She asked, "Who in the village has a lot of horses?"

Anne looked puzzled. "Well, we have a few to pull carts and for ploughing and Amos at the inn hires out the odd one..."

"No, not those sort, riding horses."

"No one, why?" Anne was looking at her strangely.

"Oh, nothing, I just thought that I heard some riders go along the road last night."

"It could be horses being taken to the railway at Newark ready to be shipped to France" suggested Anne.

"Of course." agreed Elizabeth thankful for this explanation, "I'll be waiting by my gate tomorrow then, at about what time?"

They agreed a convenient time and Elizabeth bade her goodbye. As she walked slowly up the farm track swinging the key in her hand a thought made her stop in her tracks. The horses couldn't have been ones being shipped to France for she had heard them coming back later just before she fell asleep.

Mary Peters was dusting her dresser when Elizabeth arrived home.

"Oh," Mary looked startled, "I didn't hear you come in."

Elizabeth saw that the fire was blazing merrily.

"Shall we have some tea?" she suggested.

"I'll do it," offered Mary, thinking that if Elizabeth had gone all morning without a drink she must be parched.

As she bustled about warming the pot and measuring the tea into it Elizabeth said hesitatingly, "Could I beg a favour of you Mary?"

Mary put down the cups, saucers and the milk jug on the table and turned to face her "Depends on what it is but I suppose that I can manage most things."

As Mary poured boiling water into the pot Elizabeth continued, "I would like you to come and do a few things for me each day. If we could decide on times and payment and it would be agreeable to you..." Her voice petered out as she saw a frown appear on Mary's usually round and placid features.

"Sorry, I shouldn't have asked you, you're much too busy already I'm sure. Forget that I spoke."

"No, it's not that," replied Mary quickly, "I would like to do it, really I would, it's just that I can't take your money"

"Why not, is there something wrong with my money!" asked Elizabeth quite sharply. Was the woman going to refuse because somehow she knew that Elizabeth had been in prison?

"No, no," Mary looked worried now in case she had unwittingly offended Elizabeth, "It's just that you are obviously too ill to work and as you seem to have no family and -"

"I've never worked Mary," Elizabeth explained, "I'm what you might call one of the idle rich. I come from a fairly wealthy family and my grandparents left me well provided for... so will you come and help me out...?" She gestured helplessly to the fire. "I didn't have a hot drink this morning because I couldn't face seeing to that. So I would like to pay you to come for, say two hours each morning if you could manage that?"

"Yes," agreed Mary, "I'll come straight after my Bill has left for work. He goes very early you see to milk and then he comes home for his breakfast. Then when he goes off again I could come then, about half past seven that would be. I could get the fire going and not wake you until you were ready to be up."

"Fine, that would suit me."

"I'll start tomorrow then, shall I?"

"I think you started today," smiled Elizabeth, "Now let's have that tea."

The little pony moved much more sedately with Anne at the reins than when David had brought her here that first night. The sun was still bright but there was that unmistakable feel and smell of autumn this morning Elizabeth thought as they breasted the hill and began to descend towards the huddle or rooftops in the hollow below.

"Is that the Minster?" Elizabeth asked and gestured towards the large grey towered building.

Anne nodded, "I'll take you round it if you like, but not today though, we have enough to do with the shopping and the doctors. We'll come back another day."

"Lovely," replied Elizabeth. She was really interested in old buildings and especially old ruined abbeys and monasteries. The thought of the church jogged her memory and she asked as diplomatically as she could if Anne knew about the untidy state of the village church. Anne replied that she was not at all surprised.

"It's always the same when those three women who are on the rota come together as they have done this week. I mean they are all right if they do the brasses or the cleaning or the flowers with someone else because then they will be reminded by the other two, but put them together and they all forget to throw out the cut off flowers and put away the cleaning cloths. I'll go and have a look myself this afternoon."

Elizabeth did not reply. That's not what I meant she thought. She felt worried that it would now be Anne who would find the door broken and that horses had been in there.

Elizabeth was quite exhausted by the time all the shopping had been stowed in the cart. Anne had insisted in introducing her in every shop; the grocer's; the butcher's; the draper's and even at the dressmaker's where Anne had taken material to be made up into dresses for the later stages of her pregnancy.

Elizabeth apologised to the doctor for arriving with Anne but he just smiled and asked her to take a seat and he would attend to her shortly. Doctor Andrew Grant was a tall, cadaverous looking figure with a shock of jet-black hair and the blue-shadowed chin of a man who needed to shave twice a day.

"Say ah," he commanded holding her tongue down with a metal spatula. Elizabeth shuddered at the cold feel of it in her mouth.

"Does that hurt?" He enquired

"No, just my throat."

"Finding it painful to swallow?"

Elizabeth nodded in confirmation She felt worried because she thought that he looked angry.

"Umph," he said sitting down at his desk again, "Disgraceful - shouldn't be allowed."

"I'm sorry doctor," Elizabeth rose and made as if to leave, "I won't trouble you any further."

"Sit down woman!" Now he really did sound very cross Elizabeth thought so she subsided into the chair again.

"I'm not angry with you. I'm angry with the so-called doctors who did this to you - how many times?"

When Elizabeth didn't answer he repeated.

"How many times were you force-fed Miss Bateman? The truth now."

"I can't honestly remember. The first time it just seemed to go on and on in a haze of pain. The second time. Well only a few days and then they let me out because of that new act; we called it the Cat and Mouse Act...."

"Yes, I know all about that. You've been in prison and on hunger strike twice."

"Well three times actually. If you count right at the beginning when I went in for just a month."

"I don't know Miss Bateman whether you are a very brave woman or a very foolish one but I do know that you are a very ill one. I shall give you a soothing mixture for your throat to take before meals so that you will be able to eat a little more comfortably and a general tonic." He stopped and looked hard at her. "But you must rest. And I mean rest in bed. It is not just lack of food which is causing this tiredness, your heart is not good, not good at all Miss Bateman. Come and see me again in a fortnight or sooner if you feel worse."

Elizabeth thanked him and when she had paid and received her two bottles of noxious looking medicine she wondered what he would have said if she had told him that she did not really want to recover too much in case the police even here found her and sent her back to prison. She couldn't go there again, she would rather be dead.

❖

For the next few days Elizabeth got up late, ate the food that Mary prepared for her and took Doctor Grant's medicines. Each afternoon she rested in bed. Sometimes with a book but more often just watching the play of light and shade on the crooked ceiling and listening to the everyday village sounds. She could pick out now certain villagers by their voices or by the time of day they went along the road. Only in the evening did she hear the horsemen, but she never caught a glimpse of them no matter how hard she tried.

One morning the postman brought her a letter from her brother. She opened it with trembling fingers.

'Dearest Sis' she read. She looked at the date at the top. Still in England three days ago. But then she began to read and her heart thumped. 'Great news,' he had written, 'the magic order has come, we are to make immediate preparations to entrain tomorrow morning. No official information as to our destination but it must be France! Now keep your chin up, it is a great thing to be going to defend our country in her hour of greatest need. I am doing it for you to keep you safe...' Elizabeth stopped reading . Oh, John she thought, you are doing it because you think it will be a great adventure and that you will come home in a few months covered in glory. You can't wait to go. You think that if you don't get there soon it will all be over before you get to the front. But it's not like the skirmishes we've had in the Empire before. It's not even going to be like the Boer War and that was bad enough. This is a fight to the death between the greatest nations in Europe. Sadly she continued reading. 'The best thing you can do is to keep cheerful and to get well again .I won't forget to write as often as I can and you must give me all your news, He had signed himself 'your loving brother'. There was a post scriptum under his boyish signature which read, 'I've asked the parents at least to write to you now that you are again a respectable woman; for my sake if not for yours. Will you forgive them if they do? I hope so.'

Oh John, Elizabeth thought , tears coursing down her cheeks, dearest Johnny, always cheerful, always compliant, always the peacemaker. And that was why she felt that it was so wrong that he was going to fight .She had always been the one who got into trouble by going her own way, doing the daring things , not any more though the fight had all been knocked out of her. But now he was going into a fight that she believed would be far worse than even her worst imaginings. She feared for him, his bodily safety initially but also for his mental and spiritual well-being.

She folded the letter carefully and put it in her writing case to await a reply this evening. She decided that when she saw Mary the following morning she would ask if her husband could come and move her small writing desk from the sitting room which she never used into the living room. She went through to check that it would fit in one of the corners.

She opened the sitting room door. Everywhere was flooded with sunlight. She felt a dampness seeping through her silk slippers. Looking down she saw that she stood not on the red turkey carpet but on a carpet of what smelled like camomile. There was a little path made of uneven stones bordered with lavender, clumps of thyme, marigolds and other sweet-smelling herbs and flowers. A hazy figure in a dark dress with white collar, cuffs, cap and apron was bending over cutting herbs and putting them in a basket. Their scent perfumed the air, the sky was a very vivid blue and everywhere looked as if it had been newly washed. Mingled with the scent of the herbs was the sweet smell of wood smoke..... Elizabeth shaded her eyes to look at the woman who did not seem to have noticed her. The woman's features were indistinct, she was humming a half-remembered tune as she worked. Elizabeth walked along the path towards her....... and walked into the sitting room window. I must have banged my head and knocked myself out she decided picking herself up from the carpet minutes later. I dreamed that scene. I imagined it. I did. Didn't I? But it had been so clear Elizabeth could have painted that garden, so clear and so real, except for the woman, except for her.

❖

Elisabet Bayteman, humming as she filled her herb basket sensed that some one was watching her but didn't look up. She had been aware of a presence in her cottage for some days now . A curious presence not a fearful one. But she would ignore it and above all tell no one. These Puritans were too quick to cry witch about anyone who seemed in the least bit odd. And I would certainly qualify as odd thought Elisabet as she stood up with difficulty on her one good leg, easing her weight from the other twisted and malformed one. I grow herbs, I make medicines and I live alone. Walking with her uneven but sprightly gait Elisabet made her way back inside to collect her shawl. I must hurry she told herself and get to Widow Kychin's house and back for she had salves and potions to make this day .

Widow Kychin's cottage was in the neighbouring village of Winkbourne. There were two ways that Elisabet could get there; across the footpath which bisected her neighbour's fields or up her own strip of land to the narrow track which ran above and eventually joined another wider track to Winkbourne village. She decided on the latter as the day was moist and the fields were muddy. She added a few apples, three duck eggs and a honeycomb to the bottle of soothing syrup for the widow's cough and the jar of goose grease to rub on her chest. Elisabet loved this walk up the gently rising ground and never tired of the scenery for the view changed with the weather and the seasons. When she reached the path she turned to look behind her . From here on a clear day she would be able to see the great towers of the Minster church in Southwell. A fitful sun was edging out mistily from the clouds , sparrows twittered and quarrelled in the hedge which bordered one of the few fields already enclosed in the village. All around her lay the ridge and furrow of Sparrowthorne field ; stubble now that the corn had been cut. No one was about except the boy watching Goodman Wright's few sheep grazing the stubble at the far side of this great field. Elisabet followed the path across the ridge and then where it divided took the right-hand fork to Winkbourne. The path skirted a small wood of tall trees before dipping into the valley. Elisabet soon saw the roofs of the cottages, she could even see smoke issuing from Widow Kychin's chimney. Hefting her basket onto her other arm she entered the village.

Widow Kychin was a small, round, apple-cheeked woman with two small children. She kissed Elisabet's cheek and wrung her hands helplessly.

"Elisabet, Elisabet, I'm so glad that you have come, sit you down do."

Elisabet sat down on a three-legged stool in front of a fitful fire. She could hear coughing from above. The widow explained that both the children were ill in bed and that she was in the process of making them some gruel. She exclaimed when she saw the linctus and the goose grease and again for the presents of the honey and apples. Some of the former she added to the two steaming wooden bowls. Elisabet helped her carry them up the crooked stairs. The room above was barely high enough for Elisabet to stand up in. The children; a boy of about five and a girl a few years older were together in the one bed which dominated the room. They greeted Elisabet with hugs and kisses and the steaming food disappeared rapidly, so rapidly that Elisabet felt that too little good, hot food might be more the cause of their illness than anything else. She said nothing of this to the widow who was having a hard enough time as it was to make ends meet without anyone interfering. With chests rubbed and cough mixture taken Elisabet helped cover them over ,noting how poor and thin their one coverlet was and how, despite the fire down below, how cold the room was. Elisabet knew that kind neighbours had brought little bits since Goodman Kychin had died within two days of piercing his hand with the broken end of a pitchfork three years ago, but they had often little enough themselves.

She bade the Widow goodbye and as she walked home she resolved to return the next day with more eggs and a blanket that she had had woven from the wool she regularly spun. Her journey back was longer as she detoured to collect cob nuts, pick mushrooms and the last of the blackberries that hung wetly from their long, arching tendrils. She filled the top of her basket with pieces of sheep's wool that she found caught on twigs along the way.

The afternoon was well advanced and there was still water to draw from the well, the hens to feed as well as making her salves. She needs must milk the cow and feed her horse before the light failed. Elisabet ate bread and cheese as she went about her tasks, humming to herself between mouthfuls. Eventually she was finished and ventured round to her herb garden. The woman was gone, but not completely; she was still nearby, Elisabet could sense her. All her life Elisabet had seen and heard things hidden from others. Once when she was a small child gathering rushes by the stream in Netherfield she had heard the sounds of swords clashing, bloodthirsty yells and cries and the groans of those in pain. The sounds of battle coming from across the track in Southwell Field, there was no one there. Running home in fear she had blurted it all out to her father. She remembered how grave his face had become. He had not said that she was foolish nor a day-dreamer. He had taken her on his knee and explained to her how dangerous it would be if she told her story to anyone else. That if she saw or heard anything of the like again she was only to speak of it to him and no one else must ever know. When, childlike, she asked him why he explained of the fear of witchcraft which was abroad. Of how she must not draw attention to them as there were still some in the village who remembered the story of their ancestor ,Thomas, the monk; many who suspected them of leaning towards the old religion. It was dangerous to be different he admonished. So as the years passed Elisabet had heeded her father and told only him of the woman in the dress gathered high under her bosom and the little girl with her doll who she often saw at the edge of the pond. But this new person she had never met before, was she another Elisabet too and if so where had she been until this time?

Glad that Mary had been and gone and was not on hand to witness her foolishness Elizabeth closed the sitting room door and decided she would go and lie down for a while.

Lying on her back on top of the eiderdown Elizabeth considered the strange things she had seen and heard. The horsemen, the weeping, the sad state of the church. Anne had not seen this when she had gone in the afternoon, only a week's dust and some dying flowers. And now the woman in the herb garden. Was she hallucinating, dreaming, or seeing... ghosts? After a while she fell into a dreamless sleep, only to be woken by what could be described as loud whispering right under her window.

"I will go father," A youngish male voice.

"You will stay and tend the farm .The king has no need of lads to fight his cause." An older , angry, male tone.

"But Newark has declared for the king, father and we are, aren't we?"

"Yes, my son , but we must not lose our land; if we do not till it then the lord will find someone else who will."

"Like Abel , you mean father?"

"Exactly like him . We should then be landless beggars . Do you understand?"

"Yes father." The younger voice held resignation but there was still a hint of rebellion under the compliant answer.

The voices stopped abruptly, Elizabeth listened for footsteps. There were none. She rose and moved to the window and looked down through the open casement. The road was empty.

George Weaver and Bill Peters stumbled down the steps of *The Spread Eagle* inn. It was a bright, moonlit night and their footsteps sounded hollowly as they made their way along the village street.

"What's she like then, this new woman?" George asked.

"All right I suppose." Bill Peters hadn't really looked at her closely even when he had gone the second time to move the desk, he had just placed it where she had indicated, took the proffered silver threepenny piece, touched his cap and left.

"Well, is she young, old, or what?" George, a big bull of a man, took off his cap and rubbed his thick, black, curly hair; a gesture of his when he was displeased.

"You'd not be much use if I were the police and she were a wanted criminal."

"Do you think she is?" asked Bill, trying to change the subject.

"Could be I suppose," George replaced his cap, "more like she's come away 'cos her man's joined up."

"Why should she do that then?"

"I dunno, but you know nowt anyhow."

"My Mary said that she'd come up here from London for her health."

"I knows that already, my Amy said."

"Well why don't you ask her what the woman's like if she knows so much."

"I will when I gets home. Useless lump you are, Bill Peters."

"Not that useless that she didn't ask me to move her desk then."

"Did she? Why?" George stopped.

"I dunno do I, she didn't say did she?"

"Like I said, you don't know owt Bill, useless you is...." George's voice died away as he walked in disgust to his own front door.

Bill, closing his quietly so as not to wake his son Benjamin, smiled in the darkness. Let George think what he wanted .He wasn't going to gossip about this Miss Bateman. She had given his Mary a bit of a job and that meant more money coming in and if she had come here for peace and quiet then she ought to get it .He and Mary weren't going to trumpet her affairs, even if they knew them. And she hadn't given big George threepence for moving her desk even if he did think he was the strong man around. And thought Bill she did ask if I would come and help her again if needs be so she must trust me, so there George Weaver.

CHAPTER FOUR

For the next few days Elizabeth tried to keep watch by the window in the evenings for the horsemen, without avail. She wrote a long letter to her brother describing the village and her new and restful life. She ordered a hamper to be sent to him by a well known London shop which advertised ‘staples and delicacies’ which could be sent to the troops at the front.

Mary’s husband, Bill, moved her writing desk so that there was no need for her to go into the sitting room again and when she attended the church service on Sunday all seemed as normal; flowers tastefully arranged on the window ledges; woodwork shining and smelling of bees wax polish; brass and silver on the gleaming white altar cloth. So she had persuaded herself it had all been due to her ill health. Indeed she felt so much better, less tired, eating quite well and sleeping much more peacefully. The tonic, rest and the country air are working she thought. Even though she had had no communication from her parents as John had hoped and no further word from him in France she felt so much more hopeful and cheerful about the future and put all her earlier fears down yet again to illness.

That night as she undressed she examined herself in the mirror. Yes, she did look better. Her cheeks had a healthy glow, her blue eyes sparkled, her dark, brown hair looked glossier and curlier. She froze. But that’s not me! She gazed horrified at the image in the mirror. She leaned forward the better to examine the face that looked back at her through the mirror. It’s like me but it’s not me. My eyes are grey not blue, my hair is a much lighter brown, wispy, rather than curly.

“Who are you?” she asked in a frightened whisper to the face staring out at her. ”You’re not me so who are you?”

There was no answer. Had she expected one? As she stared, horrified but fascinated , she wondered if it was a trick of the light for the face seemed to waver, shimmer and then blur and she recognised herself again. She was very afraid.

“Am I going mad?” she said aloud.

And then she heard the horsemen. “Oh no!” Throwing her hair brush down she leaped to the window and tripped on the edge of the rug. Feeling herself falling she made a grab for the narrow mantle piece with her right hand , missed , and clawed at the wall in an effort to break her fall. She slithered to the floor and sat there a minute her heart pounding .They had gone, the hoof beats were dying away into the night. In her hand, her right hand, was a thick wad of wallpaper and plaster which she had torn from the wall as she fell. Getting slowly and gingerly to her feet and finding no real damage to her person she looked at the mess she had made of the already loose wallpaper.

She had torn a long swathe off to the left of the fire place about six inches wide and running from shoulder height to the floor. Underneath the wall was now brown. She tapped it. It was wooden and hollow. Going downstairs to fetch a knife she wondered who had boarded up and plastered over the left hand alcove and why. Well she was going to find out. It took her a good hour to scrape off all the paper and lift the plaster in pieces with the blunt and now ruined knife. Wide panels of wood were revealed. These would need more than a knife to remove them Elizabeth knew. She sat down and thought about this new problem. There was a large screwdriver that Mary's Bill had left. Would that do? It was going to. She inserted the flat screwdriver blade between the crack of the two middle panels and using it as a lever went up and down the gap. There was a sudden cracking noise. Not of the wood splintering as Elizabeth first thought but of two long, narrow doors opening up on either side. It was a cupboard.

Elisabet Bayteman heard the bedroom cupboard open. She felt cold and shivery for now the unknown presence was in..... Not just in the house but inside her life.....

Inside was surprisingly dust free. Well not really surprising Elizabeth thought when it had been sealed so completely until now, there had been no way until now for any dust to get in. She wondered how long it had been hidden. There were two shelves. The top one was bare. The second one held a pile of clothes. Gingerly Elizabeth lifted the top garment out; a leather sort of jacket; then under it a piece of lace and at the bottom a blanket. And under that a large wooden cross on a leather thong. On the bottom of the cupboard beneath the carefully folded clothes was a rusty sword and two metal objects ; spurs, but strangely shaped like a butterfly's wings..

Also on the floor of the cupboard was a wooden box. Elizabeth lifted it out carefully, it was quite heavy. She raised the lid. Inside were two books. The smaller top book had a cover of beautifully tooled leather, a little faded in places and worn. She opened it gently. A picture of deep blues, bright reds, emerald green and gold glowed up at her. The colours shone in the dim room, echoes of a more flamboyant and vibrant age. There was black writing on the facing page which was not she surmised as she peered at it in English, it was probably in Latin for she thought that what she held in her hands was a medieval book of hours of the sort owned by wealthy persons or the church.

The second book was twice the size with a wooden board front and back and looked crude and home made. Elizabeth saw as she flipped through the pages inside that they were a greyish, brown colour covered with tiny writing; in English this time. Turning back to the first page, to see if there was a title, she read, 'Elisabet Bayteman, her book.'

Elizabeth sat down on the floor trembling. Nearly the same name as hers. Was this the woman in the garden? Was she the face in the mirror? Turning the page she read with some difficulty, 'Now that I can read well Father has said that I may write in my own book and has made this for me....' The strangely formed E s ;loops and curls in odd places and a letter shaped like a long looping F , which turned out to be an S made deciphering the script difficult at first but the writing was neat and even and soon Elizabeth found that she could manage it quite well.

'Father says I must keep my knowledge of letters hidden for it is not for the likes of us to be able to pen a page of words better than the minister or the lord of the manor. I am only to show myself able to write my name and even that with difficulty.' There was a lot more in this vein and then at the bottom of the page a neatly drawn family tree.

Thomas, the monk (1502- 1578) == Mary Bayteman

I

Thomas Bayteman b.1560== Elisabet Petters (1586-1612)
I
Elisabet Bayteman Born 1612

It was a strange one, Elizabeth thought. She read on the next page. 'Father says that I may have the book that Grandfather Thomas brought from the Abbey at Welbeck There will be no son for him now and it will be my charge to keep it safe. There was a lot about how the Grandfather had with the other monks been turned out of the abbey by King Henry's men. He had walked into Hockerton still wearing his habit of undyed, Cistercian wool and found refuge with the Bayteman family who had lived in a house on a bit of land in Sparrowthorn Field. He had helped to rebuild part of the house in bricks which had been made a little further up the road just inside the village boundary. He had married the daughter, taking the family's name as his own. Elizabeth wondered why he had not reverted to his own name and if he had told them about the book of hours which it said he had 'rescued from King Henry's wicked men '.The art of reading had been taught to his son with instructions by the old monk before he died that it should be carried on to the next generation always in secret for it would have made this already different family more odd if as labourers they had been able to read and write; Latin as well.

The next entry was dated; January 10th 1638 . It said starkly. 'This day I buried Father . He now lies in the churchyard with Mother, Grandfather and Grandmother. I am all alone.' She was twenty-six now Elizabeth worked out and obviously unmarried. That too was strange. She continued to live alone for in the sparse entries that followed there was no mention of a husband.

With a sigh Elizabeth closed the book. She would read more tomorrow. Now she must tidy up the mess she had made. For some reason which she could not put sense to she did not want Mary to know what she had found. Picking up all the wallpaper she screwed it into balls and fed them into the downstairs fire which was still just alight, poking the black ash until it mingled with the glowing coals. Then she swept up the plaster and shovelled it into an old pillowcase. This went into the bottom of the cupboard for the night. She would think about how to get rid of that tomorrow. Perhaps dig a hole at the top of the garden and bury it. She swept the carpet and dusted the furniture as a fine, white dust lay over everything. Finally she put everything except Elisabet's book back in the cupboard and closed the doors. How could she disguise the existence of the cupboard? Did she need to? Yes, she decided for the moment she wanted to keep her find a secret. Eventually she just lugged the silk-covered dressing screen from the other front bedroom and placed it in front. It would have to do for now. The ceiling was so low that only about a foot of the cupboard showed above and to disguise this she hung up three dresses from some black hooks conveniently sited in the beam above.

Completely exhausted Elizabeth undressed and flopped into bed. But sleep was elusive. There were too many impressions and thoughts swirling around in her mind. Uppermost was the question , why was Elisabet Bayteman who had lived here two hundred and fifty years ago making herself known to Elizabeth Bateman of 1914 ? What connection was there besides the similarity of name and her presence in this cottage? And was that all there was ? Or were they in some way related? Elizabeth couldn't see at the moment how this could be at all possible. As she finally drifted off to sleep Elizabeth decided she would only find out the answers by reading the rest of the book and checking up in the church registers.

CHAPTER FIVE

Elisabet stirred the iron pot slowly, savouring the warmth of the fire. The days were getting a chill on them now. She added a good handful of oatmeal to thicken the pottage. While this bubbled away she fetched a mug of cider from the barrel and a piece of oaten bread from the wooden bread ark in the pantry. This pantry lay at the back of the large room and was the only other room on the ground floor. Its small window had a lattice of reeds. Hanging from its beams were flowers and herbs drying and strings of onions. On three short shelves Elisabet kept a number of pottery jugs and bowls as well as some wooden dishes and on a wide bench running around two sides of the room were wide bowls, a chopping knife, two pewter plates and mugs and a large jar of honey. On the floor were two wooden half barrels, three large baskets, her barrel of cider and two sacks; one of peas from her garden which she had dried and the other of oats from her neighbour. She put her wooden bowl and spoon ready on the table. Tomorrow, as she did every week when she had something to sell she would harness her old mare to the cart and go to the local market to sell her goose and hen's eggs, herbs and salves, butter and cheese.

Once the pottage had thickened Elisabet moved the pot away from the fire on its pot-crane and spooned two generous ladlesful into her bowl. She supped it noisily, breaking pieces of the bread off and cramming them in her mouth. As she ate she glanced with pride at her twists of coloured wools neatly twined round their spindles. Mustard yellow dyed with weld flowers, dark-brown walnut dyed wool, a pale orange dyed with onion skins and a good blue obtained from woad leaves. All this would go tomorrow to the weaver to be woven into cloth. In the corner stood Elisabet's great wheel ,her treasure, a spinning wheel, with its basket of foamy wool ready to be spun and another basket which needed washing and combing with the prickly-headed teasels. The wool she collected piecemeal from where small clumps had become tangled in bushes and the odd hedgerow which had been planted in the old queen's time to enclose some of the fields, not many here thank goodness as in some villages. She also exchanged some of her honey for wool from the sheared sheep in Spring. Most men here had a few animals as well as still tending their own strips.

There were also some tallow candles she had made by dipping bundles of tied rushes into melted fat but also some wax ones which now hung from the wooden frame to set. These would go to market together with pots of honey from her black bees. Wiping the last of the pottage carefully from the bowl with the last of the bread Elisabet sighed and rose from her stool. Time to sleep, she needs be up early on the morrow.

The squeak of the trolley wheels moved along the corridor, footsteps stopped at her cell door, there came again the grating of the key in the lock. She was being forced back, held down. Clamp your mouth shut. A hard metal object trying to prise apart her lips, rasping as it tried to breach her teeth. Pain flooded her head but if she unclenched her teeth they would force that vile tube down her excruciatingly painful throat. Her mind screamed.... Elizabeth awoke, sweating, shivering. Where was she? The room was dark. Not morning then. She felt, rather than saw a shadowy presence in the room moving towards the window. There was a pain down her left arm and a tight iron band around her chest, she gasped. Suddenly a grey light flooded the room. There was a sound of wood creaking. Silhouetted against the small grey square of window was the figure of a woman.

"Mary?" Elizabeth whispered, "Mary?" And receiving no answer again, "Is it you Mary?"

In France, Captain John Bateman waited in the cold, dim light of early dawn surrounded by his men. He checked his watch. The rum ration had been given out, some men had received its warming liquid gratefully, others whom he suspected were unused to spirits by reason of their youth had choked and spluttered as they drank. Bayonets had been fixed. Any moment now the sergeant would blow his whistle. John checked his revolver again, it seemed such a paltry thing with which to lead men out into battle across the so long stretch of flat ground and towards the coils of barbed wire which wreathed the front of the enemy trenches like a veil...

Elisabet was awoken by the crowing of her cockerel. Rubbing her eyes she knelt down by the side of her bed to say her morning prayers. Taking down the wooden shutters from the window it seemed that some other person still lay in her bed, she rubbed her eyes again, whatever it was, was gone. She dressed and went carefully down the narrow, wooden stairs to the larger room which lay below. Putting a handful of straw and twigs in the hearth , she struck her flint once, twice, three times. A spark appeared and the waiting tinder caught light. Watching the weak flames grow stronger she added some larger twigs gently until she deemed that the flames were strong enough to add some bigger pieces of log and leave it to burn. Elisabet broke her fast with a piece of bread and a cup of cider and then went out to feed the hens and geese and collected their eggs. Outside the door were two tall wigwams of thin logs and a pile of cut ones stacked under the overhang of the eaves. Then there were plots of cabbage, leeks, onions and garlic with grassy paths between them before she reached the hen loft. She collected about a dozen brown eggs, laying them in the straw lined basket and scattered the hens' food. They came squawking and flapping down the tiny ladder as she made her way to the orchard above where the geese are kept. Here she added six goose eggs to the basket and then went through the trees to the quiet corner of the garden where the woven straw bee hives rested on their wooden stands. The honey had already been collected but she liked to visit the black bees each day to tell them all the events of the village. After leaving the eggs ready in the cart with the other things to go to market Elisabet went with her wooden bucket and drew water from the well which lay in front of the cottage on the opposite side of the road. This was left in the pantry where it would stay cool until her return .Elisabet was fortunate to have an old horse which she tethered on the grass at the side of the road and a much repaired cart . She was going to take her two neighbours' wives to market with her as she usually did and would receive in return a share of wood when their husbands coppiced the trees and a bag of oats when the crop are harvested. All was now ready. Elisabet went to lead the horse between the shafts.

Elizabeth awoke much later, the sun was up and light glinted between the curtains at the window. Struggling weakly she heaved herself up into a semi-sitting position and was trying to arrange the pillows more comfortably behind her when Mary bustled into the room. She drew back the curtains and came towards Elizabeth.

"I thought that I had better see if you were awake," She looked anxiously at Elizabeth who she thought looked dreadful. "Not feeling too well? You stay there ." As she spoke she fluffed up the pillows and made Elizabeth comfortable. "I'll fetch you a nice cup of tea and a bit of toast. "

She hurried away. Elizabeth could hear her moving about down below her. She didn't want to move. She felt weak and ill. She dimly remembered the nightmare. Had the woman at the window been part of it she wondered or had she been awake then?. At least Mary had not noticed the cupboard. She lay back tiredly until Mary returned with the tray and the welcome words,

"A letter for you, now have something to eat and drink your tea while it's hot and then lie still and you'll soon feel better. I'll see to everything," and was gone.

Elizabeth sipped her tea and looked at the familiar round boyish handwriting. A letter from John! Hastily putting down the cup so that the tea slopped in the saucer she tore open the envelope and tea and toast forgotten began to read.

'Dearest Sis,' John had started, 'I received your parcel the same morning as we left Rouen. It was extremely welcome as the train journey was a very trying one with a lot of stops. Sometimes we were able to get out and make tea and cook food in the billy cans. We then detrained and have marched on average about fifteen miles a day. I know that it doesn't sound that much but it is for the men, the weight of their packs is a colossal, sixty pounds in all, and the great, rough cobble stones that you get at each end of every village here are very uneven and quite slippery for men in hob-nail boots. If a young lad falters I take his pack and rifle for a bit and try to encourage him as if I am not exhausted myself. I make no sign, just a joke now and then but how I would give anything to fall out and rest on the grassy bank at the side of the road. However the long and tedious march has ended and we have at last reached the area we have been imagining for the past weeks. We are now within the sound of the guns and at night it is like trying to sleep through one vast and continuous thunderstorm. Tomorrow we shall be moving up to the front line trenches and when we arrive I will send you a field post card if I am too busy to write because you will want to know that all is well. Try not to worry about me; I am with a splendid group of men. There is a lot of laughing and singing in the ranks, sometimes uncouth and not very respectful to the higher military authorities, dear Sis. But my men are in good heart and so am I. Could you please send some sweets, (the cheap, boiled ones that last a long time when sucked) for the men welcome these and some beef tea squares. Will you send out a lot of both as soon as you are able so that I can share them with the men who do not get any extra delicacies

Please write soon,

Your loving brother, John'.

Elizabeth folded the page thoughtfully. John was by now right at the front. Had there been a big battle? , she must find out and she must ask Mary how she would get the things that he had asked for as soon as possible.

When asked Mary said that she had not heard anything but that she would bring Elizabeth the daily newspaper from home later in the day and Elizabeth had to be content with that. She also promised that when she went in to Southwell the following day if Elizabeth was not well enough to go she would get the things that Captain Bateman had asked for and post them at the same time. Elizabeth promised to write a short note later in the day to include in the parcel and write out the address that John had given. Assuring Mary that she would remain in bed until she felt better Elizabeth lay back and opened Elisabet's book. She turned the old pages carefully until she found her place and read, 'the King has been at Newark again. He comes often and many have been healed of the King's Evil,(Elizabeth wondered what on earth that was,) at his touch. 'Elizabeth's knowledge of dates was hazy but she guessed that the king mentioned must be Charles 1 when she read the next entry. 'So it has come to war at last. The King raised his standard at the bottom of the castle hill in Nottingham the carter said who passed through Southwell yesterday. He had come through Newark which has declared for the king and is very busy preparing its defences. Men are pouring into the town and even the townspeople are arming themselves . The carter wonders if they will make the bridge below the castle impassable, I hope not for it is a newly repaired one these last nine years, taking cart loads of timber and much money to rebuild.'

The were further entries after this about the village which meant little to Elizabeth as she had no knowledge of the people mentioned. Then she noticed that on one of her weekly visits to market in Southwell, Elisabet had recorded that, 'many were talking about the great victory won by the King's army over Parliament at a place called Edgehill and were expecting the men of Parliament now to be subdued and peace to ensue.' She closed the book. So the other Elisabet had lived through a war too, a civil one, Elizabeth wondered if she too had had a relative in the thick of the fighting. She decided that she would don her wrapper and go down and sit by the fire that Mary had lit. The day was surprisingly chill even though the sky was blue and the sun shone. Elizabeth did little but sit by the fire, eventually eat the broth which Mary had left for her and then in the early afternoon read the paper which Mary sent at lunchtime with a tousle-haired boy with grubby knees. There was no news of any great battle and only a short list of casualties. Elizabeth breathed a sigh of relief. Perhaps John was safe for the meantime.

Benjamin Peters ran as fast as his grubby knees could carry him, scuffing up dust from the edge of the road as his little feet pounded along. He had just been coming out of Sparrow Cottage after taking

Miss Bateman the paper when he had heard the school bell. He would be late. As he raced on he wondered what this' new Miss' would do to him? Mr Ratcliffe would have given him a stroke across his hand with the cane for sure but Mr Ratcliffe had gone to be a soldier a month ago.

The 'new Miss', Miss Olivia Mason watched in amazement as the small dust storm revealed itself to be Benjamin Peters. He skidded to a halt in front of her , head down , panting noisily.

"When you have your breath back Benjamin perhaps you would kindly tell me what is amiss," she asked mildly.

Benjamin fought to control his breathing . His eyes travelled from her black, shiny, buttoned boots to her long, blue skirt ,neat, high-collared blouse and up to the slightly amused face regarding him quietly.

"Please Miss," he gulped, "I'd to take a newspaper to the new lady's cottage for mum."

"You have a whole hour for lunch, Benjamin. Surely you could have managed to do it in the time."

"Yes Miss, sorry Miss." Ben scuffed his boots in the dust. He was in for it now. It didn't come. No 'go and stand by my desk' which meant the cane. Instead Miss Mason asked,

"And how is Miss......Bateman, isn't it? She's been ill hasn't she ?"

"Yes Miss, quite poorly, Miss."

"Is she in bed?"

"No Miss, sitting by the fire. My mum's doing everything she can for her, Miss".

"Thank you, Benjamin. In you go now." Ben could hardly believe it. She's a soft one he was thinking when the quiet voice of his teacher came from behind in firm tones. "It will not happen again Benjamin. Do I make myself clear?"

"Yes Miss, thank you Miss." And then he preceded her through the porch and into the schoolroom beyond.

Elisabet was glad when they breasted the hill and could see the roofs of Hockerton peeping between the trees at the bottom of the

slope. Her good leg ached as it always did after taking the weight of the twisted leg for most of the day. She felt weary and longed for the remainder of her pottage to warm her chilled body.

"Where did he say?" Alis Smalles' voice broke her reverie. "Where was the great battle?"

"It was Edgeheath," piped up Ellen Wright, a small, round, know-it-all. She always knew everything and rarely got any of her facts right.

"No, Edgehill, I think he said," answered Elisabet, clicking her tongue to encourage the mare to move a little faster.

"That's what I said, Edgehill," persisted Ellen. "A great battle and a victory for the King and now we can get back to how we were."

"Where were we?" Alis was bemused.

"Yes, it's all over now," Ellen replied with confidence.

"Pray God that you are right." Elisabet murmured.

Her two neighbours nodded and lapsed into silence. They crossed the wooden bridge over the dumble, the mare's hooves making dull thuds on the planking and began to climb the short rise past the church.

"Nearly home." Elisabet remarked more cheerfully.

Mary went to Southwell the next day and sent off the parcel. Elizabeth arranged through Mary also to have a daily paper delivered so that she could keep abreast of the war news now that John was at the front. She spent the next week resting as Anne had been up to see her and had threatened to fetch the doctor to her if she did not. She slowly began to recover from her exertions with the cupboard. The thought of the bag of plaster upstairs kept reminding her that she would only rest for a few more days and then she must bring it down and bury it in the garden. She wondered from time to time why she didn't want to tell Mary and ask for her husband to come and remove it for her. There seemed to be no valid reason except that she had a strong feeling that it was imperative that she should keep the whole thing secret. Anyway it wasn't very heavy and she need only dig a shallow hole.

CHAPTER SIX

"Not there," commanded a quiet voice as Elizabeth bent over to loosen the earth at the edge of the pond with a trowel. "The trooper is buried there."

"Here?" Elizabeth pointed to the ground with her trowel.

"Yes."

I'm talking to a ghost and she's answering me . Why am I not afraid? Elizabeth straightened up and gazed at the woman standing passively by her side. It was the same woman that she had seen in the herb garden , only much more clear and distinct. She could see the coarse weave of her dark brown dress, the dark curls escaping from the white, linen cap, the blue eyes and the healthy, glowing skin--- the woman in the mirror.

"Are you Elisabet Bayteman?" Elizabeth asked gently.

"Yes" The reply was like a sigh. "And are you also?"

Elizabeth smiled and nodded, hoping to be able to ask about the book they she had found upstairs, but Elisabet was fading into the trees of the orchard, wavering, quivering and was gone.

Disappointed Elizabeth picked up the pillow case of plaster bits and hurled it into the pond. It sank with a splash and a gurgle . The lily pads closed over the patch of water momentarily exposed. Elizabeth wondered who the trooper had been and why he had been buried here and not in the graveyard at the church. She turned away. Bill had scythed down the grass and weeds in the garden and Elizabeth thought that when Summer came again it would be lovely to have a seat out here in the sun and dappled shade from the nearest fruit trees. Here she would sit and dream and read and become strong and positive again.

Going along the path to the house Elizabeth was startled by a piping male voice. she looked around.

"I'm here, gal!"

Standing on tip toe so that she could see over the hedge Elizabeth saw a little gnome of a man in the next garden. Her neighbour whom she had never met before. She wondered where he had been hiding himself. Under a toadstool the silly thought came unbidden to her mind . He looked ancient, his back bent like a wind-blown tree.

"You been poorly, gal?" His eyesight was obviously still good.

"Yes, but I feel a lot better now."

"You will here, lovely here, been here all me life, only went away once, didn't like it."

"Oh." Elizabeth wondered how old he was.

"No, didn't like it so I come back sharp. I can remember the old king , when I was a lad."

"Can you?" Elizabeth wanted to ask which king , hoping that it wasn't King Charles.

"Yes I remember King William, then Victoria, my she was there a long time. Then that Edward and now George. I lived the other three out but I shan't live this one out no doubt. Called to see if you would like eggs--- lovely brown eggs I've got. Want some?"

"Yes please if you have some to spare."

"Wouldn't ask if I didn't." He handed her a chipped, blue bowl over the hedge with great difficulty as he was scarcely the height of the hedge himself.

"Want me bowl back though."

"Of course, Mr, er"

"Samuel, Samuel Turner."

"Thank you Mr Turner, er how much for the eggs?"

"Now then gal, it's a gift, to get you better .I shall come and take tea with you when you are well ."

"That would be lovely, when....." But he had gone and Elizabeth was talking to empty air.

Holding the bowl of speckled, brown eggs carefully Elizabeth went down the slope to see Mary coming round the side of the house carrying a covered basket. She saw the bowl of eggs.

"Oh, good, Old Samuel's eggs are quite the best for taste in the whole village, I don't know why. You'll be wanting one for your tea I'll be bound.?"

Mary was hurrying inside and putting her basket down in the pantry. She took out a loaf and a small pie on a saucer.

"New bread," she said rather unnecessarily as the aroma was unmistakable ."just out of my oven so we'll let it cool a while and an apple pie. " She took a stone jar out next with a narrow neck and a cork stopper. "A drop of cream to go with it. Delving further down she brought out a dish with a lid. "And a pat of Mrs Enleigh's butter."

"What a feast, " exclaimed Elizabeth, looking at the sweet-smelling loaf, brown eggs and yellow butter.

"Wholesome too, soon have you well, eating this, food for the gods this is." Mary filled the kettle.

"Shall I make tea now?" She went through into the living room. "Ben's been home and had his tea and gone out to play with Jimmy, his friend so I'm in no hurry." She set the kettle on the trivet and poked the fire. "And he was saying that his new teacher, Miss Mason, was asking after your health."

Elizabeth wondered if anyone in this community did not know about her and she had a sudden pang of fear. Would anyone have recognised her from a newspaper photograph, would anyone inform the police if they guessed or knew that she was hiding from them here? She thought that she had put such fears behind her but now.....

"I said that she said that she might call on you one evening."

"Sorry," said Elizabeth , realising that she had been far away and had not heard a word that Mary had said.

Mary repeated it, thinking that for a moment Elizabeth had looked as worried and haggard as the day she had first come. As Mary cut and buttered bread and boiled her egg in a small saucepan on the fire Elizabeth laid the table and almost just to change the subject, asked, "Do you know anything about the Civil War, Mary?"

Mary paused, spoon in hand as she went to lift the egg from the pan, and considered.

"A bit, I suppose, about around here anyway. Newark was besieged three times because it was a very important place."

This was news to Elizabeth because although she knew that the king had precipitated the war by ruling without Parliament and taking obsolete taxes like Ship Money she did not know any details. She had heard of Cromwell's New Model Army and the two great battles at Marston Moor and Naseby and that to her shame was all.

"Was Newark really an such an important place?" she asked thinking that Mary must have got it wrong. That she was making the place important because it was local. It had seemed such a small, mean place ,admittedly it had been dark when she had passed through.

"Oh yes, Newark stood where any army had to cross the river Trent in the east and there was a lot of marshes around the town then so it was difficult to get round it, the King often came to Newark before the war and stayed in the castle, it was his. The queen came with troops during the war and Prince Rupert raised one of the sieges because the king asked him to."

"Gracious you are knowledgeable," remarked Elizabeth. She sat down at the table and tapped her egg with the spoon. Goodness she thought for the first time in months I feel hungry and she broke into her egg with gusto.

"I'm not really , the man at the library in town could tell you much more."

"Could he?" Elizabeth chewed thoughtfully, wondering if it would be wise to show herself in the town in daylight. "How could I get there?"

"Oh Amos at the inn will take you, well anyone really on Wednesday, it's market day you see. I sometimes go. I could come with you if you like and take you to the library." She wondered if Elizabeth would think her forward for this suggestion.

"That would be lovely Mary-- this Wednesday do you think? I'm sure I'm much recovered and I think the outing would do me good."

Jonah, Amos' jack-of-all-work at the inn had been up since just before dawn clearing out ashes from the inn fire and the kitchen range and laying and lighting the latter. He had collected and washed the used mugs from the night before and as he swept the floor a smile spread over his bony face at the remembrance of George Weaver's antics as pint by pint he had got steadily more drunk the previous evening. It was a good thing that he had Bill Peters to take him home.

Putting the brush away he made for the back door and donned his wooden soled boots and tweed jacket. His best jacket, a present from Amos who had found it had been left behind one night and no one had ever returned to claim it. It was a bit short in the sleeve and he could only fasten the middle button now. Mrs Amos said that he shot up like a weed overnight. The wool tweed was lovely and warm though and it looked just right when he was driving the carriage to Newark market.

Jonah was eager to get out. He took four carrots from a bag in the pantry; now for the best task of the day. He pulled the door shut quietly and went up the rising road , entering a field gate on his left. Turn Close this corner field was called and it included the land on which the inn stood. Jonah thought it was called that because the road turned the corner at the bottom. He stood just inside the gate and feasted his eyes on the one black and three brown mares which stood cropping the grass at the far side of the hedge-rimmed field. He called quietly to them and they lifted their heads and came trotting towards him. He stroked each velvety nose and gave each brown horse a carrot from his pocket. The black mare was nudging him gently with her head and as he gave her the carrot he reached up his arms and put them around her neck, laying his head against hers.

"Bess," he whispered in her ear, "My beautiful Bess."

As Jonah leaned on the fence stroking Bess' velvety nose he thought again of how lucky he was to live in this place and with such a kindly couple as Mr and Mrs Amos. Life has not always been kind to him. His mother had died within two days of his birth and a local woman had been brought in as wet nurse for him and to tend the house. Within six months his father had remarried, a tall widow with suspiciously black hair and a high colour called Mrs Clements. His father, Jonah realised was besotted with her and had no time for his daughter, Selina nor his baby son. Jonah's eldest sister, Matilda was already grown up and married. As the years went by Jonah like Selina began to realise that Mrs Clements, as they always called her, despised them or at least had no care for them whatever. She would attend the local chapel three times each Sunday and put a gold sovereign on the collection plate and invite her friends back to the house for a supper while her stepchildren were sent to their rooms having had nothing. When Selina complained to their father Mrs Clements asserted that they had already been fed and that they were both greedy children. When their father was at the shop which he owned in Nottingham the next day Mrs Clements took a stick to both of them promising more of the same if they dared ever again complain to their father. Selina and he knew that their father would not listen to them anyway so there was no point anticipating further beatings. The two children clung to each other; stole food from the kitchen whenever they could and vowed that when they were old enough they would leave.

One day however the thirteen-year-old Selina came home from school to find him eating orange peel which he had found in the gutter. When she had remonstrated with him his heart-rending cry of, "But I'm hungry Lina," made her determined to do something at once. She stole enough money from her step-mother's purse to pay the train fare to send him to her elder sister and she went to live with the large, unruly family of a Catholic school friend. As soon as she was fourteen Selina found herself a job in a shop and sent back the money she had taken with a letter to their father. He never received it. Within a month of the two children leaving he had dropped dead in his shop of a heart attack. Mrs Clements had sold the shop and the house and left the city.

Jonah lived only two years with his elder sister before she too died in childbirth and her husband sent him to an orphanage. It was here Mr and Mrs Amos had seen him and took him in. When he had eventually told them his story they had tried to find his sister and had even taken him on the train to Nottingham; but he could remember nothing, not even the house he had been born in and really he did not care for there had only been heartache for him there but he would have liked to find his sister Selina.

Elizabeth was ready when Mary came towards the gate. She merely pulled the door shut, realising after only this short time the sense of not locking it for then she did not have to carry the large key around in her bag. The dust at the edge of the road was damp and ribbons of mist swirled above the fields. The air had that dank, late Autumn chill and every spider's web was a pearl raindrop confection.

Elizabeth was warmly dressed in a wool skirt and a long jacket with a big fur collar .She noticed that Mary's black skirt was fading with age as all cheap, black garments did and that her coat was ill-fitting and mended at the cuffs with a band of not quite matching material, to cover the frayed edges Elizabeth surmised. The two women chatted in a friendly way. Elizabeth already valued Mary's common-sense approach to life and her open kindliness. Mary had admired Elizabeth from the first day that she had unpacked her bags and realised what had happened to make her so ill. She had never spoken about it ,it was not her way , perhaps one day Elizabeth would tell her and until that day Mary was content to leave her thoughts unsaid.

"There's Jonah, all ready," Mary announced, pointing to the large old-fashioned Victorian carriage and four horses standing patiently in front of the inn.

"Shall we be the only passengers?" Elizabeth enquired as they neared the conveyance, "and is that Jonah?" She inclined her head towards the young lad holding the near side front horse's head and thinking that he didn't look old enough to be in charge. Mary saw the look ,

"It's all right," she reassured her "he's not as young as he looks and he is a wonder with horses."

Elizabeth was surprised how quickly they seemed to arrive in Newark compared with the night time journey she had made some weeks ago. Many of the trees and hedges were bare of leaves and the fields were ploughed. The landscape was a study in brown. She could see the spire of a church, Mary told her it was the spire of the parish church, across the flat fields and soon their road joined another. Mary explained that this was the Great North Road and then they were crossing a railway and a bridge over a river. A badly ruined castle stood battered guardian on one side.

"There's not much left." Elizabeth pointed to the ruins.

"No," agreed Mary, "Parliament's men made the town's people take it down when the sieges ended."

"So why is there any of it left?"

"Well plague broke out and the troopers left." came the terse reply.

Elizabeth wondered if plague had been a good or a bad occurrence for the town, as it had got rid of their enemy. 'Trooper,' Mary had said, just as Elisabet had.

"What did you mean by trooper?"

"Oh Parliament's men, Roundheads if you like."

Elizabeth was surprised by the bustle and busy atmosphere of the place. They made their way from near the castle down a narrow, cobbled lane between small, old, brick cottages; crossed another road and plunged into an even narrower alley which finally brought them out to a cobbled market place, thronged with people and bright with fresh produce. The church, whose steeple she had glimpsed on the journey, towered to her left and the buildings around the square was an eccentric mix of Georgian and black and white Medieval , mainly three-storied buildings. Elizabeth was very impressed. She had expected a small, mean place from her first impressions.

They wandered around the market .Elizabeth bought oranges which Mary dismissed as too expensive but Elizabeth thought that she might accept some for Ben when they got home. They looked in the windows of the shops and when their feet began to ache and Elizabeth felt tired she suggested a reviving cup of tea.

Rested and refreshed Mary led the way back towards the castle and the library. It was a small, stone-built, Victorian Gothic building standing on the edge of the castle grounds. They entered and Mary asked in hushed tones at the desk if they could see Mr Peasebody.

They were shown through into a smaller, rather dark room and told to take a seat. From the way Mary had spoken Elizabeth expected Mr Peasebody to be a man grown old and bent and dusty from a life of study and cataloguing in the library. However a large, youngish man with a great head of golden-brown hair introduced himself as Leonard Peasebody. He greeted Mary like an old friend before asking Elizabeth how he could help her. His eyes lit up when she mentioned the four magic words; civil war and local history.

He rubbed his hands together eagerly, " I could tell you so much about that but I am sure you will not have that sort of time now so perhaps I could give you a small pamphlet I myself have written?"

"Thank you that would be kind." Elizabeth hardly had chance to get the words out before he was off. He hurried back and proffered a small booklet with a sketch of the ruined castle on the front, a lozenge-shaped badge with lettering on it and the head and shoulders study of two men entitled 'Newark , the key to the north,' by L. M. Peasebody. It was priced at one shilling and sixpence but when Elizabeth opened her bag to offer this amount he waved it away. He disappeared again and returned with a sheet of paper , closely hand-written .He explained that this was a list of general books about the Civil War if she was interested and that the last on the list was a history of Newark by

Cornelius Brown, which unfortunately was a reference book but that she might find some one around here who would lend her a copy.
Thanking him again Elizabeth shook his hand and asked if she might come and see him again if she had any more queries.

He smiled ruefully. “If you are quick Miss Bateman .”

Elizabeth raised her eyebrows quizzically. “I am expecting to be in France shortly, fighting for my king as my forebears here did. He leaned forward and tapped the pamphlet, “and just as proud to do so as I expect they were.”

CHAPTER SEVEN

When Elizabeth arrived home she felt grubby and tired. She longed for a bath. Each time she had used the tin bath before Mary had helped carry it to the living room and place it in front of the fire and then Mary had lugged the buckets of water to fill it for her and Bill had emptied it later. She wondered how she could manage alone. As she put a match to the fire she considered the problem. Watching the flames licking eagerly at the sticks and small logs she thought that if she bathed in the small back room , a kitchen she supposed it was of a sort, she could manage to fill the bath and then rush in here to dry and dress herself in front of the now blazing fire.

It was not as easy as it sounded. The tin bath , although not heavy, was awkward to get down and filling it with buckets of water from the tap took her breath away. With about only a third of the amount that Mary had put in Elizabeth decided it would have to do. She rushed into the living room, drew the curtains and threw more logs onto the fire. The bath water which had only been heated by the previous day's fire was only tepid but it was wonderfully refreshing. She lay in it until she realised that it was cooling rapidly. As she got out and wrapped herself in two large bath towels she thought she heard a sound like two doors being closed coming from the living room. Hurrying into it she knew instinctively that the room had changed. When she looked she saw that it was darker, the fire more smoky as if burning damp wood. She halted at the door, not now wanting to go in even though she was rapidly becoming quite cold, she hesitated .....felt faint.....

Elisabet knelt by the fire which was sulky and smoky. The still damp wood burned fitfully with more smoke than heat. She pushed a few pine cones in, which she collected for this purpose, from a basket by the hearth and watched as the flames brightened. Hearing a sound to her right she turned. Someone stood in the doorway. She saw that it was the strange thin woman who had been poking around by the pond. She was draped in two large pink pieces of cloth. She looked cold.

"Come to the fire." Elisabet spoke with a soft and melodious voice, "Come and be warmed." The woman came down the step, faltered and crumpled up on the floor.

Elisabet got up clumsily as her good leg had gone numb from taking her weight for so long while tending the fire. She bent over the woman. She was still breathing, but cold, so cold. And no wonder thought Elisabet wandering around at night with no clothes on . Her shoulders felt clammy where they were not covered by the strange fleecy material. Elisabet fetched her newly woven blanket made from the last sheep's wool that she had spun and tucked it around the woman tenderly. She turned once more to the fire and began to heap more logs on.

When Elizabeth came to she found herself lying on the carpet. Her eyes roamed the room; curtains at the window now, not shutters; oil lamp shedding its yellow light, no evil smelling candles, the fire burning brightly ,no large dark hole where the range now was; carpet beneath here, no oddly scattered weeds on the floor. Had she imagined the other room and the woman kneeling near the fire who she now knew was Elisabet Bayteman? She moved carefully and realised that she had been wrapped in a coarse woollen blanket. When she felt steadier and her heart had stopped thumping she rose and dressed by the fire, savouring the warmth of it and examined the blanket. It looked like the one upstairs that she had found in the hidden cupboard except that this one was new and seemingly unused. Was it Elisabet's blanket? Of course it had to be and while she had been lying on the floor Elisabet had wrapped her in it. Now, even though she had previously not felt any fear, she definitely knew that Elisabet meant her no harm in fact she had taken care of her. But what did she want? Why did she keep seeing her and how was it all going to end? She must read more of the book and see if it contained any answers .This reminded her of the pamphlet about Newark that she had brought home. She would eat first and then read it. It would give her a background, a framework with which to understand Elisabet's time.

❖

Elizabeth sat by the now fiercely burning fire and thumbed through Leonard Peasebody's booklet. It was set out with headings; first siege, second siege, the queen's visit, Prince Rupert relieves the town and so on and was interspersed with line drawings of the castle, the governor's house and likenesses of the chief participants. Turning back to the beginning she read how the town had been flooded with soldiers soon after the king had raised his standard near Nottingham castle in the Autumn of 1642 and had begun to make its remaining Medieval walls stronger by digging defensive ditches and banks. She learned how Newark was attacked in February 1643 but that the enemy was repulsed after a couple of days. The brave townspeople had rushed out to help the soldiers fight off the enemy with any weapon that was to hand and a little boy had even walked through the streets beating an old drum and shouting to everyone to come out and fight for the king. The king's sconce was then built and the town's walls and ditches made stronger.. Elizabeth wondered what a sconce was until she turned the page and saw a drawing of a star-shaped system of ditches and banks labelled as the sconce. Next she found an account of how the queen had come on her way south with men and guns for the king who was by now in Oxford. Elizabeth read on to the story of the second, longer siege, the appeal to the king for help and the daring dash of Rupert and his men and their successful rout of the Roundheads down Beacon Hill, across the river and the Roundheads subsequent surrender of many cannon and muskets. Finally she got to the end; the third long siege and the king's order for the town to surrender. She discovered that the strange diamond shape on the cover was a siege piece which had been made from flattened out silver to be used as money during the siege. When she got to the end, which mentioned the order to take down the castle as Mary had said and the plague breaking out Elizabeth felt quite sad. How dreadful that the townspeople had endured so much and fought so bravely for over three years only to have to give their enemy the prize that they had denied them for so long and at so much cost to life and property. Elizabeth wondered if men from this village had been fighting to defend the town or to besiege it? And Elisabet Bayteman, what had she thought about the armed struggle that was taking place virtually on her doorstep? Which side had she supported? King or Parliament? She would never know the full story; there would not be an account in any history book about the events in such a tiny village as this one but perhaps when she read Elisabet's book she would find out what she had done and thought. And suddenly Elizabeth knew that what that Elisabet who had lived so long ago had done and thought in her time of war was important to her, very important but she couldn't for the life of her think why. She would begin again tomorrow with Elisabet's book it was much too late now. And she would go and see if there were any records at the church about Elisabet as well. As she went up to bed Elizabeth pondered on the strangeness of how eager men and some women were to enter the fighting; no one then or now could know at the beginning what the outcome might be , did they ever consider it? No she thought not , the beginning was taken up with excitement and brave words, the war itself with brave or even cowardly deeds , it was only the end which was always sad. Win or lose the end would be desolate for those women who saw their sons, lovers, husbands and brothers go and never return.

Next morning dawned bright and sunny but extremely cold. Frost patterns obscured the window glass and icicles hung from the corners of the guttering. Hedges, trees and grass were rimed a hairy white and ice glistened on the puddles. Elizabeth watched Ben Peters sliding on the ice on his way to school and she wished she was six again and as carefree as Ben. He saw her at the window and waved as he went past. Elizabeth came down once Mary had lit the fire. The air was frosty down here too. Not with the sort of cold outside but with Mary's obvious disapproval. Eventually Elizabeth had to ask her what was wrong. Mary rounded on her.

"It's you, you're supposed to be ill, recovering,"

"Yes I am getting better, Mary, largely thanks to you," Elizabeth replied trying to placate this usually placid woman.

"Well, it's no good me taking care of you if you won't take care of yourself," Seeing Elizabeth's puzzled face she explained, "getting that bath down all by yourself, heaving water , washing in that cold, little place, it's enough to put you right back."

"I'm sorry Mary," Elizabeth truly was now that she saw how Mary was worried about her. It was worry not really anger. "I just felt so grubby and I didn't want to disturb you and Bill last night."

"Disturb us, you'd not disturb us at all, next time you just come across and we'll see to it for you !"

"Thank you Mary and again I am sorry," said a chastened but happy Elizabeth. She now realised by her outburst that Mary wasn't simply coming to clean and cook for the money, even if it helped their meagre finances, but because a friendship had grown between them. Elizabeth valued that for she had never truly had a woman friend. She stepped forward and took both of Mary's work roughened hands in hers and looking at her closely murmured,

"Thank you Mary, I value you just as much."

Mary appeared dumbstruck by her words and then she said, her voice thick with emotion, "I know why you are ill and that's why I want to take care of you --Well that's why I did it to begin with but it's more for friendship now. I won't deny that the money is a help too , but now I come because I like you Miss Bateman."

"Elizabeth." said Elizabeth and bent forward and kissed her cheek.

After Elizabeth had breakfasted and Mary had returned home Elizabeth decided to go and call on the vicar. The vicarage was a large, brick, Georgian house reached by a short drive from the top of the church lane. Elizabeth rang the bell and waited in the high porch. The vicar's wife ushered her into her husband's study and glided off silently as if on invisible wheels to go and make some tea.

The vicar , a small, round man with a red face and twinkling eyes exchanged pleasantries with her for a few minutes and then he asked if there was anything special he could do for her. Hoping that he didn't think she needed any spiritual comfort Elizabeth explained her interest in the past history of the village and asked if she could look at the parish registers.

"Certainly," Reverent Mason rose and added, "I'll bring them through from the church. It's rather cold in there and it will be very damp if you are to be sitting long. Perhaps you would like to sit in the dining room there's a fire laid there and it would be easier to lay out the books on the table." He rushed off and reappeared some minutes later followed by his wife carrying a tea tray. "Let us have our tea first, Miss Bateman ," Reverend Mason sat down in the chair next to her as his wife busied herself with pouring the tea. "I have put the books that you require out in the dining room and Dora is putting a match to the fire. It will be quite warm by the time you are ready to begin."

They sipped their fragrantly steaming tea and talked of this and that, touching on village characters and events; there were very few of the latter and that explains thought Elizabeth why everyone knows about me. I'm obviously the only interesting happening for months. Eventually the war news was bound to come up and it did when Mrs Mason , who had added little to the conversation up to this point, asked Elizabeth if she had anyone ' over there'. Elizabeth explained that she had just received a letter from her brother who was now at the front.

"We shall pray for him ," remarked Mr Mason, "as we pray for the safety of all our brave men at the front." He did not add that silently he also prayed for the Germans and their worried relatives . He also added his own plea that it would all end very soon. He did not think that either woman would understand him thinking about the enemy when their own were in such mortal peril and in this he did Elizabeth a disservice.

"Our son, David, has just gone," added Mrs Mason, "and we have had no word from him as yet."

"Try not to worry just yet" consoled Elizabeth, "I'm sure he's written , probably more than once and you will get two or even three all together."

"Yes, I suppose you are right" murmured Mrs Mason as she began to collect up the cups and saucers, "but the waiting and uncertainty are hard, so very hard."

By the way her fingers had picked restlessly at the material of her skirt all the time they had been seated Elizabeth knew that she hadn't the calm assurance in the efficacy of prayer as her husband had.

Eventually she was shown into the dining room and began to search the registers. They went back as far as 1538 so Elizabeth decided she would look for the marriage and death of Elisabet first. She found no entry of any marriage but she soon found the surprising entry of her death in 1643 and next to it was recorded the burial of 'one of her bastard twins.' Looking hurriedly through the births she quickly found the birth of twin boys to 'Mistress Elisabet Bayteman' and their names, John and James. Which one had survived? Going now from marriage to birth to death and back to birth again, slowly working down the years towards the present day Elizabeth discovered that Elisabet's descendants had lived in the village until the late 1800s. By the end of the morning she had worked out a rough family tree.

Thomas, the monk, married Mary Bayteman,
1502-1578
Their son, Thomas, married Elisabet Petters
(1560-1638)
Elisabet, their daughter, had twin sons (1612-43)
John (1643-1760) married Jane Kitchin and James died in 1643
John's son, John, married Frances Maul.
His son, John (1702-91) married Anne Green.
His daughter Elisabet was unmarried (1704-?)
John had three children: Anne (1730-31), Elisabet (1731-??) and John married Alice Peters (1734-80)
Their son John (1768-182?) married Sara??
His son, John (1803-50) married Hope Kempe (1803-??)
Their son, John (1823-61) married Mary Whaite.
His son John born 1856

And there was nothing more no matter how hard she searched the late nineteenth or early twentieth records. It was extremely unsatisfactory considering how well she had done at the beginning even though there were many missing bits! But there was no record of the marriage of the last John Bayteman nor of his death even though she had searched right up to the present year. He must have left the village . And it was infuriating that someone had spilt something dark over the page where the deaths of some of his forebears were recorded. She rose and stretched. Looking at her watch she saw that she had spent the whole morning here. Her hands were dusty and her neck ached. Closing the registers , she picked up her notebook and pencil and went to thank the vicar. He was out but his wife assured her that if she needed anything else she was to come back and they would see what they could do.

As she made her way home she saw Ben Peters skipping ahead of her. A strange thing she thought how the Peters or Petters as it was sometimes written, family had been linked to the Bayteman's and that Mary was her husband's cousin. But perhaps not, in these little places there had always been a lot of intermarriage.

CHAPTER EIGHT

Mary read with dread the headlines of the morning paper trumpeting the news of a big battle. She sat down and read the article carefully. Getting to the end of the report she thought that it may not worry Elizabeth too much ; after all it did say a German offensive and heavy German casualties. Folding the paper, she picked up her bag and shrugging on her everyday coat went across to Sparrow Cottage.

The Reverend Mason read a similar account in his paper as he sat finishing his breakfast, his wife had gone across to get the carriage into Newark. His heart was heavy by the time he had read to the end. He collected his few dishes and stacked them tidily in the sink to await his wife's return and without bothering to put on his coat made his ponderous way to the church to say what he wondered? What were words in the face of such awful happenings.

Basket over her arm Elisabet set off into the village. The four cottages of which hers was one were isolated at the western end of the village. They stood at the top of the track down to Bachelor's Button farm, named after the double flowering button-shaped buttercups which grew in profusion there. Elisabet often picked butterbur there down by the dumble, in fact she had a decoction of it for Dorcas Bylbee's wheezing with her now. She checked off mentally; tincture of barberry for Mistress Wrighte's biliousness; gall paste for the swelling on Christopher Scartcliffe's arm; a paste of cuckoo pint berries for William Ridge's gout and the juice of crowfoot for John Wilson's warts. She also had four brown eggs for Widow Neep and a comb of honey for Widow Maye's daughter Isobel.

As she walked Elisabet saw to her left the brown ridge and furrow of Sparrowthorne Field and two horses waiting to be harnessed in the yard at Sparrowthorne Farm. She waved to Mistress Hazzard standing by the open door.

Elisabet had now reached the centre of the village proper where all the houses and farms clustered around the ancient stone church of Saint Nicolas standing on a pronounced mound at the head of the road to Southwell. She called first to see Widow Neep who lived opposite the church and to give her the eggs.

"They're still not laying," commented the Widow cheerfully as she put the four eggs carefully in a bowl.

"No matter," Elisabet smiled back. She loved this small, indomitable, sticklike woman, "your pig is making up for it, he's fattened up nicely."

"Indeed and nearly ready for the killing, and you shall benefit from it ,never you fret Elisabet."

Bidding her farewell Elisabet went on down the church road to a pair of cottages leaning crookedly against each other. Here she left instructions with Mistress Scartcliffe of how to use the gall paste and with her neighbour to treat her son's warts.

Before making another call she walked further down to where the wooden bridge crossed the dumble. There were often mushrooms for the picking here. None today though so she walked to where the road to Southwell forked in Great Beck Close and was rewarded by a find of two horse mushrooms at the far side. Retracing her steps Elisabet called in to Parsonage Farm with Mistress Wright's tincture and Paisthorpe Farm with the paste for William's gout. Further along the Newark road she called at the last cottage in the village and spent some time with Dorcas Bylbee whose breathing she could hear as she neared the edge of Home Close in which the cottage stood. Elisabet helped her to swallow a little of the decoction which seemed to ease her chest a little and she was able to croak her thanks. Leaving to make her last call on Widow Maye at Burnstoop Farm Elisabet felt that nothing she could offer Dorcas except prayers would help.

The morning was quite spent when she hobbled home, her basket containing the mushrooms and payments of peppercorns, salt and best of all a gift of a complete sheepskin from Richard Wright at Hall Farm. He was a true gentleman Elisabet thought. He said that he had noticed how kind she had been to the sick and aged in the village, asking no payment for the medicines she brought them but especially to walk so frequently to Winkbourne with gifts for the two widows who lived on the estate there and then he had presented her with the sheepskin and had promised a sack of flour to be brought to her cottage that afternoon. How lucky I am Elisabet thought to have such kind neighbours. These people would not turn against her as she knew others had done in the country eager to cry 'witchcraft' if a cure went wrong. With a light heart and a heavy basket Elisabet came at last to her own cottage door.

Jonah, harnessing up the horses, thought about the phrases from the newspaper that he had overheard. Amos, sitting at the kitchen table had been reading aloud the selfsame account as Mary in her cottage while his wife had been frying his morning bacon. Words like a ' curtain of bullets from our gallant defenders of poor little Belgium' had filled him with pride . It all sounded so stirring and exciting, much more so than his own mundane existence. Place names like Wipers and Cambray sounded exotic and strange. Jonah suddenly felt that he too would like to see these foreign parts. He wondered if there were mounted troops in these battles, none had been mentioned. If he decided to volunteer he couldn't be parted from his horses, especially not from his dearest Bess. Arriving at the field where the horses stood by the gate he opened it and in a fit of pure love he flung his long arms around the horse's neck.

Elizabeth too read the leading article with fear. She turned hurriedly to the casualty lists and scanned it quickly for her brother's name. Not listed under the dead...... nor the wounded. She breathed a sigh of relief and the icicle of fear which had at first pierced her breast began to melt a little but only a little for it was quite possible that he may have been hit after this had gone to press .She knew that John must have been in this battle for she had received a field postcard from him; it had been waiting , lying on the floor when she had returned from the vicarage. She got it out again from the pigeon-hole in her writing desk and reread it. On one side it said 'on active service' and her address was written below. To the left of this was her brother's signature agreeing that 'the contents of this envelope refer to nothing but private and family matters'. He had merely crossed out everything on the printed side except 'I am quite well' and 'I have received your parcel' ,dated and signed it . As the card had somehow got wet in transit the pencilled date was difficult to read , the day completely illegible and October 1914 did not help at all to pin down exactly when he had sent it. It had said 'letter follows at earliest opportunity' but if a battle intervened then there might never be an opportunity.

❖

That afternoon a fitful sun appeared so Elizabeth wrapped herself in the blanket of Elisabet's and sitting on a wooden chair brought out specially watched Bill, Mary and their son trying to put the garden into some state of tidiness before the Winter came. Elizabeth had agreed the Bill should use all down one side to grow extra vegetables so a large, weedy patch was slowly being transformed into a freshly dug rectangle. Mary was patiently digging up weeds with a hand trowel and young Ben was picking as many apples and pears as he could reach from the low, gnarled branches of the fruit trees in the orchard where in some places they almost touched the ground. Elizabeth, dozing in the warmth, felt a small hand on hers. Opening her eyes she shaded them with her hand and saw Ben grinning down at her.

" Miss Bateman?"

"Don't bother Miss Bateman, Ben, when she's resting," came his mother's voice from across the patch of grass.

"It's no bother Mary," Elizabeth called back, "I feel quite rested now and would welcome Ben's company. "Yes Ben?" She turned back to face him.

"Will you be able to eat all those?" He pointed a small, stubby finger towards the laden fruit trees. "There's an awful lot , I've picked a whole basketful and there's millions more."

"No, Ben, I don't suppose I shall be able to eat them all myself." Elizabeth's eyes traced the sprinkling of freckles across his snub nose.

"It would give you dreadful tummy ache if you did," Ben advised solemnly.

"It would Ben," His hair as usual stood out from his head in all directions. Elizabeth watched as he pushed his hands through it; a habit of his she had noticed ;saw his mother watching him and hastily tried to smooth it back in place again. The gesture reminded her of her brother John. Fear for him returned again sharply.

"Well to save you from tummy ache I could take some away."

Mary, hearing this called, "Ben, stop bothering Miss Bateman and stop begging!"

"What would you do with them then, I wouldn't want you to be ill eating too many either you know."

"I would take them to school; one for me and everyone of my friends and one for Miss Mason as well," he added

"That sounds like a very good idea to me Ben, lets do it shall we?"

A grin spread across his chubby face and his eyes crinkled up as he laughed with delight.

By the end of the afternoon the vegetable patch was all weeded and dug over and the flower border tidy .Bill and Mary had finished picking the higher apples and pears and Mary promised as they put the assorted containers of fruit into the outhouse that the following day she would sort out the damaged fruit to be used at once. The Peters family left for their evening meal.

Elizabeth was just finishing her small plateful when there was a sharp rapping on the front door.

Her visitor was a tall, rather severe-looking young woman with wire-rimmed spectacles, carrying a leather bag which she put down with a heavy thump on the doorstep.

"Sorry to call on you at such a late hour, Miss Bateman, I'm Miss Mason the temporary school mistress." She extended her hand in greeting.

Shaking the proffered hand and inviting her inside Elizabeth asked, "Temporary school mistress?"

"Oh, yes decidedly temporary, Mr Ratcliffe left rather suddenly; he volunteered when the war broke out and I offered to step into the breach as it were, only for the duration of the war; but I must add that I am enjoying it so far."

"Do have a seat." Elizabeth gestured to her most comfortable chair and asked if her visitor would like a cup of tea.

"No, thank you, I can't stay long. Let me explain, you visited my father to look at the parish records...."

"Then you are.."

"That's right, the vicar's daughter. Anyway Benjamin Peters had mentioned that his mother had taken you to the library in Newark to look up local history so putting these two facts together I thought that you might like to have a look at this."

Here she bent to the bag which she had put down on the floor next to the chair, and hoisted out a large, very heavy, leather-bound tome of indeterminate age. "Cornelius Brown's History of Newark" she announced with triumph as she handed it to Elizabeth, "careful it's frightfully heavy."

Elizabeth was astonished, "But this is the very book that Mr Peasebody recommended."

"When I knew why you had been to the library I knew that you must have talked to Leonard, that's why I brought it."

"You know him?" Elizabeth was surprised what a small world it was in these parts.

"Oh, yes, quite well." Elizabeth noticed her sallow cheeks stain to a rosy glow. And would like to know him better she surmised but only remarked out loud, "Thank you for bringing it, I shall take good care of it please tell your father."

Miss Mason rose to leave. "I did have a second reason for coming, besides seeing if you were feeling any better that is."

Elizabeth's eyebrows rose quizzically.

"I wonder if you would come and talk to the children about London; I believe that you lived there until recently?"

"Goodness." Elizabeth's stomach seemed to come up to her throat. "I thought that I had been so careful." When she did not answer immediately Miss Mason added, "I'm sorry, I shouldn't have troubled you, it's just that the children rarely leave the village, I suspect that there are very few of them who have ever been any farther than Newark and your experience would help them to.. to.." Her voice faltered and died.

"Of course I will," Elizabeth thought of how silly it was of her to be afraid to go and speak to a few country children. As long as she was careful about what she said and didn't mention...

“Good,” said Miss Mason, making for the door, “and perhaps the girls, and the boys as well, would be interested to hear all about the W. S. P. U.”

“How did you...” Elizabeth gasped.

“I recognised you from a photograph in the ‘Suffragette’”

“You‘ve read that here?” Elizabeth was astounded .

“Of course, Hockerton isn’t quite the back of beyond you know. I’m surprised that Mrs Peters didn’t tell you. But perhaps she didn’t recognise you, it wasn’t a very clear picture and I had to rummage through all the back copies to find it and have a second look before I was sure.”

“Mary,” Elizabeth almost shouted, “Mary , what does she know about it ?”

“She reads it too- I used to pass my copies to her to read , she’s on your side as well you know. Your secret is quite safe with us!”

As she made her way home Miss Mason pondered on the condition of the woman she had just visited. Elisabeth Bateman looked exceedingly ill and it was certainly as a result of the harsh treatment she had received in Holloway prison. She wondered idly if she would have been brave enough to have endured the force feeding as Elisabeth and many of the other suffragettes had done? Although she supported their cause and had sent money and purchased the newspaper she had never even marched behind their banner. Was it because she had feared it would upset her father? Or was she secretly a coward? She would never know now she suspected but she was glad that she had not hurt her kindly peace-loving father by joining in acts of vandalism to property as she knew Elisabeth had done. He was, she knew already, mortally wounded by the outbreak of this war and would find it difficult to read of the deaths and destruction which was sure to come; was already at hand since the retreat from Mons.

Reaching the vicarage gate she sighed and tried to dismiss the dread that had crept into her heart when Leonard had told her of his decision to enlist. He was an idealist. He had not realised that this was not one of his glorious battles he could read about from the comfort of his armchair but a real life struggle to the death between too powerful nations. Or perhaps he did realise even more deeply than she did that this was the making of a different kind of history; more bloody, more cruel, more invasive of every family in the land than any of the conflicts that had ever gone before it.

❖

Elisabet jumped at the sound of a loud banging on the door. Moving as fast as she could she drew back the wooden bar and opened the door cautiously.

"Mistress Bayteman?" A large man dressed in a leather jacket and holding a helmet in his hands was looking down at her. Behind him she could see four, no six troopers in their lobster-pot helmets.

"Yes." So Parliament's men were here in her village, what she had dreaded had at last happened.

"Any other in this house?"

"No sir, no one but me."

"You make potions so I am told?" Elisabet knew that if some one in the village had told him there was no point in denying the fact.

"I do sir, to heal if need be."

"I have need of your healing mistress."

Elisabet gestured for him to enter. He ducked under the low doorway and held out one of his hands. It was roughly bandaged with a not too clean piece of rag. Unbinding it Elisabet saw an angry gash, probably made by a sword. She took him through to the small back room where she made her salves and potions. Taking a piece of cambric, much washed and now quite soft, she gently bathed the wound with alder water. The trooper winced as she applied the decoction but stood still and patient as she fetched a small pot of the freshly crushed leaves of Herb Robert and applied these to another small square of cloth , binding it firmly in place.

"Thank you mistress."

"Do not thank me yet for it is still red and hot, you must replace the compress as many times as you are able." She gave him the remainder of the pot and a wad of cloth. "Clean, fresh cloth must be applied each time, trooper."

"Captain Richard Watkins at your service mistress."

"Well Captain, take the pot and return it when it is empty. You may come again if it troubles you further."

“I am in your debt mistress,” he hesitated but Elisabet said curtly, ”Just deal kindly and courteously with my neighbours Captain and you will not be indebted to me.”

“That I will mistress.” He turned on his heel and left. As the door closed behind him Elisabet sank on to the nearest stool with a long drawn-out sigh of relief. Her legs were trembling and her mouth dry. She had spoken to and indeed treated one of the army she had so feared and he had been polite, deferential almost. Be careful she admonished herself, he needed your help this time. Next time he may not be so pleasant.

Elizabeth was at her bedroom window when she heard the unmistakable sound of horses’ hooves again. Standing so that the curtain hid her from view she peered down .The front of the cottage where a small garden and wall normally were was now only separated from the narrow dirt track by a wide, grassy bank. To her right she could see a cloud of dust and then horsemen came into view. She counted them as they approached. Seven, all mounted on tired-looking horses and wearing high thigh boots, leather jackets and lobster-pot helmets. The large man at their head reined in as they came alongside her cottage and dismounted. Taking off his helmet and smoothing down straight, collar-length hair he strode towards the door...

She was awoken much later by a beam of moonlight on her face. So she hadn’t pulled the curtains. How had she got herself into bed? Elizabeth could not remember doing so. Rising and going to the window she opened the casement and looked out. The night air was bitingly cold. Bright stars were scattered across the moonlit sky. There was no wind, no movement, no sound, no light anywhere. Standing there getting more and more chilled, Elizabeth wondered which century she was looking out at now. It was too dark to see any details and too cold to stand here much longer she thought. Slamming shut the window and pulling the curtains she hurried back to bed, diving under the covers and lay there shivering until warmth slowly crept back and she slept.

❖

The sun rose higher and higher in the sky, melting the frost and ice which had formed in the night but Elizabeth slept on. Twice Mary tiptoed up to peep at her. Finally leaving her to sleep she wrote a note and left it on the table with the newspaper, put the guard around the fire and left for home and the many tasks awaiting her there.

It was nearly noon when Elizabeth woke. She gaped at the time which showed on the small bedside clock. Her head felt heavy and her fingers clumsy as she dressed. I've slept too long she decided as she went downstairs. Having washed and breakfasted she opened the paper. There was more news of the German attacks on Ypres and today a surprisingly long list of casualties again. She brushed her hair vigorously and knotted it at the nape of her neck. Deciding that it was too late to do much she may as well sit by the fire and read Elisabet's book.

Elisabet had recorded the arrival of a small troop of Parliamentary soldiers in the village and how their leader, a captain, had come to her with an infected sword cut to be treated. Elizabeth rested the book on her lap .So the troop of men she had seen had come here, had come to this house. Was that why Elisabet had hidden this book and the other things? Had she written something in here that if found by the Roundhead soldiers would be dangerous to her? Elizabeth read on. There were many more references to the troopers; quartering themselves in the Vicarage and Manor Hall Farm . Outrage and hurt was written large on the page describing how they had stabled their horses in the church and demanded money not only from the churchwarden in this village but also in the neighbouring village of Upton to satisfy their demands.

Elizabeth closed the book hurriedly and hid it under her skirt when she heard Mary's light tap on the door and her voice call as she opened it.

CHAPTER NINE

Mary was holding out a letter and smiling, “So you are awake at last, you have had a long sleep, I must say.” She didn’t add that it had done Elizabeth good because from her drawn, white face it patently hadn’t. Mary began to fear that there was something more wrong with Elizabeth than the need to rest and eat well.

Elizabeth took the letter eagerly. Mary saw a smile light up her wan face. But then Elizabeth glanced at the envelope and the smile froze.

“Is anything wrong?” Mary asked gently handing her the letter opener.

As if in a trance Elizabeth took it and slit open the top. There was one folded sheet inside. It read; ‘Your brother has asked that we should inform you if anything should happen to him.’ Mary saw Elizabeth’s already pale face blanch, her hand went to her chest.

“What’s wrong?” Mary asked again more urgently this time. But Elizabeth was reading the only other sentence written there. It said; ‘He has been slightly wounded and is in base hospital, he will write to you from there.’ There was no signature. Such a cold, heartless missive. So they had still not forgiven her then. Their hearts were still hardened against her no matter what. She folded the sheet and returning it with shaking hands to the envelope, looked up at Mary bending over her,

“It’s my brother. He’s been wounded.” And fainted.

When she came to it was to find Mary holding the bottle of smelling salts under her nose and trying with her free hand to rub Elizabeth’s ice cold hands in turn. Elizabeth took a deep breath, coughed and pushed the little bottle away. Mary had covered her up and now she went and fetched the medicine which the doctor had prescribed.

“Nearly all gone,” she commented measuring out a spoonful and offering it for Elizabeth to swallow. “Shall I go and get some more for you tomorrow?”

"I think perhaps I shall ask the doctor to call and have another look at me here." replied Elizabeth weakly, "I don't feel at all well at the moment and he did say that I was to contact him again if there was no improvement. Perhaps I shall go down and ask Anne if I may use her telephone later."

"No, I'll pop down and do it for you ." Mary put the stopper in the bottle and went to wash the spoon. Returning she lifted Elizabeth's legs on to a stool. "But I'll stay here while you have a bite to eat."

"I'm not really hungry Mary."

"You must eat something." Mary insisted. "An egg, do you think that you could manage an egg?" Elizabeth agreed to try more to please Mary than anything. After she had eaten some of the boiled egg and had a few minuscule bites from the thin slice of bread and butter and was sipping a cup of tea Mary asked, "What's this then?" She held up Elisabet's book.

"I found it. It's a very old book written by a woman who lived in this very cottage."

"Can you read it?" Mary opened the book and peered rather short-sightedly at the minute writing, "It's very small."

"It's not too difficult to decipher it once you get used to the style of the letters, I'm only reading a bit at a time."

"And tiring yourself out." Mary sniffed, "I'll put it here then. Now you rest while I go down to Mrs Enleigh's. " She placed the book on the mantle shelf above the fire and was gone.

Elizabeth dozed by the fire. Once or twice she woke up and saw a different room. This room, but again there was the earthen floor and the weeds. The shutters were drawn back and there was a strange translucent material in the window where the glass should have been. The fire was again in a big, open hearth but now with an iron pot suspended over it. The room was strangely bare, no pictures, no mirror only a wooden table and bench. The second time she awoke in this changed room she saw that she was sitting on a wooden settle with a high back. One leg was resting on a wooden stool. It was a strangely twisted leg, bare with the misshapen foot encased in a soft soleless shoe tied with a leather thong. Looking at her hands she saw that they were rough and stained. Putting her hands to her head she straightened her linen cap , feeling , not hair pulled back but curls at each side of her face. Before she fell asleep again Elizabeth knew that for a short time she had truly become Elisabet.

❖

Mary was out of breath when she reached the farmhouse. Anne was throwing handsful of grain to her hens.

"Good afternoon Mary," she paused, "Whatever is the matter?"

"It's Miss Bateman, Mrs Enleigh. She didn't get up until a little while ago, but it wasn't a good rest because she looked dreadful. I gave her a letter which had come by this morning's post. She read it and fainted."

"Goodness, how is she now?" Anne gestured that Mary should come into the kitchen with her.

"I brought her round and gave her medicine and a bite to eat. Not that she managed to eat much of it at all. I've left her dozing by the fire. But there is hardly any of the medicine left and she feels that she wants to see the doctor. I think she does too."

"I agree," Anne moved into the sitting room where the telephone was kept, "and the doctor needs to come to her as she is certainly not well enough to go down into Southwell." She lifted the receiver off the hook and gave the number. She was soon through to the doctor's house. Mary waited while Anne explained. The person on the other end spoke for quite some while. Anne's face grew grave and still as she listened. Finally she said, "I understand, thank you." She replaced the receiver with a heavy sigh. Mary waited.

"Do sit down Mary." Anne said quietly, sinking into the nearest chair. When Mary had seated herself gingerly on the very edge of the chair opposite Anne explained. "Doctor Grant will be unable to come until tomorrow. Quite unlike him I know, but he and his wife have just this morning received some distressing news... a telegraph..."

"Oh dear," Mary knew, everyone did even after only a few months of war that telegraphs were bad news.

"Their son, Andrew - Andy - is missing."

"Not dead then thank goodness."

"No, but Mrs Grant has taken it very badly. Of course the doctor is extremely worried as well. So you see he really cannot leave Mrs

Grant this afternoon but he will be here first thing in the morning." Mary sighed. Anne continued, "You go home. I'll go up and see Elizabeth and sit with her a bit, then perhaps you would see that she is all right before you go to bed?"

Mary agreed, thanked Anne and made her way home.

Anne spent a couple of hours with Elizabeth, chatting and drinking tea. She seemed Anne thought a little better and relieved that at least she knew that her brother was being well cared for in the hospital. She saw the even this was better than not knowing what had become of him like the Grants. Eventually, satisfied with Elizabeth's promise to rest Anne left to acquaint Mary with the condition of their patient and hurry home to prepare David's evening meal.

So when Mary came just after it had got completely dark she found Elizabeth in bed. She bustled round making everywhere tidy, raking out the fire after making Elizabeth a hot drink and putting a hot brick from the oven in the bottom of the bed. Sure that Elizabeth would soon be asleep, Mary left. She did not notice that the old book had gone from the mantlepiece.

Elisabet put down her pen and stretched. Time to close the shutters. Looking out she saw there was a bright moon, a very bright moon. Good, that would make moving across the fields easier but it would also be easier for them to be seen approaching the village. Closing the shutters she looked at what she had written and remembered that remarkable afternoon.

She had gone along the path across the fields with her basket. She had collected acorns. These she would pound into a powder to stop vomiting. Nearby was a bush laden with the blue-black sloes whose boiled down juice was invaluable all through the year to those villages with bowel flux. With her basket now almost full she added leaves from the nightshade growing against the thorn bushes. There were any number of these, this large field, one of the three large fields of olden times was not called Sparrowthorn for nothing! The nightshade leaves would be bruised to release the juices and applied to kill pain and reduce the heat and redness of inflamed skin. She made her way along the top of Sparrowthorn Field to where she knew polybody grew amongst the mossy stones and tree stumps. It was one of the potions that she used as a purge. She would just pick some pennyroyal that grew near the pond in this part of the field, now enclosed, called Well Furrows. She used quite a lot of this at certain times. The village women often came for it to promote their courses. Elisabet used it with caution for she suspected that many a dead child was expelled which otherwise would have been born alive but it was always difficult to know if her patients were telling the truth.

Elizabet turned to look at the huddled roofs of Southwell and the two great towers of the Minster church which on a clear day like today were visible from here. For some reason it made her think of her Grandfather Thomas, the monk, and his arrival here. She remembered sitting on her Father's knee when a girl as he had explained how his father had told him that the king's 'visitors' had been only too ready to listen to gossip because they journeyed so fast on the king's business they had little time to verify these stories and had perhaps had no inclination to do so. Her Father had gone on to explain that the first his Father and the other monks at Rufford had realised something momentous was about to happen was when a Doctor Layton arrived at the monastery in the icy days following Christmas 1535. Her grandfather had thought at first that this doctor was merely another traveller seeking a few days shelter for he had only spoken to Abbot Thomas and one or two others, not her Grandfather, and left. But he had left a worried and strangely unsettled community behind and soon her Father said they were to learn that the abbot and six of the other monks had been accused of dreadful crimes in the monastery and doing unspeakable things to local women. Her Father had never divulged what these terrible things might have been, perhaps he himself didn't know. But he had told her that the following year four different men, some of them local gentry, had spent many days making great lists of everything that the monastery had, even the phial of the milk of The Blessed Virgin. And then Grandfather Thomas and his fellow monks had been turned out and he had come here, just a few miles away to Hockerton and married Grandmother.

Elizabet scanned the horizon over to her left . She could just make out the dark mass of Rohagh, its tall trees, roaming deer , sunlit, flowery glades, even the holy well once belonging to the abbey all gone to a greedy friend of King Henry. But he had not lived to enjoy all his ill-gotten wealth reaped from the faithful work of countless brothers and lay brothers over hundreds of years. No, her Father had remarked, God was just and had struck him down only nine months later. Elizabet sighed and turned back to walk along the high ground. It was all so long ago and now she must do her poor best to help the people she knew with the herbal remedies passed down to her from her Mother and Grandfather.

As she neared the pond Elisabet thought that she heard the sound of leaves rustling. It could not be the wind, the late afternoon was still and cold. She halted, straining her ears she heard the sound again. Not leaves, something moving on the ground. An animal? Slowly and quietly she moved towards the pond for this was the direction the sound had come from. The pond was round and tucked into the top corner of the field. It was edged with alder bushes and trees, a dark and mysterious place. From the far side came a low moan. A wounded or dying animal then. Moving with even more caution, for oft times she knew a beast in pain will lash out even at a friend if it was a domesticated animal and this was probably wild. Elisabet crept round the edge of the pond and saw in the hollow at the base of one of the trees the crumpled figure of a man.

"What ails you friend?" Elisabet asked quietly. There was no reply other than a another low moan. Weaving under the low branches, bent almost double, Elisabet came at last to stand over the man.

He lay on his front with his legs tucked up to one side and his face turned away from her. Elizabet could see that he once had a horse for the butterfly spurs still clung to the heels of his very muddy boots. Above the boots was a frill of dirty, ripped lace and his breeches were so matted with dirt it was impossible to tell their material or colour. His deep-wine coloured coat and lace cuffs were similarly damaged; Elisabet wondered if he had crawled to this spot. His long, curled hair obscured his face, his hat lay to one side, its bedraggled feather dipping in the pond's water.

Elisabet bent down and brushed his hair from his face. A youngish face, oval, but broader at the forehead than chin, which was marred with downy stubble. Using the hem of her skirt Elisabet wiped soil from his cheeks. His eyes opened, large, green eyes with long eyelashes, gazed painfully up at her.

"Help me," he whispered through parched lips.

"Where are you hurt?" Elisabet gently cradled his head. He gazed helplessly at her. "Do you know where you are hurt?" She asked again. There was no answer, his eyes closed.

Elisabet sat and wondered what to do. He was obviously a cavalier by his dress. She could not ask men from the village to help as this may alert the troopers. She must move him. The day was drawing on and already the air was colder. She must get him to shelter or he would die here of cold. And the nearest and safest shelter was her own cottage.

Her brain ticked rapidly through the obstacles she faced to get him there. He had to be able to walk, she could help him but she could not do a lot for although he did not appear to be a very tall man he was broad-shouldered and well built, a heavy man. She must not be seen coming back here again so soon so they could not attempt the move before nightfall. The only thing in her favour was that here they were at the top of the ridge above the village; it was a gentle, downhill journey.

She thought she would cover him with her cloak and come back later with a potion to revive him enough to get him down the fields and through her orchard. Once inside she could examine him and tend his wounds. She had sat so long that her bad leg ached. She must move. As she adjusted her position his eyes opened again. Putting one hand either side of his face she looked hard at him, willing him to understand.

"I shall come back in the dark. I shall bring something to make you well." His eyelids flickered. Did his understand?

"I shall cover you with my cloak until I return, do you understand?" An imperceptible movement of his head she took to mean yes. Rising, she untied her cloak and tucked it around him. Making sure that he was as well covered as he could be she put his hat on his head and said, "Rest now, it will not be long, you will soon be safe."

❖

And now, wrapping her blanket around her shoulders she picked up the leather bag. In it was a leather bottle of water, some soft cloths, an infusion of lavender flowers in a small stoppered bottle, and another bottle containing a syrup of great wild lettuce to ease his pain and a stout staff.

She saw that when she arrived at the pond the cavalier had hardly moved. His forehead felt cool as did his hands. Taking a cloth she soaked it in the lavender infusion and carefully bathed his hands and face and smoothed back his hair. As she had expected it revived him and she was able to moisten his cracked lips with water. Gradually she managed to get him to a sitting position leaning against the alder tree. Now she persuaded him to take a few sips of water and a little of the lettuce syrup.

It was bitterly cold by now and Elisabet realised that she had to somehow get him moving. Reaching for the stick she pressed his left hand around the fork at the top and putting her arm under his right one she whispered, "Try to rise, gently now, lean on me." Slowly and awkwardly he pushed himself up. Leaning now against the bole of the tree and nearly upright he rested . "Good," Elisabet encouraged him. And then a little later, "come, we must make our way down here." Elisabet pointed in the direction of her cottage, thinking that it would be a minor miracle if they got there.

CHAPTER TEN

Elizabeth, reading the diary, was amazed at the resourcefulness of this bygone woman. She saw that although darkness had fallen it was still quite early . She would go down and see if the fire was still warm, maybe she would be able to heat some milk for a warm drink. Rising she moved to the door. There was a quiet scraping creak from below. An intruder? Voices, a woman's and then a deeper male voice. Mary and Bill? Creeping to the door she tip toed halfway down the stairs and peered down into the living room.....

The journey across the fields was truly a nightmare for Elisabet and the wounded cavalier. Even leaning heavily on her and using the stick he was unable to go more than a few yards without stopping. His breath rasped in his throat and his chest heaved with the effort of dragging his wounded, cold and weary body over the furrows and ridges of Sparrowthorne Field. Slowly, oh so slowly, they stumbled along; the only sounds their own footsteps; Elisabet's hippity-hop and the cavalier's slow dragging tread. All the while Elisabet was on edge and listening for every sound, ready to dive on the ground as there was no other cover, if she heard the troopers from the village. The nearer that they got to her cottage the more acute the danger of being seen or heard became. An owl hooted softly and small rodents scurried across their path. Elisabet could now see the darker shape of the cottages against the night sky quite close at hand. They reached the top of her orchard and here they rested yet again.

"Nearly there." Elisabet whispered to the man sagging by her side. She knew his strength was nearly spent. And then after what seemed an eternity she was pushing open her own door and hearing the familiar scrape of the bottom on the flagstones and the creak of the hinges. They stumbled into the room. Elisabet lowered her companion gently on to the wooden settle, stirred the fire to life with a few twigs and lit a candle.

"This is my home, you are safe now."

"Who else is here?" His voice was soft and gentle.

"No one but me, Mistress Elisabet Bayteman." He made no answer. "Could you not trust me to know your name?"

He gazed blankly at her, "I do not remember." He said helplessly.

❖

Elizabeth, descending the remaining steps came to the living room door. Elisabet stood looking down at a man slumped on the wooden settle. She looked tired and dirty, they had just come in even though it was quite dark outside. Elizabeth could only see the side of the man's head and shoulders but by the hair and the ruined lace collar she could tell that he was one of the King's men. Slowly she realised why the book had been hidden. This man's enemies held the village, his presence here was dangerous and Elisabet's book contained his story. As she watched the scene blurred and became foggy as if a mist was rising from the floor and she saw no more. Slowly she crept back upstairs and, opening the book again, continued to read.

❖

Elisabet found a lump the size of a pigeon's egg on the cavalier's head. That she thought accounted for his memory loss. As she examined his wounds, cleaned and bound them she realised from the answers to her questions or rather lack of any that he did not remember anything before she had found him. She consoled him that he would remember as he rested and healed. She discovered a musket wound in his left shoulder. The flesh was torn and discoloured around the entry point and as there was no exit on the back of his shoulder the ball was still embedded in the wound. That was bad thought Elisabet, for it was something that she could not remove it was not visible and therefore too deeply inside. He also had a long gash down his leg and his left arm. His hands and knees were scratched and torn where he dragged himself over the ground like a wounded animal.

When Elisabet had done all she could to make him comfortable for the time being she heated him some pottage and held the bowl while he spooned it up hungrily.

"You must rest now," she said as she helped him to a mug of small beer, which he drank thirstily. She helped him up the steep and narrow stairs with difficulty and to her own bed. He fell into it and was asleep as soon as his head touched her goose-feather pillow. Elisabet covered him over tenderly and made her way downstairs to a hard bed on the floor in front of the dying fire.

❖

Doctor Grant's arrival was marked and commented on by all who saw him enter the village the following morning as he drove in, cars were a very strange occurrence here. Amos, watching the doctor's car turn the corner by the top of the Southwell road in a haze of blue smoke and dust muttered,

"Them dirty, noisy things. Didn't ought to be allowed. You'd think he'd have more sense him being a medical man."

"Is the doctor's car the only one around here?" Asked Jonah who had come to join him at the window.

"No boy, I seen a couple down in Southwell and I dare say that you've seen some in Newark too."

"One or two, they frighten the horses they do."

"Aye and folk too, like as not. Tis not healthy all that smoke and noise. Pity the doctor got rid of that nice little pony and trap that he had, well turned out little rig it were."

"Do you think that a lot of people will soon be buying them, and that they won't need horses?"

"No boy, who'd want to, except for doctor's and such like who are not like us. Folk like us know that you can depend on a horse. Feed it, groom it and it won't let you down not like them there machines , they is always breaking down so I've heard. Why even the army uses horses."

This last statement roused an uneasy feeling in Jonah's chest. He had heard that horses were being collected from their owners and taken to the war. "Will they come for our horses?"

"Mine, boy, mine, I don't know do I? If they do they do there's not much I shall be able to do about it. But how some folk in this village will get about if I have no transport I don't know, really I don't."

Jonah thought of Bess. If they came and took then he would go too. She needed him to rub her down and feed her, no one else would know how to do it properly. And he needed her because he loved her so. An orphan with no living kin that he knew of Bess was mother and sister to him, where she went he would go too.

❖

Mary waited downstairs while the doctor examined Elizabeth in her tiny room above. He had to stoop to avoid hitting his head on the low beams. His advice to continue to rest and take the medicine of which he had brought a fresh supply remained the same. He sat down on the edge of the bed and gazed at her kindly.

"What is troubling you, Miss Bateman? Can you tell me? I may or may not be able to help but even if I can't things are often better for being taken out and aired in daylight."

Elizabeth bit her bottom lip and said nothing.

"Come along, what is it?"

"Is my heart very bad doctor?"

"It's damaged and weak, certainly, it needs to be treated gently. Worry will not help you know."

"Would that cause me to see or hear things; things that I know cannot possibly be there?"

"No, why ever should you ask such a thing?"

"I think then that I must be having nightmares."

"I'm not surprised." The doctor delved into his bag. "You're worrying about your brother, aren't you?"

Elizabeth nodded. "I can't help it."

"I understand, none of us can."

"I'm sorry doctor, I shouldn't burden you with my worries when you and your wife have also had bad news."

"I think," said the doctor slowly and carefully as if trying out the words for the first time, "that having had a similar experience, shall we say, I can understand much better. I cannot tell you that there is no need to worry and if I tell you not to that would be foolish of me. But I can give you something to help you sleep and I will come and see you again next week."

❖

The days passed slowly for Elizabeth resting in bed. Mary came every day as usual and little Ben called on his way back from school. Sitting on the end of her bed he would amuse her with his tales of what he and the others had been doing all day. Elizabeth had sent a short note by him to Miss Mason assuring her that as soon as she was up and about again she would fulfil her promise to come and speak to the children. She dipped into Cornelius Brown's History of Newark, looking at the line drawings of the town from different sides, the castle, Anglo-Saxon pots, combs and shards, and aspects of other areas of the town that she had never seen but was now determined to visit as soon as she was able. She confined her reading to the earlier history, learning about Bishop Alexander, who had built the castle and procured from King Henry a grant to hold a five day fair in the town near Saint Mary Magdalene's day. She read about the sudden death of Edward's beloved Eleanor in the village of Harby to the north and the vexed question of whether the Beaumond Cross was in fact one of the 'Eleanor crosses' .She found the law suits entertaining to read and also the dreadful doings of John of Oxford who had 'fleeced Robert ffiskerton of twenty-six shillings and eightpence' and how the citizens of Newark were ' prone to stick with daggers their neighbours with fatal consequences.'

She pointedly read nothing about the Civil War period and she locked Elisabet's book away in her writing desk. Anne called most days with little delicacies to tempt her appetite and Miss Mason sent her some amusing novels with the reply to her note. The newspapers were dire to read. Headlines like 'German dash for Calais stopped by allies' or accounts like the one how Ypres, the jewel of Flanders with its rich architecture, towered, pinnacled and carved buildings was being steadily pounded, blackened by fire, battered by shells and was crumbling into ruins because of the continued bombardment. Worst of all were the casualty lists. Elizabeth was also not keen on the advertisements exhorting young women to persuade their sweethearts to join the army today! Surely, she felt a man should decide for himself without some young thing pushing him into it by clinging on to his arm, batting her eyelashes at him and wheedling him to join up.

Her brother had sent her from hospital a postcard , a cartoon type one you might have bought at the seaside before the war. There was a picture of a British bulldog and when it was inverted it said 'puts the Germans to flight' but it took her some minutes to work out that the bulldog had become a fat German, pack on back, spiked helmet on head, looking sheepishly over his shoulder as his short legs took a great leap, presumably back towards Germany. On the reverse John had written, 'this is NOT amusing at the moment!' Elizabeth didn't think so either but it was clever. The reverse side so amused Ben when she showed it to him the following afternoon that she gave it to him to take home.

The weeks dragged by. Elizabeth saw no more incidents nor heard anything. Convinced that she was recovered she took to coming downstairs every afternoon and sitting by the fire to do a jigsaw which Mary had purchased for her. The days grew more dark and dank, morning came later and night fell earlier. She had waited patiently for a letter from John and eventually it came. The battle for Ypres had ground to a halt .The German advance had been stemmed for the time being at least and John wrote that he was much recovered. This news was a double edged sword for if he was better then he would soon be back in the thick of the fighting again. He had received a piece of shrapnel in his left arm which was now completely healed and he would be eligible for home leave before rejoining his unit. 'I don't know what the parents wrote to you ' he said in his letter, 'but would you try and reply kindly to them for my sake. For if anything should happen to me then they only have you.' Elizabeth pondered this. She did not want to reply to the heartless couple of sentences her father had bothered to send. She thought of his stern face and his rigid , unbending ideas. He could not make the first move of reconciliation. It was not in his nature. But her mother, she was different. She was a gentle peaceable woman, John was like her in his ways, and I am like father thought Elizabeth with a pang of self realisation, that's why I don't want to be the first to bend either. I will. I will for John and for mother's sake. So she decided that she would write today and then when she wrote to John she could tell him with a clear conscience and quite truthfully that she was making a beginning to heal the breach for she realised that all would not be well after one letter.

He had written about the battle; of how they had arrived and had to dig holes for protection which had soon become linked to form a rudimentary trench system, of men sheltering in ditches a few feet deep, knee-deep in water and how at some places along the line where the land was too sodden to dig they had been forced to get behind a pile of sandbags and brushwood as the German onslaught fell upon them. 'I was so proud of the way my men stood and gave all they had got' he continued , 'rifle fire spat from their guns as if they had machine guns. The Germans were advancing in such closely packed masses we could hardly miss them. It was like a fairground booth where you fire at sitting ducks. I don't know what their commanders were thinking of to let them continue advancing like that, I was sickened by the slaughter I can tell you by the time I was wounded and out of it. But I am pleased to know that since I have been here we have won the battle as we have also taken a good few casualties. They were good lads,' her brother continued,' those men of my regiment, not well educated, just working class but they were long service regulars, the shilling a day men who knew how to fight. They were told to hold the ground and they did.' Elizabeth thought that it was strange that he was writing about these men as if they had ceased to exist.' I am sending you dear Sis , a small bit of shell which came calling you need not fear that by sending you this we shall leave ourselves short, no we have plenty more , they come to call on us every day. We were having tea when it came with its usual cheerful whistle, sailed over our heads and burst in the middle of the road. It fell behind an ambulance, just missing it , we thought we had been lucky but not so for it had a cheerful ,singing friend which just had to follow it. I was hit in the arm and my lieutenant in the leg. We were both carted off, he is the lucky one in a way for his wound was a 'Blighty one'. Do keep it as a souvenir'. There was then a bit about some old school chums that he had met up with in hospital and finally the plea again for chocolate and cake. He said it was to distribute amongst the chaps but Elizabeth knew what a sweet tooth he had. She wondered if he would possibly get up here for his leave. It was something to look forward to, something to get really well for.

❖

A few more days passed before Elizabeth was well enough to walk out in the village. It would soon be Christmas and John had written again to ask if she would be able to meet him in London as he thought this would be best. Elizabeth was afraid to go. She was much better now and she looked quite healthy. She could be seized by the police and sent back to prison so easily if she was recognised in London. She wrote back straight away explaining the position and went down to the post box in the afternoon murk to send it with a heavy heart for she knew that John would probably not be able to travel all the way op here in the leave time he had; she would miss seeing him. However he wrote by return that his leave had been fixed and that he would come. Elizabeth was overjoyed.

She called in at the schoolroom another afternoon, a few days before the school finished for the Christmas holidays. Anne had brought for her some little gifts and chocolate bars for the children. Miss Mason was pleased to see her well again. They talked together, watching the children at play and they decided that Elizabeth would come and give her talk in January. Miss Mason rang the hand bell and the children walked in quietly and stood behind their desks. They greeted Elizabeth with a singsong, 'Good afternoon Miss Bateman' Their eyes shone and they were smiling when she distributed the small gifts and Miss Mason also reminded them to thank her for the apples which had arrived each day by way of Ben. She left with her ears ringing with thanks and wishes for a 'Merry Christmas.' It will certainly be that thought Elizabeth, smiling happily as she made her way home.

Elisabet's cavalier rested and slowly the grazes and bruising on his hands and legs healed and faded. Elisabet bathed the lump on his head with the coldest water she could obtain from the well and this too subsided but his memory did not return or if it had he did not divulge any more details to her of where he had been wounded or who he was.

One day she asked him what she might call him as he had not remembered his name. He thought for a minute before he replied that he could remember the name John but he did not know if it was his name or not but she should use it until he remembered his own. So Elisabet had to be content with that. She was more worried about his other injuries; the two long cuts on his arm and leg were very slow too heal, much more so than she would have expected of a man of his age and general health. For he had obviously always enjoyed good health and been used to good food and plenty of it. But most of all the musket wound in his shoulder was her deepest concern as it oozed pus and was going an unhealthy shade. She had put mould from a bit of bread which she had left uneaten for this purpose on it every time she had changed the pad but to no avail. As soon as he was stronger she must get him to the barber-surgeon and that meant getting him to Newark and back. She could use her horse and cart but it would be a difficult and probably dangerous journey. And she would have to cut his hair.

One day when he mentioned the danger that he might be to her as he had seen the heads of the parliamentary troopers as they had ridden past the window Elisabet had put it to him that his hair would be the first thing that would give them away and to her surprise he told her to "Lop it off, straight away." And so she did .

"Now you look exactly like a Roundhead " she laughed.

"Then that is what I shall be. John, the Roundhead!"

CHAPTER ELEVEN

John, the Cavalier, thought about what might happen to Elisabet if the troopers found out about her hiding him. Although he doubted that they would hurt her they could make life difficult for her in a myriad of ways. So far he had been too weak to leave this small, upper room but now he felt strong enough to venture downstairs. He knew Elisabet was concerned that she could do little for his shoulder and in truth he would not tell her that each day the arm and hand became more useless and painful. Now there were times when he could no longer feel his fingers. He feared that the musket ball was pressing on a vital part which somehow governed his arm, how he did not know. Soon he must ask for more of the potion to dull the pain. But not yet. He must not worry her more for she had a great enough burden already while he was here. But he must hide the coins which lay in a heap under the bed where he had managed to tip them when Elisabet had said that she would take his coat to clean and mend it. Gold coins in this mean hovel, should they be found, would bring suspicion on them.

Waiting until Elisabet had left the cottage to tend an old woman , whom she called Widow Neap, he sat on the end of the bed wondering where to hide them. With only three rooms there was little choice. This room had a reed and plaster floor and the room below had trodden clay, smoothly polished over time by the passage of countless feet. He wondered what the little back room floor was like where Elisabet kept her potions.

Pulling on his breeches as best he could and tying them he moved unsteadily to the door. The stairs seemed steep and high but managing to cling to the wooden handrail with his damaged left arm and levering his right hand against the opposite wall he slowly and painfully made the descent. By the time he reached the bottom he was trembling like a leaf and sweat poured down his face. He sat down on the bottom step until he felt able to move. The medicine or still room was small and rather dark. There were sacks and barrels, pots and basins as well as herbs drying, soaking and being pounded. It smelled like an apothecary's shop. Looking at the floor he found that it was made of clay tiles about a foot square. Prising one up in a corner he scraped a hole by alternately using a knife and a spoon until he had a hole deep enough to hide the coins. He packed as much earth back as he could and replaced the stone. Testing it with his foot he thought that it now looked exactly as it had done. He carefully swept up the spare earth and carrying it in a bowl threw it out of the door. He had just got back to the upstairs room when he heard Elisabet return. When all the fighting was over and the King had subdued these rebels he would come back and unearth the coins and give them to Elisabet. He flopped down and without even removing his breeches, pulled the blanket over him and slept with exhaustion.

❖

"No!, no!, you can't have her, you can't!" Jonah's shouts brought the women out from Bank Cottages and Miss Mason, who was crossing from the vicarage, halted at the school room porch.

Amos was holding Jonah back with difficulty, his arms clasped around the boy's middle. His wife, Martha, stood on the doorstep wringing her hands helplessly. The sergeant, who had come to requisition all four mares looked ill at ease but he carried on harnessing them all together. As the horses were moved away Jonah went berserk

"You shall not have Bess! Bess!" he yelled as the mare was led away. Martha hurried forward to calm the boy but it seemed that as the horses rounded the corner and were lost to sight that nothing would ever console him. He broke into hard, wracking sobs, punctuated with the hoarse calling of Bess' name. Eventually he collapsed in a heap in Amos' arms and then allowed himself to be led inside.

"Get him a nip of brandy, ma" Amos instructed , stroking back Jonah's hair to try and soothe the lad.

"Don't take on so lad, we'll have other horses."

"Not like Bess." Jonah's reply was punctuated by gulps.

"No not like Bess, I grant you..."

Martha had returned with the glass of brandy which she touched to Jonah's lips. He gulped, felt the fiery liquid burn his throat and coughed. But the warmth calmed him. He drank the rest more slowly. When the glass was empty he raised his eyes to see Amos and Martha watching him. They looked worried. He wondered why.

"Better now?" Martha asked. He nodded, uncertain as to whether he could trust himself to speak just yet.

❖

Elizabeth, hearing the sound of a motor car thought that the doctor had come on one of his weekly visits to her. She rose and went to the window. The man who climbed out of the car was... it was John, her brother John! She rushed to open the door, he was just coming in through the front gate.

"John!" she cried, flinging her arms around his neck.

He picked her up and swung her round as much as the restricted space allowed, thinking how thin and light she was, like a little, brown sparrow. But she was obviously overjoyed to see him and when she stepped back to get a better look at him he saw that her cheeks had a certain pinkness, from powder or happiness, it was difficult to tell.

"Mind your head," she instructed as she led the way inside.

"It's a good thing that I'm not much taller," he observed, ruefully seeing how low the great beam which ran across the middle of the ceiling was. By the time he had fetched his bag and taken off his coat and cap, Elizabeth had the kettle singing on the trivet and the small, round table under the window set with tea things.

"I'm going to pull my boots off Sis, if you don't mind my stockinged feet? "He suited the action to the words and padded to the table.

As they sat talking and sipping, darkness fell outside the window. Elizabeth pulled the curtains and they moved to sit by the rosy glow of the fire.

"I didn't really expect you until tomorrow at the soonest." Elizabeth conceded, "and certainly not by motor car, is it yours?"

"Um." John stretched his feet out towards the fire, savouring the warmth. "Bought it in London, motored down to see the parents, just stayed the one night. Said that I would call and see you. They didn't, well Pa didn't seem very pleased that I was deserting them to come up here so I said that I had less leave than I actually have."

"Oh ,John!"

"No, not Oh John, I couldn't have stayed another night. It seemed so, so, passé is probably not the right word .Everything was still running like clockwork as if there was no war except that there are mighty few servants now. Ma's sole topic of conversation seemed to be the lack of servants and Father's was how he could conduct the war more successfully than the commanders, army, king, uncle Tom Cobbley and all. Not that I blame them, poor dears, their comfortable, settled existence has crumbled away under their feet and they are still trying to cling to some shred of normality. I couldn't have a proper conversation with either of them. They don't understand what it's like over there. ..."

"What is it really like?" Elizabeth asked.

He gazed into the fire . "It's hell on earth Sis, absolute hell, one hundred per cent hell. It won't be over by Christmas, not this one nor the next or even the one after that if I am any judge."

There was a long silence then Elizabeth said quietly, "If you want to tell me I promise that I will listen, even if I don't understand."

"I know you would," he reached over and touched her hand," but I would rather write. It's well-- not so difficult to find the right words then ."

Mary came across later with a pie and a pudding tied up in a cloth. "Meat and potato pie and a treacle suet pudding." She announced, putting them in the oven to keep warm.

"Capital!" Exclaimed John," I could eat a ----"

"A what John?" Elizabeth asked.

"I was going to say a horse but after what I've seen of horses recently I think I'll eat your pie instead."

They had a wonderful meal, finished with coffee which John had brought up with him from London. It was only nine o'clock when they had finished and John had smoked his pipe but Elizabeth could see his eyelids drooping so she suggested that he should go and unpack.

She had put sheets and blankets , with Mary's help, on the double bed in the large, newly decorated front bedroom. Mary had been pleased that at last someone was going to benefit from hers and Amy's hard work.

John was appalled but said nothing about the primitive washing arrangements and the earth closet half way up the garden. Elizabeth was much improved generally since she had been hiding in his friend's flat in London, despite its modern conveniences , and this Mary Peters seemed a treasure so who was he to find fault.

They went to bed early. Elizabeth fell asleep almost at once but John lay awake for some time enjoying the luxury of the big, comfortable bed, warmed with a hot brick . He watched the moon sail in and out of the clouds through the window opposite. It seemed idyllic for the first hour but then he began to feel irritable that he was still wide awake. He changed the pillows round, lay on his left side, his right side, pulled the blankets over his head, even after he had risen and pulled the curtains closed to cut out the moonlight he could not sleep. Finally he gave up trying. Putting the eiderdown around his shoulders, for the air was bitterly cold, he lit a candle and tip-toed downstairs. The fire had died but a few sticks, a twist of paper and some careful blowing soon gave a handful of yellow flames which he fed with small logs from the basket. He drew the chair nearer and sat down with his feet on the fender. Within minutes his eyes closed and he slept.

John awoke cold, cramped and with a pain in his neck where he had slept with his head on one side. Lighting a match he saw from his watch that it was gone three o'clock. He rose and groped his way to the window. Pulling back the curtains he saw snow falling. It had been snowing for some hours he guessed by the thickness of the covering on the outside window sill He turned to go back upstairs and was surprised to see a man standing at the other door. He wore narrow trousers which ended at the knee and a shirt with wide sleeves and tucks down the front. He was of similar height and build to himself. His hair looked as if someone had hacked it with a knife and one arm was bound across his chest with a clean but frayed cloth bandage. The two men looked at each other.

“Who are you? What are you doing here?” John Bateman asked taking a step forward. The other man’s form wavered, danced and then like smoke in the wind disappeared into the shaft of moonlight from the window.

Jonah crept down the stairs, his boots in his hand, praying that no creaking step would wake Amos or Martha. He was dressed in his clean shirt and his tweed jacket. He must make a good impression. He was just reaching for the door latch when he heard a noise above him. He paused, heart in mouth, but all was quiet once more. It had only been Amos muttering in his sleep. Jonah silently opened the door and stepped out into the night.

.The following morning , arising late, John decided that he would not mention last night’s apparition to his sister. He breakfasted and taking a rather old and rusty spade began to clear a path from the front door. He met Bill Peters doing likewise. Elizabeth watched them leaning on their respective spades and talking amicably. John saw her and waded through the deep snow to the window.

“Bill and I are just going for a drink together. Is that all right with you?” He mouthed through the window. Elizabeth smiled and nodded an affirmative.

The pub was agog with the news that Jonah had run away. Amos, pouring beer from the great casks that rested behind the bar was morose and upset as he said that his wife, Martha, had cried and cried when they had discovered he was missing this morning. John was introduced to the locals, played a game of darts and was just about to leave when the door opened and in came the missing Jonah. Amos came out from behind the bar, grabbed his shoulders and demanded,

"Where you been boy, leaving without a word, me and Ma have been that worried and upset..."

"Sorry, Amos." Jonah had not realised that they would be so upset, he could see unshed tears in Amos' eyes. "I've been to join up."

"You what!" Amos' bellow brought a red-eyed Martha to the door. Seeing Jonah she ran to him and hugged him fiercely.

"Don't you hold on to him too tight now Ma," cautioned Amos, "'cos the daft 'apporth has just been and volunteered."

"Oh no, Jonah, no!" Martha wailed. "Why? Why?"

"'cos they took Bess. I've got to go to Bess, she needs me, I love her."

Martha pulled him through the door and into the kitchen. "Now," she said sternly, "I knows you love that mare but...but," her voice faltered, she wiped a tear from her eye with her apron. "Don't you care about us? How we'll feel without you?"

"Course I do," muttered Jonah, shamefaced now, "I do, I do really, you've been good to me, only home I've ever had."

"Sit down Jonah." Martha said wearily for she could see now that he did not understand and to give him credit neither she nor Amos had ever voiced their feelings so how could he. "We picked you from the workhouse, not any other lad, you. I haven't any of my own, but I thought I had you . I thought that you were my boy, I looked on you as the son I never had, I thought that you looked on me as your Ma. I love you Jonah. Didn't you ever think about that when you went off like a thief in the night?"

"Well no, not really, I knew you wouldn't want me to that's why I snuck off. I didn't think you would be very upset ,cos I'm not your son, just a bit put out until you found someone in the village to do the jobs. I'm not your son, I'm nobody's"

"Don't you say that ever again Jonah Smith," Martha's voice was husky and fierce, "You're my lad and you have been since the first day you came through that door there. So we'll have no more of that. I'll be Ma in future, is that clear?"

"Yes... Ma." Jonah hugged her.

"Now sit down my boy and I'll get you something hot to eat, you must be starving."

❖

When John realised that Elizabeth's only form of transport had left the village he decided to put a proposition to Bill on the way back home.

"Do you really want to do that?" asked Bill, astounded at such profligacy. John assured him that he did.

"I can't take it back with me and if you can learn to handle it in the next few days to be safe enough then Elizabeth and your wife and anyone else in this village will have the means to go to Southwell or Newark whenever they please"

CHAPTER TWELVE

So John and Bill went out every day for an hour or two. Bill proved to be quick and eager. He had a natural feel for the car and was soon driving with confidence. By the time Christmas day came John felt that Bill was able to handle the car competently.

Elizabeth and John went with the Peters family to the small village church, its interior festooned with locally cut holly, ivy and laurel. Red candles gleamed on the deep window sills, around the font and the pulpit. White candles shone on the snow white altar cloth and were reflected in the gleaming silver chalice .It was a simple, moving hour of well-loved carols, familiar readings of the first Christmas spoken out in the piping voices of the school children, well rehearsed by Miss Mason. After the service the villagers clustered around the font, in the porch or just outside on the gravel path to wish each other a 'Happy Christmas' . John found himself being introduced to a kaleidoscope of faces and being wrung by the hand by countless men, women and even children until his brain whirled.

Soon they were hurrying to Mary and Bill's cottage, Ben having a piggy-back home on his father's shoulders, for their dinner. Mary had plucked and stuffed a goose, prepared vegetables and put one of her own puddings on to boil. Elizabeth and John had provided crackers, chocolates, brandy, sherry for the women and cigars for the men. Replete with food they sat around the fire watching Ben playing with his presents and John thought that this was the best Christmas he had ever had. He said so, thanking Mary and Bill for making him, a virtual stranger, so welcome. Ham from the Peters' own pig , Mary's bread and pickles finished off their appetites completely. Too soon it was Ben's bedtime and Elizabeth and John rose to leave.

"I shall not see you in the morning Mary," John said, "Bill will be taking me quite early and then coming back here with the car. You are all to use it until I return, keep them to that , will you Bill?"

"I shall, Captain."

John kissed Mary's cheek in farewell. Bill wondered what he should do with the car if anything should happen to the Captain, but he did not ask, it did not seem politic to do so.

❖

Elisabet hobbled back from church on Christmas morning; the snow lying underfoot made walking doubly difficult for her. Her shoes were wet through but she had enjoyed the singing of the carols and the packed warmth and joyfulness of her neighbours.

The previous evening Watkins and his small troop of Roundheads had packed up their kit and ridden off. It had then been a communal village effort to clean and decorate the church ready for this morning. Elisabet had cut holly, with its bright berries, from her garden and decorated all the window sills. It had been worth working well into the evening for the church looked clean, bright and festive. Elisabet felt much more relaxed now the Roundheads had gone. John could walk out in the orchard now and get some air, he had been confined inside too long.

All the other villagers except the very old and housebound were off to the Hall which lay further down the road below the church for the usual festive fare and frolics. Elisabet had decided that she and John would celebrate together. She had killed and plucked a chicken, made the minced meat and fruit pies; traditionally shaped to resemble Jesus' cradle ;and marchpane shapes to look like stars. She also had cob nuts she had picked in the Autumn and a bottle of her home made elderberry juice.

John was sitting on the settle. She pulled off her cloak and hood and looked to see how the chicken fared on the spit above the fire.

"You should be making merry with the others." John said quietly.

"I can make quite merry enough here with you." Elisabet turned and smiled at him. Such a sweet smile she had.

"But here we cannot play games and dance as they will do."

"I cannot dance." Elisabet looked serious now. "It is the one thing that I would love to do, but as much as I wish, I may not, this," she pointed to her leg, "will not let me."

"Does it pain you?"

"Sometimes, more often it is the good leg which hurts as it takes more work than it should."

"Poor Elisabet." John reached over and laid his hand on her shoulder. She did not move away as he had expected, instead she turned more fully to face him. He put his hand higher and touched the curls which fell about her ears. "So soft," he murmured and, standing up, bent and kissed her.

❖

Bill carefully pulled the car to a halt in the station yard.

"You'll do, Bill," John remarked as he got out and reached for his bag from the rear seats. "Off you go home now. There's no point you hanging around here. The train will probably be late like as not." When Bill hesitated, John continued "Look after her for me Bill, you and Mary, she's very frail."

"We will Captain," Bill cleared his throat. Should he ask? But John, leaning towards him, answered his thoughts.

"Especially if , well, if I don't make it."

"You'll be all right Captain. Lightning never strikes the same place twice."

"No, Bill, it doesn't but German shells and bullets do. So if the worst happens, take care of her and - the car is yours of course." He put up his hand to silence Bill's protest. "I shall write a letter to that effect so there will be no problem." Reaching his hand across he took Bill's work-worn, calloused one in his and shook it firmly. "And thanks for everything. I would have liked to have known you better but somehow after even these few days I feel that I have known you all my life." He slammed the car door and strode quickly away.

"God keep you safe, Captain," Bill muttered to the disappearing figure.

❖

Elizabeth felt weary, she had tried so hard to make her brother's leave a happy one and she was sure it had been. The new lines etched on his face when he had arrived had largely been smoothed away by good cheer and laughter. But now all she wanted to do was sit by the fire. She must have dozed for she was awoken by Ben's voice by the side of her,

"Miss Bateman, I did knock, three times, honestly."

"I'm sure you did Ben."

"You were fast asleep. Mummy says that if I am tired I must go to bed. You should go to bed Miss Bateman." Sometimes thought Elizabeth he was a very serious child.

"Presently Ben, now you are here I would rather talk. Tell me which of your presents did you like best?"

He looked down and thought, wrinkling his brow. He leaned his elbow on the high arm of the sofa , crossing one foot in front of the other. Again Elizabeth was struck by the pose. How many times had she seen her brother stand so? Perhaps most males did, she had never really noticed. Eventually he said, "The train I think." This was a beautifully made wooden train with all the details carved by his father.

"Good, I'm glad that's your favourite."

"I really came with a message from Mr Samuel, next door." His brow wrinkled again. "Do you want any eggs? For if you do he will bring them."

"I would love some."

Ben went to the door.

"Ben, just wait a minute," Elizabeth took a painted tin of biscuits from the dresser cupboard "Would you take this to him from me?"

"For the eggs?"

"No, a late Christmas present."

Elisabet lay warm and content in the crook of John's good arm. She had not thought that anything could be as wonderful as this past night had been. She knew that what had happened was wrong. But was it really? She loved him. She had loved him since she had first seen his crumpled form lying on the ground by the pond in Well Furrows. Suppose he had a wife? Perhaps she would never know. When he was well he would go to fight again for the King but he had promised that he would come back when the King's enemies were beaten. Would he keep his promise? Would he, a gentleman, want to remember a poor, twisted creature like her? But he had said that she was beautiful; how had he put it? Inside and out. She had been ashamed and tried to hide her twisted leg from him but he had just stroked it and muttered 'poor leg' and then said, 'you were not shocked by my wounds, Elisabet when you first tended me.' She had tried to protest that it was different; that his wounds would heal in time but that she would not. She had been born like this and would die like it. 'It does not matter to me,' he had replied. 'I do not notice it. I see only my beautiful, kind Elisabet.' He had not said that he loved her but it was of no importance. Elisabet snuggled up to him. This, now this was what was important.

❖

Samuel hobbled round with the same bowl again full of eggs and plonked it on the table. "There is no call to go giving me presents," he said in his high voice. "But I do say that I does like a sweet biscuit so I thanks you kindly for them. I likes them with my tea." Elizabeth smiled at him.

"That your brother who came in the motor?"

"Yes, he was on leave. He's gone back now."

"Aye, thought so. Reminded me of a young chap that I used to know. Looked just like him, he did." And he was off. Elizabeth shook her head. He was like a troll, appearing and disappearing so abruptly. You couldn't really have a good conversation with him at all.

After twelfth night the weather held the village in its iron jaws. Ponds, ditches and the Dumble froze. Icicles hung from trees and eaves like unsheathed swords, gleaming in the weak noonday sun but still frozen in the bitter air. Inside the cottage Elisabet and her Cavalier huddled around the fire by day and warm and snug in each other's arms by night. Elisabet was kept busy preparing medicines for a score of Winter ills; decoctions of hemp root for the elderly with gouty pains, of henbane for the louse-ridden, taking hazelnut and pepper electuary for those with the head rheum, and hawkweed mixed with honey and hyssop to ease coughs. Slowly the days drew out but the cold persisted. For Elisabet these were the happiest days of her life; loving and being loved she did not notice how John winced if she touched any part of his shoulder nor that her supply of poppy syrup was diminishing far faster than she was using it.....

Elizabeth read with horror the account of two Zeppelins which had reached Yarmouth, dropping bombs and incendiaries, killing four people and injuring many others as well as destroying property. It was a dreadful thing for women, children and old people to be attacked in their homes. When she had read about German atrocities in Belgium at the beginning of the war she had never thought that civilians here in England would also suffer. A letter From John, now back in France had distressed her by its description of the pounding of Ypres by German guns. 'The heavy shelling,' he had written, 'has ruined the Cloth Hall; the cathedral is wrecked; and many of the medieval merchants' and weavers' homes are blackened shells. The countryside around is pock-marked with shell holes and denuded of trees 'He wrote that many of his old company were ' gone to a better place, the salient,' he said was 'populated with new, young volunteers and soldiers from the Empire, Canadians in this case.' But he also wrote of amusing incidents and the camaraderie between the men, the joys of a bath even when twelve men shared the same water and a jolly evening in an estaminet when it was their turn to move back out of the forward trenches.

Elizabeth had just finished her reply to him and was making her way down the path when she decided to pick a few snowdrops from the edge of the orchard. The air was cold and still, nothing moved, animals and birds hid in the warmth of hole and nest, she hurried down the path. As she neared the door her foot slipped on an icy patch on one of the flagstones there and she fell full length, scattering the snowdrops. With her breath knocked out of her, hands and knees smarting she lay for a second or two. Slowly she levered herself up. Something gleamed where her fall had dislodged the moss between the stones. Bending down carefully, for her head was thumping, she poked in the crevice. The edge of something; could it be gold; gleamed dully in the flat, grey afternoon light. She went inside and returning with a knife and the doormat, knelt down and carefully began to investigate the area around.

Gradually, clearing away the soil, she was able to get the knife beneath the object and one swift flick brought it up. A ring, speared by the knife point, quivered under her astonished gaze. Elizabeth went inside and washed it at the stone sink. It was a heavy, gold ring. Trying it on all her fingers and finding it too large she surmised that it was a man's ring, a little bent and slightly worn but a large chunk of metal for all that.

When Mary came in the evening Elizabeth showed her find.

"What a strange old thing." Mary pronounced, " You're always finding things like this."

"Yes, I am. Why do you say old Mary?" Elizabeth questioned.

"It just looks old I suppose and anyway it wasn't dropped by Sam, the cowman, and he lived here nigh on thirty years."

"Who lived here before?" Asked Elizabeth.

"No idea," replied Mary," but they do say that a witch lived here once, long ago."

"Really, when?"

"Oh, in the Civil War time, or thereabouts."

"Was she arrested and tried as a witch then?" asked Elizabeth remembering the witch trials at Pendle in the early sixteen hundreds."

"No, folks around here used to come and get her herbs and things. She were a powerful healer with the herbs it's said."

"Do you think that she might be the woman who wrote that old book I found?"

"Could be I suppose, are there any spells or potions in it?"

"Not that I've read. It's more like a diary but without any dates."

A thought crossed Elizabeth's mind. "Is there anyone you know who could tell me any more about this?" She gestured to the ring.

Mary thought for a minute. "There's an old chap down Chain Lane in Newark. He has a little shop, he lives above it. He buys and sells second hand silver and jewellery. He might know."

"We could always ask him."

Elizabeth decided she would like another trip to Newark. "Shall we ask Bill to take us in the car on-- say, Saturday? . We could make it a day out. Find somewhere where I could take the three of you for a meal.?"

"You mean Ben as well?"

"Of course I mean Ben. We couldn't leave him out"

"He'd love a ride in the motor car," agreed Mary. "I'll ask Bill then, shall I?"

"Wonderful." Elizabeth looked at the ring again. "Even if we don't find anything out about this we can have a great day out!

CHAPTER THIRTEEN

That night Elizabeth took the book of hours out of the cloth she had wrapped it in and sat in bed studying it. She wondered if 'Mary's little man' would be interested in it. She turned the pages carefully. On one side was a calendar of prayers and facing these were beautifully coloured pictures which, despite their age seemed to spring out of the page. Getting up, Elizabeth fetched a magnifying glass which she kept in a little drawer at the bottom of her jewellery box. She positioned the lamp and placing the glass over the pictures saw a Winter landscape of a town with a castle and church on a hill. Birds flew through a cerulean blue sky pursued by huntsmen. Spring showed a similar scene transformed by minutely painted flowers. Autumn depicted peasants in the fields, golden trees and horsemen setting out from the town. There were between these seasonal scenes drawings of the Virgin and Child, the crucifixion and the resurrection all painted with the same sureness of touch, precision of line and glowing colours. It was a little masterpiece. Elizabeth laid it carefully on the bedside table. She would consider whether she would take it tomorrow was her last thought before she fell asleep.

Elisabet had spent the day scouring her pots, bowls and plates with horsetails. The water in the wooden tub on her bench she now carried outside and emptied into the sinkhole. Then , taking a broom , she swept the floors and strewed them with sweet herbs and wormwood. Sitting by the fire she stirred the rabbit, herbs, onions and roots bubbling in the iron pot savouring the warmth of the fire. On the morrow she had decided to wash the linen if the day was fine and blowy. Satisfied that the broth was tasty, Elisabet fetched bread and ale for their meal. The weather being fine for this late February day, John had walked up through the garden to the orchard. Elisabet watched him returning. Her heart leaped as it always did when she saw him. His hair had grown somewhat and now curled beneath his ears, such soft hair. Elisabet's knees felt wobbly as he smiled at her. A great loving smile which lit up his whole face. But in the weak sunlight she thought that he looked unwell, his eyes cloudy, the skin around them shadowed. Elisabet asked him to come and sit down and as she ladled out the broth she noticed afresh how he was nursing his injured shoulder. Eating he used his spoon and broke his bread with the other hand.

"Does your shoulder pain you?" Elisabet asked at length

He agreed that it did.

"And your hand?" He confessed that he could hardly use it. So after the meal was finished Elisabet sat him on a stool by the fire and examined the wound. The skin had grown over the musket wound but it did not look healthy. Quite a large patch of skin around the area was discoloured. She bent down, pretending to take away the bowl and cloth that she had been using, and quickly sniffed the area of discoloured skin. It smelled unhealthy, Elisabet had smelled that smell before when a man in the village had pierced his hand with a metal spike out in the fields, she recoiled.

"I must bathe this again and dress it" she told him..

She returned with a bowl of nettle leaf juice with which she again bathed the shoulder and then she applied a poultice of bruised bugle leaves.

"I must go into Newark on the morrow," she told him, quickly changing her plans now that she had seen how bad the wound was faring. "You will be quite safe here until I return. I must seek the apothecary's advice."

"But you are skilled with cures Elisabet," John put his hand over hers, "why must you consult another?"

"I do not think that it is healing well. It would have been better if the musket ball had been removed. I shall consult the barber surgeon to see if he will do this."

Elisabet thought that now the Roundhead soldiers were gone from the village and John was stronger he would be able to make the journey. But she must seek advice and arrange a place to stay for just one night before he had to make the return journey. John appeared to accept her judgement so she made her preparations for the following day. She would take herbs and produce with her to sell and hopefully return with good news.

❖

Elizabeth got in the front passenger seat of the gleaming and spotless car. Bill sat proudly at the wheel, resplendent in cap, goggles and leather gauntlets. Mary and Ben were an exited duo in the back. Ben hoped that his school chums would see him riding to Newark in such splendour. Elizabeth had decided to bring the book of hours with her and it now lay in her leather bag carefully wrapped. The air was mild, sun glinting in and out between the clouds, hinting at the promise of a warm and sunny February day. Bill turned the starting handle vigorously and drove off with confidence which made Mary, seated behind him, proud of his newly acquired ability. The car left the village behind, struggled up Wheatgrass Hill, thankful to reach the top. Conversation being difficult over the noise of the engine, they were content to enjoy the scenery, bare and brown though the countryside was. Mary spied a clump of snowdrops in Spring Wood and leaning across tapped Elizabeth's shoulder. She pointed. Elizabeth smiled and nodded back at her. They fairly sped along now and were soon crossing the river at Kelham. The Trent was grey and sullen. It had broken its banks inundating the small alder trees which grew on either side. And then they could see the tall, elegant spire of the church rising in front of them. As they crossed the river again Elizabeth recognised the ruined castle and realised that they had arrived.

Bill left the car in a newly sprung up garage on Castle Gate and he, Mary and Ben went off after arranging that they would all meet up here in two hours time. This left Elizabeth at the end of a narrow, cobbled alleyway which she saw was called Boar Lane. She went up it and crossed the road to another alley called Chain Lane and looked up and down and came back again before she saw a low-doored shop with a tiny window in which there was a tray of rings and some silver jugs on display. Elizabeth opened the door and stepped down into the murky interior.

❖

Elisabet felt that she was being very foolish to set out alone but she had singularly failed to find anyone in the village who wanted a free ride with her. 'Too far'. 'What in February?' And 'You might be attacked' Their refusals sounded like death knells. But Elisabet had to go for she feared for John's health. By the time she had left the village and the horse was plodding up White Cross Hill she had decided that once at the top she would set a spanking pace and try to make the journey as short as possible. The only place she feared was where the road curved its way through Spring Wood and the trees pressed in on both sides, always a dark and dank place even in Summer. She consoled herself that there was less likelihood of anyone being able to hide in the bare trees in Winter.

As she passed the end of the road to Southwell a man and woman were plodding along the side of the road. Seeing that they were carrying heavy baskets of produce she hailed them.

"Were they bound for Newark?" They replied that they were and when offered a ride, jumped on the cart with alacrity.

Thomas and Anne Tyler introduced themselves as villagers of Upton. They explained that they did not usually take their surplus eggs, butter and cheeses so far but they had heard that Newark was packed with the King's men and thought that they would make a far greater profit selling there. Elisabet agreed that they might and questioned them subtly for the news of soldiers. But apart from the fact that Roundhead soldiers had passed through their village they knew little more than she did. Chatting of this and that seemed to make the journey pass so much more quickly and soon they had joined the Great North Road to the north of the town.

Elisabet was stopped before the bridge by soldiers, presumably from the castle garrison, who asked her business and made a quick search of the cart. Beastmarket Hill was thronged with people, mainly men and all armed. Some obviously soldiers, others townspeople determined to defend themselves.

Elisabet took Thomas and Anne Tyler to the market square where she tethered the horse after giving it a drink at the stone water trough and proceeded to set up her wares on the cobbles nearby. There was obviously a scarcity of fresh produce in the town. And no wonder thought Elisabet with all these extra mouths to feed. Her produce vanished within the hour. She arranged to give Thomas and Anne a ride back and leaving the horse and cart in their care made her way to the apothecary's.

The apothecary dispensed his pills, potions and salves from the front room of a small dwelling on Kirkgate in the shadow of the church. Elisabet savoured the clean, aromatic smell and waited while a woman with a shawl pulled tightly around her upper body was served and clumped out noisily on her pattens. Elisabet described the wound and the smell that she had noticed emanating from it. The apothecary, a small, wizened man, with stooped back and rounded shoulders, tut-tutted, pursed his lips and agreed with her that the removal of the musket ball was urgent. He directed her to the barber surgeon further down the street and bade her good-day. Elisabet limped on to the larger premises with its red and white pole outside. She sat on a stool while a young soldier had a tooth pulled out and then explained her errand.

He agreed that he would remove the musket ball and named a price which made Elisabet gasp, but she agreed and arranged to bring John to him the following week.

Making her way along Middle Gate she opened a tall gate which led to a narrow alley between two shops. At the end of the alley was a group of three small cottages and in the middle one of these lived a friend who might agree to help Elisabet and give her and John a bed so that he could rest overnight after the musket ball had been removed. Charity, Elisabet's friend was also the descendent of a monk ousted from Rufford Abbey by King Henry's men. Her husband, a shoemaker, made Elisabet a special shoe for her misshapen foot, building parts up with thicker leather to enable her to walk more easily.

Elisabet was welcomed and offered ale. She dandled the youngest child, a baby boy named Luke on her knee while they chatted and Elisabet was glad to be able at last to trust someone with her secret. When she had explained the reason for her journey Charity agreed readily to help. All too soon it was time to leave if she was to get home safely in daylight. As she made her way back to the market place Elisabet heard the beating of a drum; the urgent beating of a drum and a young, boyish voice shouting, "Who will stand for King Charles and defend the town.!"

Townsfolk armed with old swords, muskets, sticks and staves, knives and cudgels burst forth, and Elisabet was left in no doubt that Newark was under attack.

❖

Tobias Monk, owner of the shop and sole occupant, was small, round and bald. He looked, Elizabeth thought like the picture of Humpty Dumpty in her childhood nursery rhyme book. His small, dark, poky shop was simply furnished. A mahogany counter with glass let in at the front commanded a view of the low doorway and the small window. On it a brass oil lamp with a yellow shade cast a pool of light. On the two walls at either side were mahogany, glass-fronted cabinets which held pieces of gleaming silver. Tobias Monk had dark, piercing eyes which took in the good cut and the finely woven material of Elizabeth's coat, her elegant leather boots, finely stitched leather gloves and the fashionable hat and rubbed his hands together mentally in anticipation of a good sale. He was rather put out when she announced that she had not come to buy but to consult him. His knowledge of old things she added as a sweetener was widely known.

Suiting actions to words she pulled a small, rectangular object from her bag and carefully unwrapped it on the counter. Tobias peered at the small, leather book closely before opening it with extreme care at the very edges. As he turned page after page and the glowing colours sprang to life in the lamplight he realised that here was treasure indeed. He reached the last page and with a sigh looked reluctantly away from the feast of beauty he had uncovered into the prematurely tired face of the woman opposite him.

"A beautiful Book of Hours," he whispered in awe. "A medieval treasure without a doubt made for some one of taste, piety and discernment. Possibly for a titled landowner by the monks in the scriptorium, a writing room at a monastery."

"Could you say exactly how old it is ?" Asked Elizabeth. There was a silence for a minute or two while Mr Monk considered this. At last he said: "Not really, before the 1530s. Henry Tudor, Henry VIII, dissolved the monasteries in 1538 or soon after so it would have to have been written prior to that but I can't say exactly when. You would need to consult an expert. I am hardly that, just an interested amateur as you might say."

"And what could you venture about this?" Elizabeth removed the ring from a pocket in the front of her purse and passed it to him.

He turned it this way and that under the lamp, examined it closely with an eye glass before admitting that he could tell her very little.

"It *is* certainly gold, but you knew that already, it is not marked and it is a man's ring. The size and weight would be too great for a woman's finger. It has some sort of crest or motto on it but it is too worn for me to be able to tell what it could have originally been."

"*Is* it old?"

"Three or four hundred years easily. And now Mrs--"

"Miss Bateman."

"Miss Bateman I have told you all I know so perhaps you could do me the courtesy of telling me where these things came from?"

"I found them." Elizabeth confessed and she proceeded to tell him about the hidden cupboard and the crack between the flagstones. She offered to pay him for his time but he waved the suggestion away. Elizabeth thought that if she bought something.....She asked him if she might look around and he waved his arms to encompass his merchandise like the good fairy with a magic wand.

Elizabeth looked at each object in the wall cabinets carefully and finally bent down to peer at the jewellery in the glass-fronted counter. That was when she saw it. On a black velvet cloth lay a small silver owl with garnet eyes. Each feather was carefully delineated even though the little bird was only just over an inch high. Mr Monk lifted it out and named the price. It was very reasonable Elizabeth thought turning it over in her hands. Wrapped and paid for and everything including the little owl in her bag, Elizabeth thanked Mr Monk and took her leave.

After an ample luncheon at a half-timbered inn just off the market place all four of them made their way back to the car. Elizabeth insisted that Ben sat at the front with his father on the way back while she sat behind with Mary. Bill swung the starting handle. The engine did not leap to life as it had done in the morning. He swung it again and again. Nothing. Sweat stood on his brow even though by now the day was damp and chilly. A burly man came out to see what was happening. He took over the starting handle from Bill. Still no spark of life. The two men went into a huddle. Mary and Elizabeth could only hear mutterings. Then Bill said,

"Oh dear, are you sure?" The garage man confirmed that he was. Bill came back to talk to the two women, addressing Elizabeth he said,

"He says that it's probably damp, that's why it won't start and he can't do anything about until tomorrow."

"But will he be able to get it started then?" Elizabeth enquired.

"He thinks so but what shall we do tonight?" Bill nodded his head towards his son's back. Ben was watching the man undoing the car's bonnet.

"We shall just have to find somewhere to stay ." Elizabeth rose and got out of the car.

"But the cost Miss Bateman!" Bill was shocked.

"Will be mine. I brought you all here. Now where would give us an evening meal, beds and a good breakfast in the morning?"

Bill went to talk to the garage man again. There was more muttering from behind the hinged bonnet and then Bill emerged and announced, "The Queen's Head is recommended."

"Isn't that where we had our splendid lunch?"

"The very same Miss Bateman."

"Come along, Mary, Ben," Elizabeth announced "It's the Queen's Head for us tonight."

Ben's face when it turned towards her was a picture of delight.

"Won't I have a lot to tell Jimmy at school on Monday," he chortled, thinking of his friend's astonishment when he told him that he, Ben Peters, had not only gone to Newark and back again in a motor car but had also stayed, eaten and slept there at an inn!

CHAPTER FOURTEEN

Elisabet soon found herself standing alone at the edge of a deserted market place. From somewhere away to her right beyond the houses came the sound of musket shots and shouts. Elisabet hesitated. What should she do? Her horse and cart still stood tethered where she had left them but there was no sight of Thomas or Anne Tyler. If the town was under attack then she must get her horse under cover. She untethered it and leading it by the head made for the left hand corner of the market where the buildings jutted out at odd angles for here was an inn.

She led horse and cart into 'The Queen's Head' yard and looked around. The place was deserted. Backing the cart into a corner she unharnessed the horse and led it into the stable putting it into an empty stall. She made her way as fast as she could to the inn door for the sounds of fighting seemed closer now. Once inside she realised that there was no one here either. She shouted and waited. Surely some one would come? By the time her third shout had died away she realised that there was no one to come. She would return to Charity's house. Recrossing the yard she was almost knocked down by a young boy dashing around the corner. "Have I startled you Mistress?" The lad panted, momentarily halting his headlong dash.

Elisabet assured him that he had not and asked who he was. Receiving the reply that he was the stable boy she explained about the horse and cart and that she would return in the morning to pay what was owing and then she allowed him to dash off.

As she returned to Charity's she heard shots again this time in front of her, there was a reverberating sound of cannon being fired from the castle she presumed and the unmistakable smell of black powder.

Charity's husband was out with the others on the perimeter walls. The two women sat consoling the frightened children. Elisabet rocked the baby, who soon fell asleep. The late afternoon quiet was punctuated by shots and the smell of smoke grew stronger. As darkness fell quiet at last descended and the exhausted children slept at last, Charity's husband returned only to collect bread, cheese and ale and to report that the rebels had attacked from Beacon Hill and were occupying houses in North Gate, just outside the town's defensive barricade. There had been fighting around Beaumond Cross but the armed townspeople and the soldiers had repulsed them. They expected further attacks in the night and on the morrow. In the meantime he would be taking his turn to man the defences. He kissed his wife, remarked that he was glad that Elisabet was there to be with her and was gone.

Charity and Elisabet kept a restless night together-one or other rising and looking to see if the children slept and to peer out between the shutters, unable to sleep. All was silent and still. Towards dawn Elisabet fell into a deep sleep only to be awakened a short time later by the sound of fighting. Gazing out through the shutters she could see something burning and wondered wearily if the Roundheads had indeed entered the town. She wondered too if John had also been awake this night worrying where she was. The children slept on through the noise of the gunfire until late in the morning and only awoke when all outside was quiet.

Soon after this Charity's husband returned. Elisabet knew that all was well from the delighted expression on his face. He told them how Parliament's forces had attacked many places and had each time been repulsed by townsmen and soldiers rushing from one part of the defences to the next.

"You should have seen Colonel Henderson," he reported with pride, " charging around on his white horse and directing men to where the danger was greatest without a thought for his own safety. We've beaten them off!" His voice had a triumphant ring to it.

"This time," cautioned his wife, "they may come again with an even greater force."

"We shall be ready for them. As soon as we are rested all the defences are going to be made stronger and higher. Anyhow we might go and attack them."

"Where?" Elisabet asked, speaking for the first time .Her voice surprised him, he had obviously forgotten her presence.

"Grantham, Nottingham...Mistress Bayteman while I have time let me escort you at least part of the way home."

"Thank you, I must hasten." Elisabet thought again of John. He would not know why she had been delayed and the longer she waited the longer he would be fearing for her. He had probably already imagined her being set on by rogues along the way.

Collecting her horse but seeing no one at the inn yet again she left some pennies with Charity's husband to pay on his return and escorted by him at last made her journey home. Near the castle the smell of burning was heavy in the air from the houses that had been fired. After bidding farewell to Charity's husband she made her way along the road as fast as her aged horse could muster. She wondered what had happened to Thomas and Anne Tyler and thought what an age it seemed since she had met them only yesterday morning.

Elizabeth took two rooms at the inn, a large one for the Peters family and a smaller one for herself. They enjoyed a merry meal together, Elizabeth amused by the range of expressions which fluttered across Ben's face as he took in everything to be recounted and she guessed embellished to his friends at school. Elizabeth slept well and while Bill went to check if the car was working sat with Mary in the bedroom. Ben was peering through the window into the market place still enthralled and savouring every minute of it all.

"What shall we do if the car is not mended?" Asked Mary, a worried look on her usually placid face.

"We can either stay here another night or hire a conveyance," replied Elizabeth, quite unconcerned.

"Both will cost a great deal of money." Mary's anxiety now revealed itself, thought Elizabeth, as worry about what all this would cost.

"No matter," she replied airily, "I got you here and I will get us home."

With this Mary had to be content. However when Bill returned it was with good news that he had driven the car here, the problem, damp, he explained had been solved.

Elizabeth paid their modest bill while the other three piled into the car, as arranged the previous day with Ben in front.

❖

When Elisabet drew up in front of her cottage with the horse and cart she knew that John was looking for her as the downstairs shutters moved, to give him a better view. She had barely got in the door when he was there with his arm around her, pulling her close.

"Were you afeared that something bad had happened?" Elisabet's voice was muffled against his shirt. He did not answer for a minute and then he said quietly,

"My Elisabet, my beautiful Elisabet, don't ever leave me again."

"Twill not be me who leaves," Elisabet said sadly, "It will be you, when you are well you will go back to fight for the King."

"I shall come back to you." He gazed down seriously at her, "Believe me Elisabet, I will come back to you."

"Nay, let us not make such plans .But let us sit awhile and I will tell you why I was delayed. "

So Elisabet relayed the news of the siege, adding every detail that she could remember for she saw his interest, and his pleasure when she reached the end of the tale.

"Put to flight!" He slapped his leg with his good hand, "but they will try again."

"That's what charity said," added Elisabet, "but the governor has ordered better defences to be built."

"They must also attack, battles, wars are not won otherwise." But she could see how heartened he was by the news and also that the barber surgeon was to remove the musket ball from his shoulder.

Hearing a letter drop through the letter box Elizabeth was pleased to receive another letter from John. He wrote that they had had four days rest, 'if you could call it that' she read, 'We manned the reserve trenches then marched back to eat and sleep. We inspected the men's rifles and mended shell holes in the road.' He had little else to tell her but he had included a photograph which some one had taken of him in front of a ruined building. Elizabeth propped it up on the mantelpiece. He stood, bareheaded, nonchalantly leaning back against the shattered wall one leg crossed in front of the other, grinning at the camera.

She had been rather disappointed with her abortive trip to Newark because she had really learned nothing new about either the book or the ring. She wondered if she might send the book to a friend of John's who worked in the British Museum in London. But she dismissed this idea as he was probably at the front as well now. It never occurred to her that neither article was hers to do as she pleased and that if they belonged to anyone then they were surely the property of David Enleigh as he owned the cottage. It didn't even occur that she had not even told him what she had found.

Against her better judgement Elizabeth decided that she would only find out more about the ring if she read Elisabet's book again. She was loathe to get it out. Since it had been put back in the cupboard there had been no more sights or sounds from the past. She would think about it.

The day was cold but sunny so Elizabeth decided that she would go to the school room and see if Miss Mason wanted her to speak to the children that afternoon. When she arrived the children were playing on a small piece of levelled out ground which encroached into the neighbouring field. Miss Mason was standing watching them. She agreed that Elizabeth should wait while she rang the bell and brought the children inside.

They came in quietly curious, cheeks pink from their exercise in the cold air. When they were seated Miss Mason introduced her. As twelve pairs of eyes regarded her solemnly Elizabeth suddenly felt nervous, her mouth was dry, this was more frightening than all the demonstrations and marches with the Suffragettes because here she was on her own, even if they were only village children. What could she say? Miss Mason sensed her hesitancy and addressed the class,

"Now children, think of some sensible questions that you would like to ask. Put up your hand when you have decided."

Elizabeth looked at them as they sat, some thoughtful, some curious; the girls all neatly dressed with white pinafores and ribbon tied hair; the boys variously ranging from neat and well scrubbed to one grubby and raggy child. Ben, in their midst, smiling shyly. The silence lasted for some while until a girl tentatively put up her hand and asked,

"Have you ever seen the King, Miss?"

Elizabeth had, and soon was relating to them the sights and sounds of the Empire's capital, a place she thought many of them would never see. Eventually, as expected, a tall, dark haired girl called Rose Something asked about the Suffragettes. Elizabeth tried to explain what she believed after saying that she had been a suffragette. That women had to obey the law just as men did and so they should be able to have a say in choosing those who made the laws. The boys now wanted to know what she had done. Elizabeth told them how she had sold the Suffragette newspaper, marched in processions, once holding the side of the banner, and chalked slogans on pavements.

"Were you ever arrested?" a small, raggy boy piped up, whom she discovered was called Sam. "My dad's been arrested but he only got a fine and then they let him go."

There were no shocked faces at this revelation so Elizabeth assumed that it was old news. She admitted that she had, twice.

"What for?" Sam wanted to know.

"For breaking a window," came the answer.

"Cor, that's what my dad did. It were a public house winda in Newark- he were drunk Miss, were you?"

"Sam!" came Miss Mason's shocked interruption.

"It's all right," Elizabeth turned to reassure Miss Mason that she was not in the least offended, and then turned back to answer Sam, "No, Sam I was protesting for votes for women--I was sent to prison." There Elizabeth thought I've done it now, and I was going to be so careful no to mention that to anyone. Am I ashamed of it fleetingly crossed her mind, no I'm just still afraid that they might come and take me back even from here to finish the remaining month of my sentence.

There had been a collective gasp, punctuated by Sam's, "Why miss, why was you. My dad weren't?"

"Exactly Sam, that's what the W.S.P.U. is saying, that there is one law for men and another one for women."

"It's not right Miss," piped up a clean, well-dressed boy sitting next to Sam.

There were nodding heads around the room.

"Please Miss," a small, sweet-faced girl with flaxen ringlets, "What was prison like?"

Elizabeth explained about the grim exterior and the drab , gloomy interior of the women's prison, Holloway. The degrading and monotonous regime, the uniforms, rough and ill-fitting, the dreadful feeling of being caged and forgotten.

They asked other questions about St. Paul's, Westminster Abbey and the girls about what 'ladies wore in London' and then the large, white moon face of the clock on the wall said it was time to go. Elizabeth was surprised, the time had passed so swiftly and she had enjoyed their questions and the way they listened so thoughtfully. As the last pair of boots clattered away Miss Mason asked,

"Why didn't you tell them about your hunger strike and the forced feeding?"

"I don't know," Elizabeth admitted, "perhaps because no one asked, perhaps it isn't something I would tell such young ears, perhaps because I still have nightmares about it....."

A week passed. Elizabeth did very little. The weather continued cold, dry and bright. Mary came every day and brought her news of Anne, who was well but in an advanced state of pregnancy; the birth being due within a month. She received a picture from the children with a short note thanking her for her talk and another bowl of eggs from Samuel next door. He came and went as oddly as before but he did venture one startling bit of information, which when she thought about it later she should have realised but had not.

"There was a Bateman family in this house for near on four hundred years"

When Elizabeth asked when the last one had died in the village as there were none here now he added,

"He didn't die, he left, came into some money, he did, young John. Went to live down south somewhere."

"When was that?" Elizabeth asked and was told ,

"Thirty years ago."

Elisabet was startled by a loud banging on the front door. Opening it she was struck dumb by the sight of a Roundhead trooper standing, fist poised to hammer again, on the sun-bleached wood. In his other hand he held a strip of paper. He asked sharply, "Name?"

"Elisabet Bayteman, sir."

He glanced at the paper. It must be a list of the villagers, Elisabet thought. He asked: "Art thou the wise woman?"

"Just a healer of village ills, sir." Elisabet felt afraid. Was he going to accuse her of witchcraft? She knew how quick these Puritans were to find sins and perhaps invent evil where none really existed. The trooper looked her slowly up and down, noting the dark, worn dress with its white collar and cuffs, her curls escaping around her ears. His lips pressed together. His eyes were as hard as pebbles. Elisabet gazed at him from under lowered eyelids seeing the close cropped hair, burning eyes and hard jawline.

"Only one room?" He barked out the question.

"Yes sir." Elisabet's heart bumped against her ribs, sure he must hear it thumping? He merely nodded as he consulted the paper again, turned abruptly on his heel without another word and strode away.

Quietly closing the door after him, Elisabet leaned on the wall and took deep breaths to steady herself. She rubbed her sweaty palms on her dress, letting out a great sigh of relief. I must get John to the barber surgeon in Newark and healed and safely away from here was her only coherent thought and as soon as possible.

CHAPTER FIFTEEN

Elisabet had spent the previous evening preparing the cart. Straw had been lain in one half for John to lie on. She would cover him with as many of the dyed hanks of wool as she could spare, these to be sold in Newark. Then she had placed baskets of herbs, eggs, and apples taken from the last of her winter store to hide him from prying eyes. Now she hitched up the horse and backed the cart as close as she could to the herb garden at the side of her cottage as was possible. It was still very early, barely just light, so, checking that there was no one about she decided that it was time to get him well hidden. John was waiting around the back corner of the house and he moved as fast as he was able to the cart when Elisabet beckoned. She helped him in, glancing round all the while. Satisfied that he was well covered by the blankets and wool and screened by the baskets she climbed on and taking the reins urged the horse in the direction of Newark.

She wondered if there would be any Roundheads checking anyone leaving the village as the Cavaliers had on the entry into Newark? There were none. Breathing a sigh of relief she urged the horse up Whitecross Hill and then down the gentle slope towards Spring Wood. There was a muffled sound of speech behind her and then John's head appeared. "May I sit up now?" he asked more loudly, free of the restraining blanket. Elisabet turned and laughed out loud at his red face and hair sticking on end decorated with wisps of straw.

"Aye. You look like a scarecrow." Elisabet chortled, "but if I say down then hide yourself again quickly."

However the journey to Newark was uneventful. As last time there were few people on the road, the general unrest since the beginning of the strife between King and Parliament kept most people in their own villages. It was a painful ride for John. Every bump and rut along the road, and there were plenty of these, caused a jolt of pain. He hoped that once the musket ball had been removed he would be relieved of at least some of it.

Elisabet took John and left him with the barber surgeon and was told to come back later. She argued that she could be of assistance but her help was rudely refused. She again left her horse at the inn and laid out her goods in the market.

Newark seemed even more thronged than it had before. Elisabet learned from the buyers of her merchandise that the defences were being made better. Earthen banks made higher, ditches deeper, pitfalls dug and small wooden forts erected all along the perimeter of the town. No Roundhead would get inside the town again. Even houses in Northgate had been removed so that the cannon on the castle walls had an uninterrupted view to the north.

Elisabet's goods disappeared like snow in the sun. The Newarkers were obviously pleased to buy fresh country fare. Soon Elisabet had only the two blankets she had reserved to cover John on the return journey and an apronful of coins.

Elizabeth fingered John's letter. It felt unusually thick. As she unfolded the sheet of paper contained within the envelope something soft floated to the floor. Elizabeth picked it up and opened it out. It was a silk handkerchief. The silk was an ecru colour, about a foot square, edged with a good two inches of fine, hand made lace. In one corner there was bright coloured embroidery. Lavender and pink roses made a curved spray to enhance the crossed Union Flag and the Tricolour of France, and the words 'Souvenir de France', also in lavender. Putting the handkerchief to one side she began to read the letter.

'Dear Sis,

We have withdrawn to rest billets clear of the battle zone. I cannot tell you what a cheerful sensation it was as we felt the good, hard road beneath our feet after mud, mud and mud and to see a bright moon and stars instead of star shells bursting above. When we marched into----- all the shops were closed except one where a lamp had been placed in the window on a cloth with a hand-written sign saying 'Teas' leaning against the lamp. Two elderly but charming mademoiselles served us with egg and chips. We drank weak beer poured from a large jug, it was absolutely delicious! One fellow played the dusty piano in the corner before we left..... It is wonderful to sleep in a proper bed with sheets as we did last night. We are promised a hot bath tonight, bliss!

This morning I realised that it was Sunday. The church bells were ringing, calling the faithful to mass. The sound reassured me that the world is still here only a few miles away from the barbed wire and devastation which have been our lot and is beginning to seem more real, more normal than the people , events and places you describe in your letters. Spring is coming . We can see it here where grass still grows green and trees still stand complete, their branches soughing in the wind. I have picked some wild flowers here and I am pressing them flat as well as I can. I shall include them when I next write, but for now you will have to be content with the embroidered one of the two handkerchiefs which I bought. I know that you prefer plain, white cotton, Sis, but all the fellows were buying these for their wives and sweethearts so I thought that you should have one too. You don't have to use it!'

He closed the letter with his love and hope that their parents would keep in touch with her. Elizabeth folded the letter and returned it to its envelope and considered the handkerchief. Why had he bought two? Eventually she put it on the mantelpiece next to his photograph.

Jonah was regretting his hasty decision to volunteer. He hadn't seen any horse, let alone his Bess. Added to this the food was bad and he had done his initial training in the clothes that he had joined up in and his tweed jacket of which he had been so proud was ruined. He had eventually been given a second hand khaki suit, he didn't like to think about what may have happened to the man who had worn it before him. He did not however communicate any of this in his letters to Amos and Martha. He merely described shooting on the big range, marching, digging trenches, mock battles and the general playing at war that he and his companions had been doing in England and were still doing at the training camp here in Etaps as he had learned to call it. He sent cheerful postcards which Martha used to adorn her mantelpiece and bedside table and signed himself with pride, 'your loving son.' It gave him a warm feeling inside when he read that before he sent it off. He had a proper ma and dad now just like all the other lads in his section.

When Elisabet found her way back to the barber surgeon's John was lying on a board raised on two wooden trestles. He was unconscious but moaning quietly. The barber rubbed his none to clean hands together when Elisabet drew the coins out of her apron pocket. His eyes gleamed as she counted the pennies into his hand.

"You did get it out?" She asked, dropping the last penny with a clink into his hand.

"Yes, out completely, here it is." He turned and picked something up from the scarred, wooden table in the centre of the room , dropping it into Elisabet's hand. The table stood on a carpet of straw, quite clean straw; the table itself had little evidence of blood on it. Elisabet wondered how long John had been lying there if the barber had had the time to replace the straw and clean the table.

"Was there much blood?" She enquired.

"Hardly any, very little at all, surprisingly , the musket ball was deeply embedded."

Elisabet thanked him and moved over to where John lay. His face was deathly pale, his hair matted and wet, beads of sweat stood on his brow. Elisabet felt his hands. They were cold and clammy. Taking a cloth from her bag she wiped his face. She rubbed his cold hands and stroked his hair, speaking to him to arouse him. Eventually his eyelids fluttered open and he groaned.

"Hush now, 'tis done." Elisabet soothed him. She gave him a dose of her poppy juice syrup for the pain and gradually helped him into a sitting position. When he tried to put his feet to the floor Elisabet realised that he was in no condition to walk to Charity's house where she had arranged for them to spend the night. So, leaving him once more she hurried to collect the horse and cart.

Elizabeth had once again to see the doctor so she had arranged for Bill to take her in the car instead of the doctor coming out to the village as she was sure that she had at last begun to feel a little better.

However once in the doctor's surgery and the examination over she realised that he did not agree with her as he repeated the medicine and the advice to rest .He obviously thought that there was little change in her health but she knew that she did feel better. Perhaps it was the frequent and cheerful letters from her brother; perhaps it was the fact that from what he had written it seemed unlikely that he would be a participant in any major battle at present or perhaps it was the warm, sunny, spring-like weather. She decided to visit the Minster while she was here and give Bill some time to do a few errands for Mary and himself.

Walking down Church Street she paused to look back at the ancient facade of The Saracen's Head Hotel at the junction. She was interested to see it as she had read in the history book of Newark which Miss Mason had lent her that King Charles I had come to Southwell in 1646 and had stayed there for a short time before going to the Scottish camp at Kelham where he had ordered the garrison of Newark to surrender, thinking that he would receive help from the Scottish army. They had however turned him over to Parliament. So much for all the brave attempts to defend Newark Elizabeth had thought as she read it. She stood and perused the display in the three windows of J. H. Kirkby and Sons Ltd. The Minster she saw as she turned to cross the road was faced on this side by a number of very tall elm trees. The Minster itself was a fine, majestic sight with its two pepperpot spires of herring bone cladding to her right and the square central tower. To her left was an almost round part jutting out and beyond this a courtyard surrounded by elegant houses which Mary had told her was Vicar's Court , the houses of the Minster clergy. Crossing over she went under the arched gateway, down the path which cut through the graveyard and into the huge north porch.

Inside she marvelled at the massive Norman pillars supporting the nave and the intricate carvings in the hexagonal chapter house. The whole building gave out a feeling of profound peace and well-being. Elizabeth supposed that nine hundred years or so of prayer and devotion had permeated its very stones. She lowered herself gratefully into a pew and watched the rays of sunlight striking the stained glass in the windows and making a myriad of coloured facets reflect on polished wood and illuminate ancient stone. She idly watched a man whom she presumed was a church warden trundle a great, wooden wheel barrow down the side aisle nearest to her and stoke a large, round stove. There were several of these along the walls at each side. She sat and meditated, thoughts dancing in and out of her mind; prayers, hopes, wishes for the people in the village she had so recently met and could now call friends as well as for herself, John and lastly for her parents. She realised as she rose a little stiffly that she was no longer angry with her parents, it was like a great icicle had been removed from her heart. She thought that she even understood why her father had been so angry, he had just not understood and had most probably regretted his words many times afterwards but like her he was stubborn and proud and would find it almost impossible to retract. She was younger, she must be the one to make the first healing move. She would write to them again; a loving, dutiful and apologetic letter as soon as she arrived home at her cottage.

John, the cavalier, spent a restless and painful night. Charity had insisted that he was put in the best , indeed only, bed. Hot stones were used to warm the bed for even though the night was far from chill he shivered and these would hopefully warm his chilled body. He tossed and turned, muttered and groaned. He was alternately cold and clammy and then hot and feverish. By the time day dawned Elisabet was truly worried at his condition and had decided to remove the dressing and replace it with one of her own. She was dismayed to see that the cloth next to the wound was quite unclean and shocked by the condition of the wound itself. She knew that most surgeons and healers would scoff at her idea that wounds of all types healed better if cleansed and if tended with clean boiled cloths and clean hands but Elisabet knew from her own experience that it was so and her mother who had been renowned for her tending of the sick had taught this too. The barber surgeon had cut roughly leaving the jagged, angry flesh, discoloured and unhealthy looking. There was little sign of bleeding on the dressing, which further worried her for surely such crude cutting should have caused a fair amount of bleeding. Now she suspected that she knew why all had seemed too clean when she had gone in the room after the operation. The surgeon had not in fact cleaned up any blood for there had been none to clean. She cleaned the whole area as gently as possible and added a poultice of bruised nightshade leaves, padding it and binding it firmly with clean cloths brought especially for the purpose. During the course of the day John's condition appeared to improve, the fever was reduced by distilled blackberry and dandelion water. By nightfall he was sleeping peacefully.

Elizabeth spent her evening writing to both John and her parents. Feeling happily tired she went early to bed. Standing at the window about to close the curtains she wondered about continuing the reading of Elisabet's book. Should she ? Would it cause the hallucinations or whatever they were to begin again? As she dithered there came the sound of horses' hooves outside, pulling back the curtains she peered down into the moonlit road. Eight, ten, twelve men on horseback, helmets shining dully in the moonlight, troopers, Roundheads! She drew back hurriedly into the room. Her hand held not a curtain any more but the smoothly worn wood of a shutter. She was wearing not her own cotton nightdress but a dark coloured, coarsely woven dress with a white collar and cuffs. She lifted the skirt with the other hand, strange, leather shoes, a twisted leg and foot. Who am I? The thought rose in her throat with panic. Elisabet Bayteman was the unwanted answer. No, she thought, I am not she - but she knew that she was. She moved awkwardly across the room , through the door and slowly hobbled down the steep, bare wooden stair ,in her hand she held an evil smelling tallow candle which barely illuminated her unwilling steps as she made for the rear room. Here there was a strong medicinal smell and she could see that someone had been pounding herbs. The book lay open on the wooden surface of the bench. The page was partially blank and the ink was still wet. A quill and ink pot lay beside it . Elisabet bent over to reread what she had just recorded.

'This day we arrived back safely without any alarums from Newark. John is in much pain still but thanks be to God and Our Blessed Lady his fever has subsided and he sleeps quietly. I do not know if I should accept the ring. Did he truly understand what he was saying or was he merely bemused with poppy juice? Elisabet turned the page back. Here she had written, 'the trooper did come back again . I have told him yet again that I do have only the one room and that it would also be unseemly to place one of his men here in a house where a single woman is living alone. But I am much afeared that he might one day wish to enter the cottage and check the number of rooms and so find John.....He went away but I like not the look in his eyes as he stares at me. His gaze begins at my throat and travels slowly down my person to the ground. Can he see what I have so far successfully hidden from all, including John? Can he look through cloth and sinew and see sin? Elisabet looked at the ring again. It was a heavy, gold ring with a creature resembling a running deer and a word which was worn and indecipherable inscribed under it .John had pulled it with some difficulty from his finger and taking her hand in his had put it on her finger. It was much too big. She had tried to give it back to him but he had folded her fingers around it and said softly,

"Elisabet I want you to keep it, until I return. It is a family ring....."

"You have remembered who you are?" Elisabet asked.

"Not completely, when I am certain I shall tell you. But it is my family's ring. These letters," He pointed to the words under the deer, "these say that I love you and I mean that. Put it on a cord Elisabet until I return please.."

So to please him she had threaded it on one of her pieces of coloured yarn and tucked it into her dress. She knew that he meant what he said now but he was weak and ill and did not really understand what he was saying. When the fighting was over her would realise that he , a gentleman could never marry a nobody like her. She would keep it for now but when he was well enough to leave she would somehow contrive to pack it into whatever he took with him....She could feel the ring now under the fabric of her dress. She closed the book and hid it in a basket. Elisabet rose and climbed back upstairs. Elizabeth got wearily into bed.

CHAPTER SIXTEEN

Sunlight poured through the half open curtain illuminating the shallow hump of Elizabeth sleeping soundly in the bed. Mary drew back both curtains noticing as she did so that the screen which had once hidden the cupboard door was pulled to one side and that the door was ajar. She closed it and pulled the screen back into place. Tiptoeing to the bed she put the cup of tea which she had brought up with her on the bedside table carefully and bending over the still form said quietly, "Miss Bateman, a cup of tea for you."

Through a fog of sleep Elizabeth heard the voice and wondered if it were Elisabet calling her. But no she thought I am Elisabet. Opening her eyes she pushed herself up on one elbow and gazed around her with something like astonishment. Where am I she wondered? For a minute she did not recognise the room and then she registered Mary's anxious face looking down on her. Pushing herself up she waited as Mary arranged the pillows behind her until she was sitting comfortably and silently handed her the tea. Elizabeth sipped it gratefully. Eventually she found her voice. "Thank you Mary, what time is it ?"

Mary looked at the tired, colourless face and remarked that it was nearly midday.

"It can't be! Surely I have not slept so long," Elizabeth seemed very upset, " I have much to do and I cannot lie a bed all the forenoon."

"Well, you have," Mary remarked and wondered why Elizabeth was speaking so strangely. Mary added silently to herself that Elizabeth didn't look any better for her long sleep. She said out loud, "I have heated you a bowl of soup, do you want me to bring it up or will you come down?"

Elizabeth agreed that she would come downstairs and after Mary had gone she dressed slowly as she drank the rapidly cooling tea. She felt strangely light-headed and her fingers were clumsy as she fiddled with the tiny covered buttons on her blouse cuffs. They defeated her entirely so carrying the now empty cup she descended the stairs to ask for Mary's help.

❖

Elisabet, pouring water through her wood ash collected over the past few days for the purpose of making lye, looked gratefully up at the clear blue sky above. When she made her soap this time she thought she would add lavender to some and rose petals to the rest to scent it. Scented soap would smell lovely and it would sell well and for more money than the usual kind. She was sorely in need of money after paying the barber surgeon. Not that she regretted the actual spending of the money but she did question the way the man had treated John's shoulder. The wound continued to worry her as well as the recurring fevers which John was experiencing. He did not seem to be getting well and she had tried all the salves, potions, cleansing waters and poultices she possessed. She would try mould. Last evening she had dampened a piece of bread. She would leave it until the mould was grown enough to scrape off and cover the wound for she had been told by her own mother who had been a skilled healer and had taught her all she knew that the mould was a magical thing which would feast on the evil humours within the wound. She hoped it would for she had used it before and it had not helped. It was her last real hope. That and her continuous and fervent prayers.

As she stood dreamily watching the water draining through; the morning sun warm on her back she heard footsteps. Turning to face the path she saw with a sinking heart the trooper who had called twice coming around the corner from the direction of the herb garden. She wished him God's day fearfully. He made no reply to her greeting, merely stood, tall and dark against the morning brightness, his shadow long and menacing on the ground. Again she felt his gaze travelling down her person. She forced herself to speak.

"Is there ought amiss?" She enquired.

Still he made no answer. He stood as still as the great oak in the far meadow for what seemed like a lifetime to Elisabet. Then without a word turned and left the way he had come. His heavy footsteps died away. Elisabet's knees felt weak. She moved with the gait of an old woman inside to sit on the bottom stair tread. What did he want?

❖

Martha saw the postman on his rounds and waited for the gentle thud of mail dropping on the floor before she replaced the potato she was peeling in the bowl as carefully as if it were glass, wiped her hands slowly on her apron and went to pick it up. She never knew whether to be glad or worried these days at what the post might bring ever since she had heard from her sister of the tragic deaths of two young soldiers. There were two letters and one had Jonah's writing on it. She shouted to Amos who was sweeping up round the back and sat herself down at the kitchen table holding the unopened envelope in her hands. Only when Amos was seated did she carefully slit it with a knife and pass the one folded sheet to him as carefully as if it were ancient papyrus. Amos unfolded the paper, looked at it a minute, cleared his throat and read aloud.

'Dear Ma and Pa,
We went on a speshul train to the port. They give us tea, sandwitches, an appel and sum cigarets. I have gave mine to my pal, Jimmy, hoo smokes'

Here Amos stopped as Martha said, "Well now, fancy that he's made a pal already."

"He's a friendly lad you knows mother," agreed Amos. He cleared his throat again and continued reading.

'We are at a training plase called Base Camp at ---'

He stopped reading.

"Go on Amos," Martha implored him. "Where is our lad?"

"Well," Amos replied, scratching his head in wonder, "I dunno, they have crossed it out."

"Why?" Martha asked.

"Well..." Began Amos feeling his way, "in case it should fall into the hands of the enemy, yes that's it, in case they should read this letter."

"Fancy that, the Germans thinking our Jonah is so important that they want to know where he is. Well, carry on, read the rest."

Amos continued to read the little that remained. 'In about a week we will go up the line.' "Whatever that might mean." He added.

Elisabet sat on her stool by the fire. Gazing into the flames she wondered what to do next. John's wound had seemed to heal but now she saw that the mould was not doing any good. The flesh around the wound had always seemed discoloured but now as he lay with his arm beside him, the shoulder unbandaged, the arm could be seen to be so greatly swollen that it no longer resembled an arm. If Elisabet so much as touched it he gave a strangled cry. The skin of the arm was patched a reddish purple with a yellow-green area around the healed entry wound in the shoulder. Elisabet knew that the wound was poisoned. She had tried everything and now she knew that she must cut and try to get the poison out that way. Could she do it? She had never done anything like it before. There had never to her knowledge been anyone in the village with an injury remotely resembling this one. When she had been a child her mother had treated a man who had stuck a hay fork in his hand at harvest time but despite her ministrations Elisabet remembered that he had died quite soon. John she thought must be very strong and tenacious to live this long with what was beginning to look like a mortal wound. There was no one she could ask for help, no one she could trust to stay silent. She must do it herself or John would surely die. He may die anyway she thought even if I do it but I shall never forgive myself if he does die and I have not tried this final way to help him. She collected her sharpest knife and some stout lengths of cloth. Taking a pail of clean water she mounted the stairs with dread.

He was lying on the bed moaning softly. She knelt down beside him.

"John, dearest John." His eyelids flickered. "I must cut your shoulder. It will hurt. It will hurt most dreadfully. I must tie you. She took the final strip of cloth and tied it around his mouth, kissing him tenderly as she did so.

She had to hold his shoulder and at the touch of her hand his eyes sprang open and he gave a muffled cry. Jaw and teeth clenched Elisabet made two cuts either side of the puckered wound, enlarging it so that a great spurt of yellow pus erupted. Her tears were blinding her in this act of torturing the man she loved. She tried again. More pus spurted forth. She laid down the knife. She could do no more. She could not bear his strangled screams or his thrashing against the binding strips so she washed the now enlarged and suppurating wound, finally bathing it yet again with one of her herb potions she had already tried.

She removed the gag and the binding strips and fetching fresh, cool water bathed his face and body. He was cool and seemed to have drifted into a natural sleep. The arm was still grotesquely swollen. Elisabet took away the bowls and cloths and returning lay down beside the bed with one blanket serving as a covering and another as padding on the hard floor and prepared to wait out the night. She would not sleep she was certain..... Towards dawn she took a look at the figure on the bed. Was it her eyes or that she was still shocked by what she had had to do? She was sure that the figure was that of a woman, the woman she had seen before. The woman who broke into her life from time to time recently. She moved the blanket away and gave a sigh of relief. Of course it was John. She was just upset and imagining things. She lay down again and this time she slept.

Mary was extremely worried about Elizabeth. She looked much worse since her outing to Southwell and she had been reading that old book again. She had seen Elizabeth push it hurriedly under her pillow again today as if she were trying to hide something shameful. Mary had taken up her evening cocoa. She seemed furtive, different somehow. It wasn't natural. It wasn't right at all Mary thought for a person to have so much interest in someone so long dead. Mary had taken up the book that Miss Mason had brought hoping to interest Elizabeth in some real history and surely that book must be all right for Miss Mason was the vicar's daughter. Elizabeth didn't seem interested in it, quite oblivious in fact. Tomorrow, thought Mary, I will ask her if she wants me to return it to Miss Mason and ask her to lend another book or even come and visit. Mary made her way home in a slightly less worried frame of mind.

Elizabeth was reading avidly how Elisabet had 'operated' on the cavalier's shoulder. She wondered if she too should volunteer to do some nursing of the wounded when she was feeling better?

❖

Elisabet had fewer ills to tend in the village now that the weather was warmer and for that she was grateful. Whenever she went through the village that trooper seemed to be about. Just standing, watching. Not moving. Watching, not speaking. Watching her with an uncomfortable interest. Elisabet began to be wary of venturing out. She weeded and tended her herbs and wondered if he ever went out of the village. She was feeling afraid to venture out further afield to collect herbs. In the fields there was not always someone within calling distance as there was in the village now that the ploughing and sowing of oats, wheat and barley was finished. She was afraid that the trooper meant her harm of some kind.

John's arm was not quite as swollen she thought but it was still discoloured and painful. She was running out of poppy juice, she must go out collecting soon for other herbs to dull the pain.

When Mary suggested returning Miss Mason's book she was surprised at the vehement reply that Elizabeth made that she was not finished with it yet. Mary was determined however to call on Miss Mason and see if she would come and talk to Elizabeth and give her some other interest apart from that old book. She would go this very afternoon. She waited for Ben to come home from school. He did not burst in through the door as usual full of beans, news and questions but came in quietly with his hands deep in his trouser pockets.

"Hands out Ben," admonished his mother.

He didn't respond immediately. Instead he said slowly, "Mum, I know Miss Mason is a miss so she hasn't got a husband but she has got a brother like Miss Bateman, and her father is the vicar and -"

"And so Ben?" Mary raised her eyebrows, wondering what was coming next.

"And so why is she suddenly so sad?"

"Is she Ben?"

"Yes, she wasn't this morning. It was after dinner, she came back and her eyes were all red and her face here and here," He pointed to his own cheeks, "was all blotchy and she kept sniffing and blowing into her hanky. She said it was a cold when Violet asked her what was wrong."

"Cheeky young madam," Mary interrupted.

"But it came on very suddenly if it was and I don't think it is 'cos, well it was like you looked when grandpa died."

Mary was amazed at the powers of observation of her young son. She gave him bread and jam and a glass of milk. Leaving him to eat it she put on her hat and coat and made her way down to the vicarage.

As she neared it Miss Mason came out of the school room door and crossed the road. Close to Mary could see what Ben had meant and that Miss Mason had been crying. She was sure that somehow he was right. When Mary asked if she could speak to her a minute Miss Mason invited her into the vicarage. She led her into a drably furnished room whose window overlooked the graveyard.

When Mary was seated Miss Mason listened without comment and when Mary had finished she agreed that she would go and visit Miss Bateman but not this evening as she had had some very distressing news and would not therefore be the best company for an invalid. She continued that she would definitely go tomorrow.

Mary expressed her sorrow at Miss Mason's bad news.

"It was not a close relative," Miss Mason gulped, "but you knew him Mary....Leonard Peasebody"

"Mr Peasebody from the library?"

Miss Mason nodded.

"But he... he can only have been in France ...."

"For a very short time," Miss Mason finished for her. "He had only been in the front line for a few days. I had a letter from him only yesterday. Then, well his mother sent a message, it was here when I came back for dinner. He was killed a few days ago..." She began to cry softly, fumbling in her pocket for a clean handkerchief. Mary gave her a clean square of neatly hemmed cloth which was her handkerchief and sat uncomfortably listening to the muffled and choking sobs. Miss Mason finally wiped her eyes, blew her nose and said,

"I'm sorry Mary.....I will see you get this back washed and ironed." She put Mary's hanky in her pocket. "It's just that...well, we had become engaged before he left. No ring as yet, no announcement, just an understanding until he came home on leave and now..."

Mary rose. "It is I who should be sorry to have come. Ben said that something was wrong. I'm sorry too about Mr Peasebody. Such a lovely, clever man, such a great loss to you, his family...." Her voice petered out. "I'm sure that Miss Bateman will be shocked to hear this news, she was very taken with his knowledge. Well, goodbye Miss Mason, I'll find my way out."

Mary walked slowly and sadly home. As she walked she thought about Mr Peasebody and Miss Mason. What a waste she thought angrily. A waste of two lives; one ended brutally and the other shattered emotionally.

Elisabet had been spinning all evening while John slept above. From time to time she rose and moved as quietly as she could to check that he slept soundly still. Returning to her spinning each time she felt pleased with the growing hanks of wool hanging from the nails along the end beam. Eventually with a satisfied sigh she was finished. Tomorrow she thought she would wash the linen if the day was fine and blowy.

Elizabeth reading the journal was surprised at the number and variety of tasks that her Stuart counterpart had accomplished. Besides cooking, cleaning and mending Elisabet had recorded making soap, collecting herbs, making medicines, milking, gardening, going to market, making candles. She must have worked from daybreak to dark to accomplish all this and to take care of a badly wounded man as well. The burden must have become intolerable at times. Elizabeth put the book under her pillow and began to dress. Sunlight made a golden ladder through the window on which dust motes ascended and descended. The birds sang noisily. Elizabeth opened the window breathing deeply the cool, sweet, early morning air.

❖

Elisabet descended the stairs awkwardly, trying not to trip over the bundle of sheets in her arms. She had already set out the buck tub and the under tub on the flagstones near the back door. Carefully folding each sheet she set it in the tub, placing sticks to hold the folds apart. It was some time before she had them folded and placed to her liking. She straightened up. Going to her herb room she took a ball of dried fern ash and added this to the tub. She filled it with water from her two wooden buckets. While the linen was soaking she made two journeys across the road to refill the buckets and then sat down to wait for the dirt to loosen.

As she sat daydreaming she saw out of the corner of her eye a figure standing in the garden. Afraid it was the trooper again she rose hurriedly. It was a man, quite a tall man, as tall as her cavalier. Rather like him in build and the way he stood leaning against the wall. It was not him: the clothes that this man wore were strange and drab. His hair was short but his features and green eyes were so similar.... Very afraid now that this was some shade from hell come to fetch her John Elisabet ran as fast as she could without thought for waking John. Rather she did want him to be awake for awake he could not be taken stealthily into death. She looked round the door. He was propped up on the bed. He grinned at her.

When she eventually got back downstairs the figure had gone. By midday the sheets were washed and rinsed and were stretched out ever the smaller trees and bushes to bleach in the sun and Elisabet's back felt as if it were broken by all the bending, lifting and water carrying. Pleased with her efforts she went inside to search out bread, cheese and small ale. She had completely forgotten her fright and the apparition she had glimpsed earlier.

CHAPTER SEVENTEEN

Elisabeth was as sad as Mary when she was told by the latter of Mr Peasebody's death the following day. She wondered if all wars and battles had always been so for womenfolk waiting at home or was this mechanised conflict in some way different from all the horrors that had gone before. In size maybe but for each individual woman who suffered it had always meant heartbreak. She still felt tired and listless, the doctor's medicine seemed to be achieving little. She thought that she would go and sit in a chair in the sitting room where the morning sun streamed through the easterly window. She took her book; an often read favourite from her school days; 'Emma,' and made herself comfortable. The village was quiet, she could hear the clock's slow, measured tick from the other room, sparrows quarrelling outside the window. Presently her eyes closed and she slept.

Rudely awakened by heavy, clumping footsteps her eyes opened to see boots; tall, brown, leather boots with wide, cuffed tops at the side of her. She squinted up from her sitting position on the bed of camomile to see a tall man in a leather jerkin, sash around his waist, white, plain collar to his shirt and a face which seemed carved from stone, topped with short, cropped hair looking down at her. She saw her dress, shoes, twisted leg......she tried to rise. The trooper made no attempt to help her. Brushing down her skirts she inquired through parched lips why he was here.

"To make thy acquaintance mistress." came the slow, quiet but slightly ominous reply.

"You have already done so," responded Elisabet turning away towards the corner of the cottage. When she reached the door she glanced back and saw with dread that he was following her.

"I come to make a much closer acquaintance."

"And I am busy." Elisabet replied tartly, anger at his persistence overcoming her fear.

"Busy sleeping on the bare ground like the common jade thou art.?"

"How dare you!" Elisabet's cheeks had two spots of colour.

"I dare mistress for I have come to avail myself of thy services."

"You are ill?" Did he after all only require medicine Elisabet wondered.

"Why no mistress, unless thou wouldst say that lack of a woman be an illness."

"Then I can do nothing for you," All the while Elisabet had been edging closer to the safety of her door, now she reached out to open the latch. If I can get inside quickly she thought in panic and draw the bolt..... He put a restraining hand on her arm. Elisabet tried to pull the door but found his other large hand pinioning her wrist and forcing her hand back.

"Let go sir, you are hurting me"

He twisted her round violently and pushed her back against the wall, jarring her spine on the rough, protruding corner bricks. With one hand, holding her pinned against the wall, he fumbled to undo the laces of her bodice. Elisabet thumped him ineffectually with her free hand. He stopped and slapped her face first one way and then the other making her head spin and her teeth rattle. Momentarily stunned Elisabet slumped against the wall. She felt his rough hands ripping her bodice laces open and thrusting beneath her skirt. That was when she screamed. Screamed, kicked, tried to bite, gouged with her fingernails. But he was stronger, more determined.

. Her strength was ebbing as they struggled and his repeated attacks were succeeding. Elisabet heard through her panic, over the rasping of her own breath and the trooper's grunts a noise like the squeak of the door opening and its grating on the flagstones. Suddenly the Roundhead slumped against her, his grip loosened, knees buckled and he slumped at her feet. Dazed, confused, bruised and bewildered Elisabet looked down and saw a sword protruding from his back and holding on to the door jamb was John, her Cavalier.

Ignoring her ripped dress she stepped over the body of the Roundhead and rushed to ease John's fall as his knees bent and he folded into a sitting position against the door. They sat on the flagstones, Elisabet's arms around him without speaking for sometime, each just drawing comfort from the other. Eventually Elisabet said quietly, "He is dead John."

"Good, I meant him to be. I saw what he was intending to do to you as I opened the door, I heard your screams."

Elisabet gasped, "Do you think anyone else did?"

"Mayhap they did, find something to put over him, cover yourself with a shawl," he began to raise himself painfully, "I shall go inside in case anyone has heard and comes to see what is amiss."

Helping him inside and putting on her shawl Elisabet stood at the door, her mind racing. What could she cover him with which would not look odd? Logs, small sticks, pile them over him where he lay against the wall. Moving the logs from across the small yard was easy but putting them on his body made her stomach churn and bile rise hot and sour in her throat. She was hot and queasy by the time the task was accomplished. She stood back to view the newly constructed wood pile from all angles. No. Nothing of him could be seen even with careful scrutiny. It would have to suffice for the moment.

She went inside to wash herself, stripping off her dress she stood in her shift, shivering now and scrubbing at herself with a rough cloth soaked in cold water from her bucket until her skin was red and sore and the feel of his brutal hands was erased. Taking needle and thread she mended the rents in her bodice, luckily these were not too large, the dress was of closely woven, strong wool and it was mostly the lacing that was broken. When she had put in new laces and redressed she saw a length of coloured wool on the floor. Bending down to pick it up she saw it was the wool which she had used to tie John's ring around her neck. The ring was gone, search as she might in her clothing, on the floor, in the water bucket and outside the door there was no sign of it at all. It was for Elisabet the last straw which caused her to break down and sob and sob and sob.

When Elizabeth awoke it was to find her cheeks wet with tears. The sun had moved around and the room felt chilly. Picking up her book that had slipped on to the carpet she rose stiffly, rubbing her eyes and stretching she thought that either it had been a very vivid dream or more likely that she had slipped into Elisabet's life once again. She wondered about the dead Roundhead, she would read more of the diary and find out.

Opening the book and turning the pages she saw that she had read almost to the end. There were only four more closely written pages she realised. She wondered why. It never occurred to her to go straight to the end. She read slowly, keeping the account in the order it had been written. The writing here was very uneven.......

Elisabet found John lying on the bed exhausted and in obvious pain. Although since she had cut open the wound and released the evil humours there the swelling of the arm had gone down somewhat she noticed that the discoloured patches were slowly growing in size and the pain he experienced seemed to increase with it. Elisabet made him comfortable and watched him fall into a drugged sleep. She knew that he was having too much of her poppy juice, but nothing else would ease his pain. She dreaded to think what she would do when it ran out.

She went back downstairs and sat spinning by the light of the fire. It was a soothing rhythm and the growing hanks of wool gave her a feeling of satisfaction and contentment. She hummed softly as she worked, turning over in her mind how she would tackle the question of the death of the Roundhead when she went to arrange for the vicar to bury the body.....

John woke in the darkness. There was a strange, unpleasant smell and stretching out his arms he felt cold earth and sacking around him. Sweat broke out all over his body. He had been buried alive. His fingers scrabbled against the wet clay, the earth trembled and shook. He was not completely buried he could see the sky, night sky, he felt rain on his face. Not buried then, in a hole. Hands stretched in front of him he walked forwards. He was standing not lying. Not buried at all. People were not buried standing up. The hole was deep and narrow and stretched out on either side. There was a loud crump, a screaming whistle, bright, huge stars burst above him, growing and falling.......

❖

Elizabeth read on. She was now quite at ease with the script which Elisabet used and had little difficulty deciphering it except when she came to a part where damp had mottled the page. What a strange story. Elizabeth sat back and thought about what she had just read. The fire was glowing and all was still and quiet except for the sound of the coals settling. Elisabet had been prepared to go to the parish priest and ask him to bury the dead trooper but the Cavalier had prevented her from telling anyone. When Elisabet had tried to insist that the man must be given a Christian burial in the churchyard John had warned her that she would in all probability then be accused of the Roundhead's murder. So what was she to do Elisabet had enquired? John had said that they must get rid of the body as soon as possible before someone from his troop started searching for him. Elisabet at first thought of putting him on her cart and taking the body out of the village to hide it in one of the many ditches but John had vetoed that too as much too dangerous with troopers and villagers about. Eventually they came to the conclusion that they could only bury him safely somewhere in Elisabet's long garden, but where? Elisabet walked up the garden searching for a likely spot. Not too near the house, not in the orchard there were too many tree roots for a deep enough hole to be dug. So where? Near the side of the pond the ground had a roundish hollow where some years ago Elisabet's father had removed the roots of a large, diseased tree, digging out the massive root ball had left this depression. If they could just make it a little deeper...it would be ideal.

John instructed Elisabet to make a rope harness to fasten around his waist and chest. After they had moved the covering logs the other ends were firmly tied around the body. Bent almost double with the strain John slowly hauled the macabre burden up the slight slope of the flagstone and grass pathway. As he heaved and pulled the Roundhead was dragged slowly behind him with a sickening, rubbing sound. Elisabet, following behind thought that she would hear the noise in her mind as long as she lived. John was exhausted by the time the pond was reached. Elisabet fetched bread, cheese and ale and they rested in the orchard trying to ignore the spectre behind them as they gulped down sustenance to fuel the digging of the hole. When they had finished Elisabet took her spade and enlarged the hole as best she could. John watched, unable to help her, he could not even hold a spade let alone dig with it. When they judged the hole deep enough Elisabet replaced the harness around John and the body was hauled the last few feet to his final resting place.

Elisabet and her Cavalier stood with their heads bowed while they repeated what words they could remember of the burial service. Then Elisabet used the spade again to cover him over while John stamped down on the newly dug earth to compact it. Now the depression was gone, earth level, no trace that any trooper had been in the garden except for this patch of new, dark brown earth, Elisabet and John now disguised this with loose grass, fallen leaves and the odd dead branch. Standing back and surveying their work they were satisfied that they had done all they could. Completely drained of energy and emotion they made their way wearily back to the cottage. Elisabet felt guilty. She did not really know why, but she did. It seemed somehow to be all her fault that the Roundhead was dead and she did not like the shabby way in which they had buried the body. She did not mention any of this to John, nor tell him of the loss of the ring. Tomorrow morn while he still slept she would rebuild the log pile in its original position and then she was certain that she would find it.

At the bottom of the page Elizabeth stopped reading and stared into the fire. She didn't find it, Elizabeth thought, because I did. How did she miss it? Elisabet had known approximately where to look. It would surely have caught the sunlight in the crack; it would not have been so deeply embedded then. So why didn't she find it?

CHAPTER EIGHTEEN

Captain John Bateman stepped outside the dugout. For some strange reason the night was quiet and rain fell gently. The trench system here was well organised, deep trenches in three lines; front line, support trench and reserve trench with barbed wire entanglements in front where no-man's-land lay. His dugout was quite close to the communication trench that led back to the safer rear areas. Beneath his feet were wooden duck boards and in front the fire step. He leaned back against the sand-bagged wall and stared up at the night sky, not a star to be seen, he thought about Elizabeth and his parents and home, he worried more about them than he ever did about his own safety. He had a fatalistic attitude to that. He was jerked out of his reverie by a star shell bursting overhead....

Jonah was in the front line now, he had sent Amos and Martha a field postcard and was now sitting in a funk hole with a stub of pencil trying to write a letter. He had never been good with his letters and it was always a burden to write but now it had an added horror. He was in a dilemma for he was petrified and even more afraid of showing it to his fellow soldiers and of writing something which would worry them at home. He decided eventually after much licking of his pencil to say that he was in clean, dry trenches with a field of poppies behind and that the stew was good. That he was safe and well and was pleased to receive the parcel. That would do he thought , nothing there to worry them. He stood up and putting the pencil stub in his tunic pocket began to fold the sheet of paper carefully. A German sniper had already lined up his rifle and could not believe it when the Tommy just stood there while he took aim, squeezed the trigger and fired.

Elizabeth stood at the edge of the pond waiting to get her breath back. She thought back to the last time when she had walked up while Bill and Mary were tidying the garden. She hadn't been as out of breath coming up the slight rise then. Perhaps she should get more exercise. But she had noticed that recently if she stood too long her ankles became quite puffy and she had to sit down with her feet on a stool for the swelling to subside. She sat down now on an old wooden chair that Bill had brought up for this purpose when he came to do the vegetable garden. The April sun turned the now green leaves to an even brighter green, the grass had lost its dead Winter look with a small forest of new, pale spikes and clumps of taller, broader leaves dotted here and there. Bluebells soon thought Elizabeth happily. She gazed at the neatly dug vegetable plot with its fine tilth and lines of black cotton criss-crossed to prevent the birds from taking Bill's seed which he had begun to sow now that the weather was warming up. She studied the pond, concentrating her gaze around the edge and wondering if there was any clue to where Elisabet and the Cavalier had buried the Roundhead. They had filled in the depression and the ground around here was so uneven it would be impossible to see if there had been a disturbance a mere year ago never mind three hundred and fifty years ago!

"Morning Miss." Elizabeth turned to see Bill. He touched the rim of his cap.

"Morning Bill."

"You don't want me to clean out that old pond when I've done planting do ya?" He pointed to the weeds at the side and the flat, plate-shaped lily pads.

"Not really, I was just sitting and noticing how uneven the ground is around this side of the pond. I wondered why."

"Ah, that would be where it's shrunk."

"It was bigger once?" Elizabeth had not thought that the pond might have changed shape.

"Oh yes, before old Sam came here it was. Not that I can remember, mind, but I do remember my old dad saying that it was a strange place, oval shaped the pond were then. " He sketched an ellipse in the air.

"Why was it filled in?"

"Well, I don't rightly know, miss, but my dad said that old Sam when he was a young man was doing something, don't remember what, near the edge and he found an old stone. Laid flat in the ground it were, about three feet tall and about this wide," he held his hands about eighteen inches apart, "with a curved top," he sketched an arc in the air, "and it had a cross scratched on it."

"A gravestone, here?" Elizabeth wondered if it had anything to do with the trooper's burial.

"That's just what it looked like my old dad said and Sam found a lot of rubbish under it."

"What sort of rubbish?"

"Don't rightly know, bits of metal, bits of bone. He said that it were an old rubbish dump so he used it as one, for rubbish of his that is and then put soil on the top. Over the years he gradually made the pond smaller and smaller..."

"What a shame," commented Elizabeth quietly. Now she would never know, would never find anything because she suspected that old Sam or rather young Sam as he was then had found the stone which covered the earthly remains of the Roundhead. She looked around trying to remember where she had been standing when the other Elisabet had said, 'Not there that is where the trooper is buried' She rose and walked to near where she thought it was.

"Could the stone have been found here?" She pointed to the ground at her feet.

"Don't rightly know Miss," Bill admitted, pushing his cap backwards from his forehead, "but I can show you the old stone he found, it's been leaning up against the wall ever since, never found any use for it you might say," Bill turned and walked back towards the cottage. Elizabeth followed more slowly but with rising excitement.

Bill went to the corner of the wall where Samuel's outhouse abutted at right angles. Here was a large water butt, Bill pulled it forwards, grunting with the effort for it was a good half full, so that he could get his hands behind it. With much more grunting and a few silent curses as he scraped his knuckles against the uneven bricks he drew out the stone. He brushed leaves and dirt from it with his hands and picked off a couple of large striped snails. Finished his rudimentary cleaning he pulled it along the flagstones and leaned it against the cottage wall. It was exactly as he had described it and indeed in the centre was a faintly scratched cross.

"It certainly looks like a gravestone," said Elizabeth crouching down to get a closer look.

"It does that Miss, a rough one I'll admit but why would it be up near the pond here and not in its proper place in the churchyard?"

"I've no idea," Elizabeth lied, still studying it.

"I'll be getting on now Miss if you'll excuse me," Bill touched his cap again and made his way back up the garden to his vegetable patch.

Elizabeth rose and went inside to fetch the small hearth brush and began to clean the stone more carefully. Soon the cross stood out more clearly and then she saw some other scratchings below it. She felt carefully with her fingers, closing her eyes to concentrate as a blind man might feel his way along an unfamiliar wall. Yes, they were in a pattern. Excited now she returned inside once more to fetch the largest piece of paper she had from the living room and a soft pencil. Holding the paper as steadily as she could and trying to keep it taut across the area of the scratches she rubbed slowly across with the pencil. Gradually the scratching showed up as whitish marks. Finished she held it up to the light. There was certainly something there; an R, squiggles, then an N, something else and then an H, a gap and finally A D. Underneath was a six with a long, curved top; a four and a three.

Going inside with the paper Elizabeth sat at the table and wrote the letters and numbers down clearly at the bottom of the sheet, leaving gaps for those she could not decipher. Frowning with concentration she looked at the figures, could the one be missing so that it would be a date, 1643? It would fit with Elisabet's story. Elizabeth sat back and thought. In her writing Elisabet always referred to the man as the trooper or the Roundhead as if she had never known his name. Elizabeth wrote the word Roundhead putting the modern letters under the scratchings and squiggles. That was it! Roundhead 1643! Elisabet had somehow tried to give her enemy and attacker a proper grave!

The telegram form had fluttered to the floor. Amos stood like a graven image, immobile, seeing nothing. Martha bent down and picking up the single sheet saw typing interspersed with hand-written words. She read slowly.

Dear Sir,

It is my painful duty to inform you that a report has this day been received from the War Office notifying the death of (no.) 29031 (rank) Private (name) Jonah Smith (regiment) Southwell Company 8th Sherwood Foresters on the twenty-eighth day of March 1915 and I am to express to you the sympathy and regret of the Army Council at your loss. The cause of death was killed in action.

If any articles of private property left by the deceased are found they will be forwarded to this office but some time will probably elapse before their receipt and when received they cannot be disposed of until authority is received from the War Office.

Applications regarding the disposal of any such personal effects, or of any amount which may eventually be found to be due to the late soldier's estate should be addressed to 'The Secretary, War Office, London S. W.' and marked outside 'Effects'

I am, Sir
Your obedient servant, Major ------------
Officer in charge of Records
No. 1 --------District.

Mr. A. Smith
Turn Close,
Hockerton,
Notts.

After reading it carefully and slowly again out loud of all the communication only three words hung in the air 'killed in action'

"Must 'ave made a mistake," she muttered, peering at the scrawled signature. "Our Jonah don't know no Majors and 'e's only just wrote and 'e didn't say 'e were in action, must be a mistake...." She thrust the paper in front of her husband's unseeing gaze. "Amos it's a mistake int it ?"

He did not answer. Her voice rose as she repeated the question, flapping the paper more and more wildly every time she screeched 'mistake.' Soon she was screaming senselessly and flapping the telegram across Amos' face. He moved then, folding his arms around her, pulling her close to him and said in a thick, choking voice,

"Nay Martha tis not a mistake, our Jonah is dead."

❖

Elisabet woke suddenly. Fingers of sunlight poked through the closed shutters making bars of yellow across the dim room. She rose awkwardly from her makeshift bed on the floor. As fast as she could she made for the stairs and the outside door. She only just reached the sink-hole in time. Her body shuddered as she retched. Eventually with a vile taste in her mouth she made her way slowly to her herb room and poured a mug full of water from the bucket which she sipped slowly. Wetting a cloth in the same bucket she patted her face and neck. She sat down heavily on the stool. She still felt nauseous. She counted slowly on her fingers first backwards and then even more slowly forwards. No, there was no mistake. Her courses were late, very late. Her gaze strayed to the array of potions on her bench. No, she would take nothing to promote them. If this was a baby as she believed it to be then it was her beloved Cavalier's child and she would do nothing to harm it. Even if he recovered and went back to fight for the King and did not return as he had promised her he would then at least she would have, God willing, something of him. Smoothing her hair back she rose and reclimbed the stairs.

Before lunchtime the news of Jonah's death had reached all corners of the village. There was general shock for although a number of the younger men had gone to France this was the first casualty and in such a small village it naturally affected everyone to some degree or other. There was also grief as well as sympathy for Martha and Amos who were well liked but especially as everyone knew that they had taken Jonah from the orphanage and treated him like a son.

"He only went cos they took the horses," was the general comment as villager after villager shook their heads in disbelief and dismay that young Jonah would never drive them to Newark on market day again.

Mary wept and Miss Mason told the children not to return to afternoon school. She sat at her high desk and turned back the pages of the old register to find Jonah's name. He had only attended the school a short time but he had no absence marks besides his name and the previous teacher, Mr Ratcliffe had written in the log book beside his name, 'a cheerful and willing lad,' on the last day before he had left to help Amos full time at the age of thirteen. Full time. Miss Mason wondered if Jonah's few short years of life since could be called 'full time.' She closed the book with a heavy heart and replaced it and the register in the cupboard. She locked the outside door and with determined steps made her way across the road to offer what comfort she could to the grieving couple.

As she neared the door she heard Amos muttering, "Bloody horses. He would never 'ave gone if they 'adn't taken the bloody horses. Won't be any more bloody horses in these 'ere stables. I shall 'ave one of them noisy, dirty motor cars so I shall. You can't love one of them. My lad wouldn't 'ave gone if they'd taken a bloody motor car!"

CHAPTER NINETEEN

Elisabet spent an anxious week every hour expecting the banging of a leather-clad fist on her door and the demand to enter and search for the missing Roundhead. She kept to the cottage and garden, checking constantly that the grave was undisturbed by foxes. Each time she added something to the patch of newly-turned earth; mossy stones on the edge nearest to the pond; clumps of spring flowers dug up from the top of her orchard and grass from where it grew near the new hedge that bounded an enclosed part of Sparrowthorn field. The April sun and alternating rain showers helped the disturbed roots take hold and disguise the raw earth. Early one morning in the second week since the trooper's death Elisabet heard horsemen outside. Heart in mouth she peered cautiously through the shutters and saw with relief the Roundhead troopers riding out of the village. She wondered where they were heading.

Between worrying about a possible search and trying to disguise the trooper's grave Elisabet had done little but tend to John. He seemed to alternate between bouts of fever and pain and shorter and increasingly fewer times when he could leave his bed and struggle downstairs. Elisabet was now sleeping almost permanently on her makeshift floor bed and was still rushing downstairs every morning to be sick in the sink hole. She wished that she had some powdered acorns left to stop this vomiting but these she had used to help a sick child just after Christmas. Today she thought as she washed herself I must go to market. The previous evening she had loaded the cart what produce she had; eggs, three young cockerels, some spun and dyed wool and bunches of herbs picked from her garden. She had had little time to make many of her potions but she did have a good basketful of her soap scented with lavender and rose petals to sell.

John looked a little better today she thought later as she backed her horse into the shafts. But she must be as quick as she could for she did not want to leave him alone too long.... She would light a candle and say a prayer for him at the Minster, or perhaps not for such things were being frowned on now and might actually cause trouble for her and ultimately for John. Mounting the cart she clicked her tongue and flipped the reins turning the horse's head towards the Southwell road.

❖

John the Cavalier dreamed that he was in Hell. He knew in his fevered mind that it was Hell but not how he had come to be there. Perhaps he had come in the great explosion which his half conscious mind had both heard and seen. He was in a desolate landscape, his ears battered by noise when suddenly the whole hill in front of him was thrown up into the air as if by the gigantic hand of a roaring devil. It was followed by yells and screams as around him a myriad of drably clad figures ran towards the great abyss where the hill had been. He struggled mentally to awake as his strangely numb and seemingly invisible body moved forward slowly in their wake. The evening light was eerily swirling with smoke and dust, he walked on the corpses of men, disfigured and defiled with blood, clay and dirt, unrecognisable as human, features blown away and horses, horses lying mutilated... if this was not Hell then he knew that it was the gateway to it.

Captain John Bateman was back in the front line trenches in the Ypres salient after his all too brief period of respite. At about half past four that afternoon he and his brother officers had had their tea of tinned peaches and milk ruined by heavy German shelling.

"Damn the Jerries to hell!" exclaimed Lt. George Smithers as a large lump of the dugout roof fell into his portion. John Bateman decided to take a look outside in a brief lull in the shelling. The men were keeping their heads down, many crouched in funk holes. A lieutenant of the Royal Scots came hurriedly down the communication trench,

"The village is a mess, dead men and horses," he remarked conversationally, "there is a stream of locals coming down the road, old, young, kids, animals; all fleeing from the shelling."

"Let's get inside," John replied, leading the way back into the dugout. He stood at the entrance listening to the heavy shell fire to the north west that was increasing in volume every minute as the sun began to sink. In the failing light he could see a flash and shrapnel whirling and here and there the light of a rocket. But where the British line joined the French trenches there was something strange, a curious low cloud of yellow-green smoke or was it fog...? Suddenly down the road came a galloping troop of horses, the riders goading them frenziedly, followed by another and another until the road was a seething mass of men and horses overlaid with a pall of dust. Obviously something dreadful was happening. The men were now also standing watching, dumbstruck. Then on the breeze came a pungent, nauseating smell that made John's eyes smart and his nose tickle. Men continued to stream down the road in a mad charge. John saw that some horses were carrying two or three men. Across the fields raced mobs of infantry; throwing down their rifles and equipment so that they would not impede their headlong flight. One dark-visaged Algerian stumbled yards from where John stood. He was frothing at the mouth, eyes bulging in their sockets. He fell writhing into the trench.

The Cavalier came to with a start. He was wet with sweat, his head was pounding. With his good arm he pushed himself into a sitting position and slowly swung his legs over the side of the bed. He was deadly afraid. He knew that he had been given a foretaste of Hell. Was that his destination? Slowly in his lucid moments in the last few weeks he had come to accept that he would not leave this cottage to go back and fight for the King. He had surreptitiously looked at his arm hoping that Elisabet would not notice his concern. He knew that the poison was spreading. He knew that there was nothing more his good, brave Elisabet could do for him. She could not save either his arm or his life. His mind drifted back over what he could remember. Little cameos had flitting in and out of his mind's eye for a week or so; himself as a small boy playing with a wooden sword, dressed in splendid attire when King James had briefly visited his family home, the sweet flowery smell and rustle of his mother's skirts...then a grown man, his father proudly waving him 'God speed' as he left to join King Charles' army...following the charge of the dashing Prince Rupert on a jet-black steed...the exhilaration of the ride, feeling invincible, victorious...the ambush along the road...musket shots... A hot, burning pain in his shoulder...coming to a muddy ditch, making his painful way across country, over fields, through woods, towards the King's town of Newark...collapsing by the pond.....Elisabet....Elisabet...with a smile on his face and feeling deathly tired he lay down again and slept.

❖

Elisabet had sold all she had taken and bought salt, a new sharp knife and a cooking pot and was ready to return home. She turned the cart down towards the Minster and tethering the horse to a tree made her way to the north door. Inside all was cool and dim...and bare. She saw that even the beautiful crucifix on the altar, the lace-trimmed cloth and the silver candlesticks had been removed. There was no chance of lighting a candle for John here either. She slipped to her knees to try and form a prayer for his healing. No words would come. Her mind remained blank. Fearing that this was the answer to her unvoiced plea she quietly muttered a 'Hail Mary' and an 'Our Father,' crossed herself and rose to leave. A man in the dark, sombre clothes of a Puritan had been watching her and as he put out his hand to touch her arm she jumped in surprise.

"Oh sir, I did not see you there."

"No, Mistress for sure you did not and what you said and did was not advisable" his tone was low and measured but looking up at him fearfully Elisabet saw that his eyes regarded her kindly.

"I know not what else to do sir, no other words would come."

"I know and I see you are heavily burdened with worry and trouble."

"Indeed I am sir, one whom I hold dear is very sick and like to die."

"I shall pray for you both," came the kind reply before he turned and was lost to view behind a pillar.

Elisabet returned home and straightway went up the stairs to see how John fared. He seemed to be sleeping peacefully but Elisabet was conscious afresh of the strong, unhealthy smell which permeated the room. The smell of herbs, sickness, sweat and underlying these the stench of corruption and death.

She returned to unharness the horse and remove her purchases from the cart, meagre as they were. As she made her way back Alys Smalles came out of her cottage and hailed her,

"You alright?" Alys asked, "I've not seen you at all for some time, you well Elisabet?"

"Yes, thank you Alys, just busy that's all."

"You look peaky." Alys was like a dog worrying at a bone, "you should rest. Glad to say them troopers have gone again. Come here they did wanting bread and ale and cheese. I got no spare I told them. Mind your manners says one. Well, I says you're not a gentleman I can see. Oh you like gentlemen do you? He sneered. Them with curls and love locks, them Cavaliers. He made it sound like a rude word Elisabet. Don't you talk like that about the King's loyal men to me I says not when you is standing in my garden, be off with you I says and I flapped my broom at him so I did...." She stopped for breath.

"That was very brave of you, Alys," remarked Elisabet, desperate to get away.

"Didn't think what I was saying at the time I was so mad. Still am when I thinks about it"

"Did you want me for ought else Alys" Elisabet enquired.

"Ah, yes I wondered if you might have some of that soothing syrup you make for my chest?" She rubbed herself above her ample bosom.

"I'll go right now and bring you some." Elisabet moved in her ungainly way across the road and was soon back at Alys' door with a small, corked pottery flask that she gave to Alys. Alys thanked her and offered a parcel wrapped in sacking. Quite a large parcel, drips of blood fell from it.

"A little good meat," Alys winked at Elisabet, "for your cooking pot 'cos I knows you have an extra mouth to feed."

"How do you....?" Elisabet let her shocked voice trail away.

"Alys knows, Alys sees. But Alys don't say nothing." Her neighbour replied cryptically.

But had Ellen Wright seen or anyone else in the vicinity? Would they say anything if the Roundheads returned to the village?

John had been writing in Elisabet's book. He had woken after his short sleep and felt the urgent need to set down all he could on paper. He could only find her book so he had written a few lines trying to explain what he remembered. Already he felt ill, very ill. The pain, strangely, had all gone for the first time since the musket ball had been fired at him and found its mark. He felt strangely light and floaty. Looking out of the window he realised that it was nearly sunset. A strange, evil-looking yellowy-green mist like the winter fog that creeps over the fields was advancing across his line of vision. The drab, man-shapes were there again, strange, devilish shapes with dark faces like the demons which took men to Hell with their fiery pincers in the Doom paintings on the church wall of his youth. They had once been painted over but the white had flaked away leaving a partly obscured vision of Hell. These figures came through the mist like those Doom demons had peered through the flaking lime wash. But these were coming towards him, choking and coughing.......there was no sound other than this, just the deadly, silent fog advancing, advancing and enveloping everything, including him.....

John Bateman heard a shout. "Gas, gas!"

He could see men coming towards him, gasping, choking, mucus and phlegm on their faces, eyes streaming. Shells began to burst overhead, machine guns rattled.

"They've broken through!" shouted a voice with a Canadian accent, "the bastards have used gas, they've broken through"

Captain John Bateman drew his revolver and gave his last order, "Fix bayonets, fix bayonets!"

When Elisabet returned she found John slumped over her little note book, the quill still grasped in his cooling fingers. He had been writing. She eased him gently until he was lying flat on the bed. She closed his eyes with her hand and arranged his arms and legs straight. No need to worry about hurting him now, he would never feel hurt again. Elisabet, stony faced pulled the blanket over him until it reached his chin. She could not bear to pull it right over his face she did not want to consign him to the darkness just yet. She had failed him. All her so-called skills had been of no use; she hadn't even been with him when he died. She had failed and deserted him when he had needed her most. And that hurt. Hurt with a pain so sharp that she was unable to cry or feel any sort of grief which would have been a lesser hurt. She slowly descended to fetch cloths and water to clean and prepare him ready for burial. Ice had entered her heart, winter had fallen on her, a cold dead, eternal winter of the spirit.

Elizabeth, reading the book had come to a few lines of writing in a different hand; thick, black writing, masculine and curly. Was it the Cavalier's writing? It was difficult to decipher after Elisabet's neat script. She read it with difficulty. So he had been a cavalry officer and had served with Prince Rupert. The last sentence was barely legible and tailed off to little more than a scrawl. It said, 'I have remembered who I am dearest Elisabet, I am Edward, John, Marmaduke...' Oh no, thought Elizabeth for the next few words were so badly smudged that she could not read them! Only in the middle of the smudge could she make out one word, 'Earl' and then the writing tailed away. Underneath Elisabet's neat script resumed the story, 'I came home from market and found John dead this evening.' That stark phrase told all. There was nothing more at the bottom of the page.

Elizabeth had put the book away in the cupboard. She was no longer sure that she wanted to read the remaining page. She would eventually she thought if only to find out what Elisabet had done. She already knew some of what had happened from the entries she had found in the parish registers, the cavalier she guessed was under the entry 'John the souldger' and Elisabet's death and that of her baby son was only six months later in the November.

There had been no recent communication from either her brother or her parents so she sat by the fire to read the daily paper. War news was hardly to be avoided. The British and French had made a counter attack in Artois; the British against a ridge called Aubers ridge and the French at Vimy. Many women had gone into the factories to make shells for the army as well as taking over the driving of ambulances. Elizabeth thought idly that at least this abominable war was giving women a chance to prove what they could do. Surely after it was over they would be given the vote. Suddenly she realised that all she had endured as a suffragette she did not really care. The vote had now become for her at least no longer very important. The lives of hundreds of thousands maybe millions of young men of all nationalities, friend or foe, were for her now much more valuable and all she really desired was that the fighting should stop. She closed the paper with a sigh. She did feel so tired all the time. She would write a cheery letter to John and then make her way up to bed.

CHAPTER TWENTY

John Bateman senior, Lord Chartington, sat drumming his fingers on the deep shine of his dining room table.

"You must go," his wife insisted, "you cannot allow Elizabeth to read her only brother's name in the casualty list of some newspaper."

He did not answer. His fingers though had stopped their drumming and he now reached for his gold watch chain which hung across his portly stomach. Taking out the watch he opened it up and consulted the engraved dial morosely. His wife waited saying nothing. She knew that to urge him further would be counter productive. She had learned over many years of their married life that her stubborn husband could be cajoled but never pushed. He must always be allowed space to make the final decision himself and in his own time. The silence stretched out. He considered. Never a man to make up his mind in a hurry but when he had decided he rarely wasted any time acting on his decision. He had acted rashly and harshly he knew that now when he had cut Elizabeth out of his life and affairs after her first arrest. He should have taken more time. He knew that throughout his life whenever he acted in haste he always had regretted it afterwards. He should have taken more time to study the problem, talk to her... He regretted what he had said and done as soon as the words were uttered and for some time he had pondered how to rectify the breach. But he was a proud, stubborn man who hated to admit that he was in the wrong, hated to apologise or to be seen to be even changing his attitude...but she was his daughter, now his only child. She had loved her brother. They had always been close and she had written loving and dutiful letters home even though he had never replied. He suspected that her mother had.

He cleared his throat, mentally squared his shoulders and announced, "I shall take the later morning train, ask James to arrange it for me."

His wife rose quickly smiling as she made for the door.

The following morning Elisabet had persuaded Alys and Ellen's husbands to carry John's body down to her still room. They had removed the back door from its hinges to use as a bier but even so it had been an awkward and difficult manoeuvre down the steep and narrow stairs. For two days Elisabet worried about the burial. Then late on the second evening she made her way down to the vicarage and knocked timidly at the great oak door. The vicar's wife showed her into a dusty room to the right of the front door and bade her wait while she fetched her husband. Elisabet stood on the bare, grimy boards and looked around. The oak shutters were open revealing real glass in the windows. Elisabet was not sure she would like it especially in good weather for the light that came through the glass had a strange greenish tinge as it penetrated the small diamond shapes. The walls were panelled to shoulder height and the fire grate was large, empty and had a great, carved surround. There was a desk and a chair in front of the window, the former heaped with papers, quills and books and the latter padded with an embroidered cushion. There were two book cases either side of the fire with many large and equally dusty leather-spined books. A clock ticked loudly on the mantle piece, I certainly would not want that thought Elisabet making such a noise and giving me a constant reminder of my life ebbing away. Elisabet wondered if John's house had such elegant rooms?

The door opened and the vicar came it carrying a small candelabra.

"Well, Mistress Bayteman," he declared loudly, putting the candlestick down on the desk, "I hope this is important as you have disturbed me at a very late hour, a very late hour indeed." He sat down. He did not invite Elisabet to sit, indeed, there was no other chair in the room.

"Yes sir, I do believe so," Elisabet replied timidly.

"Tell me then," he said more quietly seeing her distress, "and I will see what I may do to help you."

Elisabet began to explain how she had found the wounded Cavalier, nursed him, taken him to have the musket ball removed but despite all her efforts he had died. Now she did not know what to do as she did not know his full name nor where he came from. When she had finished the vicar was silent for a moment before replying,

"I think mistress that he must be buried here and fairly soon. Perhaps we could lay him near your parents?"

"Yes," agreed Elisabet, "I can pay for the grave to be dug and for your services now if you wish." She fumbled in a little leather purse which hung from a belt around her waist. The vicar held up his hand to prevent her.

"No, I think that we can forgo that Elisabet, if only to show that the church is as caring as you have been towards a stranger. You have been very brave to hide him all this time under the noses of our Parliamentary friends."

So they arranged the details of the burial for the day after the morrow and Elisabet left feeling thankful that soon John would finally rest peacefully beside her family.

John Bateman senior alighted stiffly from the train at Newark and hailed one of the few carriages for hire there. He remembered the journey with remarkable clarity, a journey he had last made in reverse thirty years ago. The village of Hockerton had changed little in this time, no new houses had been built but this he did not find surprising with the slump in the farming there had been up until almost the beginning of the war. And Sparrow cottage had changed not one jot. He paid the driver, tipped him generously and asked him to wait a moment while he ascertained if anyone was at home. The sharp rap with his cane on the door brought a strange woman to face him.

"Yes?" She smiled at him.

"Is Miss Bateman at home?"

"Indeed sir." Mary moved to one side to allow him to enter.

"One moment" He walked back to the carriage and told the driver that he could leave.

The door was wide open now. As he stepped into the familiar, small, low-ceilinged room Mary asked, "And who shall I say you are sir?"

"Why John Bateman, I am Elizabeth, Miss Bateman's father."

Mary fairly shot up the stairs to the room above where Elizabeth, resting on the bed, had been wondering whom the male voice down below belonged to.

John Bateman sat down and surveyed the room. He wondered what trick of fate had brought his daughter here, to the very cottage in which his family had lived for hundreds of years, where he himself had been born and lived for half his present life span. He heard with a pang of sadness the light, tripping tread of his daughter as she came down the stairs. He had missed her so much. And then she was there silhouetted in the low doorway.

"Father!" She came forward hesitantly.

He didn't answer. He rose and strode across the room towards her and enveloped her in a great bear hug which she remembered so well from her childhood. How thin she was, how small and frail in his arms. Anger filled him. What had they done to her in prison?

"Father?" He looked down at her. "Is something wrong?"

He led her gently to a chair, sat her down and pulled up another chair to sit in front of her. He reached for her hand sand covered them with his big, warm ones.

"Elizabeth..." His voice broke and choking back his sorrow he croaked, "it's John, we had a telegram yesterday." Was it only yesterday it had come?

"Bad news then?"

"I'm afraid so, you must be very brave Elizabeth. John is reported-"

"Wounded again?" Elizabeth hoped against hope.

"John is reported... Killed in action."

Elizabeth gasped and fainted.

It was a beautiful May morning, the morning they buried John, the Cavalier. Elisabet followed behind as his body covered with one of her blankets and still on the door was carried down to the church. The burial service was simple, stark and moving. Then outside Elisabet stood by the freshly dug hole as the final words were said over the earthly remains of her Cavalier. Soon she was alone watching as young Alfred shovelled earth back into the hole and firmed down the mound.

❖

Elizabeth had been put to bed by an anxious Mary and her father summoned the doctor. John Bateman waited nervously while his daughter was examined upstairs. When the doctor came down he offered him a seat and waited for his prognosis. As he listened John Bateman realised just how ill Elizabeth was and how damaged her heart. He instructed the doctor to call every other day and more often if required until he was sure she was recovering and instructed that all bills be sent to his address.

After the doctor had left he arranged for Mary to come for much longer each day and paid her accordingly. Learning from her about his son's car he asked if Bill could take him to Southwell so that he could send a telegram to his wife and arrange for some delicacies to be sent to tempt Elizabeth's appetite. Secretly he was planning to get her home as soon as she was able to travel and also wished to engage a nurse for this eventuality.

Elisabet sat on the bright new grass at the edge of the orchard and noticed how the clumps she had planted on the Roundhead's grave were bright with spring flowers. Some of the trees in the orchard were white and pink with blossom and the ground beneath was like a blue mist with its carpet of bluebells. All this beauty and her John lay in the cold earth with a brown, bare mound of soil above him. Tears misted her eyes. He would have flowers too. Tomorrow she would go and plant his grave with bluebells, cover the ugly, scarred earth with them like a blue cloak.

And how would she fare without him? She had known and loved him for such a short time but it seemed like for always. It was forever. Back in the cottage she went upstairs and took all the coverlets and blankets away and cleaned every bit of the room. His leather coat, lace collar, sword and spurs she placed in the little cupboard near the window. She folded the blanket that she thought of still as his over them and closed the door firmly.

Downstairs again Elisabet kept her hands busy and her mind blank as she washed and scoured. By nightfall no trace of John or smell of sickness was left in the little upstairs room, all was sweet and clean. And empty. And soulless Elisabet thought as she fell into a dreamless sleep.

Bill had arranged to take John Bateman to the station at Newark. He had stayed with Elizabeth now for four days and she seemed somewhat recovered. He had promised her that as soon as she was strong enough her mother would come back with him and they would take her home. Elizabeth agreed to please him. She did not want to go. She could not leave here. Here was home now. Here had always been home. She had come home to where her family was to where her other self was and illogically to where she believed her brother was. So she waved her father goodbye, smiling and trying to look happy. She turned back to re-enter the cottage and she knew, knew as if a voice had spoken the words out loud that this was where she would remain. Always.

Two days after the Cavalier was buried, Roundheads came back into the village. Elisabet was shocked when she saw them ride in as she was tending her herbs. What if they asked questions about the new burial mound in the churchyard? What had the vicar written in the burial book? She had to know. Rubbing the wet earth from her hands as best she could she made her way to the vicarage and was told by his wife that the vicar was in the church. She expected to find him at his devotions but he was standing with the burial book open on a small table placed at the back of the church. His quill was poised in his hand as if he was about to make an entry. He jumped as the heavy door creaked open and turned guiltily. When he saw it was Elisabet he gave a sigh of relief.

"Do not fret Mistress, I know why you are here. As soon as I saw the troopers ride past. I thought that it might be expedient to make an alteration to what I had previously written. I have already amended the entry." He pointed to the book. As Elisabet bent forward to see more clearly she gasped, "But all it says now is John the Souldger," she whispered, "and I saw you write..."

"You saw this." The vicar held out a crumpled sheet.

"Is that...?"

"The original entry? Yes. I have cut out the whole page so close to the binding it will never be noticed. Everything you told me that you knew of his identity is gone."

The entries for 1643 were neatly re-entered on the page again with John's entry below them. All it now said next to the date was John the souldger.

"What if one of the Roundheads asks who he was?" Enquired Elisabet.

"Then Mistress I shall say that all I know is that I buried the body of a poor soldier who was found near the village. And that is the truth is it not Mistress?"

"Yes." Whispered Elisabet, "That is certainly the truth if not the whole truth."

❖

Elizabeth sat down and wrote all she had learned about the cottage, its inhabitants and its contents since she had been there. As she wrote she felt sure that her father knew this place well too. Things he had half said, things he had known without being told and the reaction of Old Sam next door when they had met. She would write a letter and include these pages in it hoping he would be willing to explain his connection with Sparrow cottage.

Before the letter was sent however she got confirmation of her suspicions from Samuel when he called round with the same chipped bowl full of yet more brown eggs.

"It were nice to see young John agen." He remarked plonking the bowl down heavily on the table.

"Please sit down," Elizabeth invited, "and tell me everything, right from the beginning."

She waited while Samuel made his old body comfortable in the chair opposite and cleared his throat.

"Well," he began, "I don't rightly knows the beginning as it were...." He told her what old Mrs Bateman had told him when he had first lived in the cottage next door. "Her did say that it were family knowledge that were passed down from one generation to another that they 'ad been in the cottage since before King Henry was on the throne....the one that 'ad seven wives, or were it six, I don't rightly remember. Her told me that in all the childer they allus 'ad a John and an Elizabeth, must 'ave made conversing difficult I says to 'er. Anyways I were told by folks in the village an all that the Batemans were odd because there were a titled man and a monk or such like back in their family." He paused and looked into the fire.

"And is that all she said?" Elizabeth felt disappointed for she already knew this much.

"Aye, mind you they left in a strange way."

"Oh," Elizabeth realised that here might be something new.

"Aye, young John, him that was 'ere a bit ago...well 'e suddenly came into money, likewise 'e 'ad money to leave the village and I 'eard that 'e 'ad bought 'imself a fine new 'ouse somewhere down south."

"When was this?"

"1884!"

"You mean that my father left here in 1884 when he came into money?"

"That's right and yer ma as well."

Elizabeth asked if he knew anything more about her family and the time they had lived here and he told her that there had always been rumours and superstitions about the cottage. Pressed to say more Samuel said that the older village folk had always thought that there was treasure buried here and that it was guarded. Elizabeth enthralled now by these bizarre tales asked him who guarded it. Samuel admitted that he himself had neither seen nor heard anything but that some more fanciful folk had from time to time seen a tall man dressed in black and others had heard the sound of heavy footsteps, booted steps going round the house. What to make of these tales Samuel was not sure but he added recently he had heard her talking and a man's voice answering. That would be when my brother came Elizabeth reassured him. Oh no, he replied your brother wasn't here then. When Samuel had gone Elizabeth added a few more lines to her letter, adding some of what he had told her and awaited eagerly her father's reply.

Elizabeth, looking through her leather case opened the tissue paper packet to reveal the oval, green, purple and white brooch. Memories came rushing back. The optimism of the Liberal victory in 1906 and the moving of the HQ to the Strand in London, taking part in deputations to Parliament, and rallies in the Royal Albert Hall and Hyde Park. Taking the campaign to the streets and the fear that she had felt when first addressing a crowd from a kitchen chair. She remembered looking around her furtively the first time she had chalked on the pavement and standing selling the 'Suffragette'. But these early fears paled into insignificance by the side of the sheer terror she had experienced when she was first arrested and imprisoned. Looking at the brooch's colours reminded her of the tricoloured merchandise in the window of the Woman's Press Shop in Charing Cross Road where she had worked for a time in 1910 ,the camaraderie of the other women , the feeling of solidarity, the rightness of their cause.

Elizabeth sighed . Exciting days, a time of personal fulfilment on the one hand and heartache on the other. Her parents, her Father mostly, had tried at first to persuade her and then to bully to renounce her involvement in the cause of women's suffrage, even her dear brother had not understood. She recalled vividly one afternoon when she had been parading through the streets in Brighton as one of the 'parasol brigade' selling their newspaper ,just last April, that he had seen her and come up to her and coolly remarked that he hated to see his sister walking in the streets like a 'common lass'. He had been instantly sorry as soon as the words were passed his lips she knew by the guilty reddening of his face. But the words had been uttered and had been heard not only by her but also by the women with her. How she would now give anything if he could only say those words to her again . Any words no matter how hurtful....tears trickled silently down her cheeks. As she rewrapped the brooch she thought sadly that things were different now. Women taking all manner of men's jobs so that they could be released to fight at the front. And she a useless invalid. Would she, Elizabeth wondered if she were well do a man's job? Would she want to know that by so doing he would be part of that carnage that the casualty lists in the newspapers were now revealing? She didn't know. It was an academic question anyway.

. She laid the brooch with the little owl one she had bought in Newark. Mary would value both of these; one as a reminder of a cause she would have loved to espouse and the other of an interesting if not completely carefree day. Elizabeth lay back exhausted. So little effort these days caused such long debilitation. She put both brooches on the table beside her, pulled the blanket up to her chin and slept.

Elisabet went across the churchyard to John's unmarked grave. The bluebells which had been in bud when she planted them a few days ago were reviving with the rain and standing upright again and coming into flower. She turned away and hobbled down the churchyard steps. Hearing rough male voices she paused in the shadow of the mound on which the church stood. Down the church road where it crossed the stream by the little wooden bridge about a dozen horsemen had halted and dismounted. By their dress they were the Roundheads that she had seen earlier. She slipped quietly away.

Once home she considered the cupboard. She would not dispose of John's things nor her commonplace book and the book of hours but where could she hide them so that they would be safe. She sat on the bed. Bury them? No, that might cause them harm from the wet earth and burrowing animals. Under the earthen floor downstairs would be just as bad. Try as she might she could think of no other dry place, but she must make the cupboard safe. She would make it disappear! She would put daub over it and then it would look like part of the walls.

Elisabet had never mixed daub before but she had seen her father do it, so taking a wooden tub she mixed some chopped straw with water. She had a little lime so she added that and then clay and stirred it well with a big stick. She was hot and sweating by the time most of the lumps were mixed in. Carrying the heavy tub inside was impossible so she conveyed smaller amounts of the mixture in a smaller bowl and starting at floor level she patted it over the closed cupboard door and smoothed it down. Up and down the stairs she went and with each new application a little more of the door disappeared until all was covered.

Standing back to survey her work she thought that it was still rather uneven so she smoothed it again with water before cleaning up all the mess on the floor. Her hands were red raw with the lime so she washed them and smeared each one liberally with her thick mutton fat salve. She had already washed out the bowl and the tub, the former she returned to her still room and the latter she up ended in the garden exactly where it had been before. All she could do now was to wait and hope that no one came and wanted to go into that room until it was all dry and lime-washed to match the rest.

CHAPTER TWENTY-ONE

John Bateman senior sat at his big, mahogany desk preparing to answer his daughter's letter. He had not been completely surprised by her finds. He had always known parts of the story, passed down the generations, of their ancestor Elisabet and the wounded Royalist. He picked up his pen and began to write what he knew of the family history and what he himself had found. Occasionally he stopped and gazed out at the magnificent gardens of his country home, kept immaculate before the war by an army of gardeners and their boys, now it looked much less clipped and regimented. He rather preferred it this way, more like Sparrow Cottage garden, much more natural. He would tell the remaining old man and the two young boys to concentrate more on the vegetable plot. Fresh vegetables could be given to the convalescent soldiers who his wife Amy wanted to house in the other wing of the house. Yes, they would do that now.....

He included what he had written in a caring and concerned letter to Elizabeth, addressed and stamped the envelope and putting on his coat and whistling to the two springer bitches decided he would enjoy a walk to the village post office.

Elizabeth sat reading Elisabet's book...the last page now, which was loose and discoloured all down the inner edge. She thought how resourceful Elisabet had been to plaster over the cupboard. She had written little after this and what she had was merely notes. 'Went to church, milked the cow and made cheese, went to market' and then 'the horse died.' Poor Elisabet, Elizabeth thought for now she had no transport but perhaps this did not worry her three hundred year name sake as much as it might do me. She made no further reference to the Roundheads at all but had noted, 'placed stone near trooper's grave and covered it with soil and grass.' So she had been the one who had done it. She had been determined to give him a sort of a grave. Then near the end of the page, the last few lines, minutely written and squashed in at the bottom it said, 'twins born, am not alone now' and then, 'James died today' and lastly, 'ill with fever, aunt Petters has taken baby John to care for him.'

Finding the notes that she had made from the burial record Elizabeth saw that the last entry had been written only four days before Elisabet was buried. She must have died soon after. But... thought Elizabeth this is not possible how could she have written this in the book when she hid it in the plastered over cupboard months before. She felt frightened by this inexplicable notion.

She turned over the last leaf in the book expecting to find a virgin page but instead there was more writing. It was not Elisabet's writing. She read with relief and with dawning understanding of what had happened. It said, 'to whoever may find this book in the future, I discovered it hidden behind the wall while cleaning and looking at the writing which I have found difficult to comprehend I see it was written by my ancestor Elisabet Bayteman and matches exactly a sheet which has been passed down over many years inside the family bible. Therefore, before I return it to its original place I have taken the liberty of gluing this in at the end. To you who may be reading it I am also Elisabet, Elisabet Bayteman 1751'

Elizabeth turned again to the notes she had made from the registers and soon found this Elisabet. She had been born in 1731, almost a hundred years after the woman who had written the book and there had been no record of her death. Elizabeth sadly closed the little book. Who would think that anything so small could contain such great courage and heartache? She felt like crying, Elisabet had become so real to her, she had been Elisabet she felt. It was through me Elizabeth thought that she lived again in a way. And then she looked again at what was written by the Elisabet in 1751. Did 'I am also Elisabet' mean that the names were the same or that finding the book she had also relived the story?

❖

Cicely and her husband arrived late in the evening. David met them in the yard as the car pulled to a halt.

"Good journey?" He enquired of the frosty air as neither his sister nor brother-in-law had alighted yet. Eventually what David considered to be a vast amount of luggage for such a short stay was unloaded and stacked in the hall. When they were finally gathered around the sitting room fire, drinks in hand Cicely remarked, "Not much has changed, David."

"Oh it has." Her brother argued. He had never agreed with his sister even when they were children. She never saw below the surface of things, never understood the heart of the matter, never took time to consider in David's opinion.

"There are a lot of changes and none for the better that I can see."

"You always were an old pessimist David." Laughed Cicely, holding out her glass for a refill.

"I can't see much in the village or in the world at large come to that to be optimistic about."

"But we're beating the Hun, old boy" this was Geoffrey, trying to jolly the conversation along.

"Are we, are we really or is it the newspapers who just say we are? I just don't think that we can go on losing men the way we have been doing so far, why we have had two killed from here already."

"Two!" Cicely laughed.

"Yes," said David angry now, "two, and that's two too many, we can't afford to lose even two from a community of only sixty-six! There are a good few at the front as well who may not come back either."

"Oh, David don't be such a bore." Cicely had had enough of this war talk, "You've got a darling daughter...."

"Yes," David smiled, "So I have, a toast to her then." He refilled their glasses.

"Is Elizabeth invited to the christening?" Cicely asked Anne.

"Yes, of course and I expect quite a lot of the villagers will come along too."

Cicely dropped her voice to a whisper. "Don't tell David but..." She looked across to where the two men were talking quietly together to be sure he was not listening, "but I'm ashamed now that I foisted her on you."

"But why?" Anne's voice rose in alarm.

"Hush do, well she's been in prison, not once mind but a couple of times. And" she paused dramatically, "she's wanted by the police. She didn't say anything of this to me. Intimated that she wanted to disappear because of an unwelcome suitor."

"Why is she wanted?"

"Suffragette." Cicely lowered her voice further "wanted for smashing windows and the like. Dreadful goings on in London I don't mind telling you and she's one of them."

"Not now surely?"

Misunderstanding Cicely replied, "Well some of them are backing the war effort I know. They think that it will get them what they want when it's all over but that dreadful Sylvia Pankhurst is still standing on platforms spouting her left wing pacifist ideas."

Anne did not know how to reply to her sister-in- law's venomous tone so she merely said, "Elizabeth is very frail you know. We don't see very much of her. She isn't any trouble really."

"Umph!" Cicely put down her glass, "may I go and see the little one?"

Anne, thankful for a change of subject, readily acquiesced.

❖

The small Norman church was full the following morning for such a joyful occasion. Anne with the help of Mary Peters and her neighbour had placed leaves and dried flowers in every niche and cranny as well as the flowers on the altar and around the font. Cicely, swathed in furs, shivered as she entered. What a cold, damp place this had always been. She remembered sitting shivering through interminable sermons in her childhood and hoped that the vicar would keep it short today with a small baby present.

"Hello Cicely," said a quiet voice behind her.

She turned and gasped. Elizabeth had looked ill in London but on this cold cheerless morning she looked so fragile, ethereal almost...as white and papery as the honesty leaves in the vase behind her.

"Good morning Elizabeth." She smiled, "is the country air suiting you?" She wanted to rail and shout that she had been tricked, she wanted to say 'why didn't you say that you were hiding from the police?' But she knew that whatever Elizabeth had done she was now too ill to go back to London, let alone to prison. Instead she said, she hoped in a kindly voice, “Come and sit beside me,” and taking the stick like arm she shepherded Elizabeth to a seat at the front.

Elizabeth sat meekly through the service, standing, sitting and kneeling when those around her did. But her mind seemed cocooned in cotton wool, her thoughts slippery and elusive. On the very edge of her vision shapes intruded, at the limit of her hearing were other voices. When they turned at last to the font and Cicely and her husband as godparents moved to the back of the church Elizabeth felt the shapes and voices move too.

Mary Peters watched her anxiously from across the aisle wondering if the slightly swaying figure was going to faint.

Then Elizabeth saw her... her other self, her alter ego, her ancestor. Elisabet stood at the font, a baby in each arm. Two cloaked women either side seemed to be supporting her. Even from this distance Elizabeth could see that Elisabet’s face gleamed with sweat and her eyes glittered feverishly. The church was cold, icy, as the vicar spoke his words became puffs of vapour.

“I’m ill,” Elizabeth thought.

In a daze both women heard the vicar name the two baby boys John and James Bayteman.

Elizabeth opened her eyes cautiously. Where was she? Who was she? Cicely was bending over her, her rather vapid face anxious.

“Elizabeth, are you alright?”

Elizabeth focused on Cicely’s silly frothy hat, the crow’s feet around her eyes, worried, caring eyes....

“Yes.” She whispered, “I just felt a bit faint.”

Cicely held her gently. “It’s all done now, the baby’s christened, Geoffrey and I will get you home. You don’t want to go back to that cottage do you?”

“Yes.” Elizabeth said more strongly now, “Please Cicely just get me there, Mary will take care of me.”

❖

Aunt Petters will take care of me thought Elisabet. Alys had come across during the difficult birthing of her twin sons. Alys had mopped her brow, held her hand, told her to yell, push and had finally delivered the babies. When she had tried to thank her Alys had said simply,

"You'd do the same for me Elisabet. Alys knows."

Elisabet just wished that Alys had washed her hands for now little James was hot and feverish, mewling fretfully and she herself felt strangely ill....

❖

Elisabet lay sweating and freezing in her narrow bed. Bright sunlight illuminated the whole room. The newly plastered wall was almost unnoticeable now after the passage of six months. She dozed and then woke suddenly. Someone was there in the room. A dark figure stood blocking the sunlight from the window. As he moved towards the bed and turned she gasped. It was John. He was immaculately dressed in his leather coat with snowy white frills of lace at collar and cuffs. His skin was tanned and healthy. His hair curled beneath his wide hat with its jaunty feather. Bending over her his long-lashed green eyes crinkled as he smiled at her.

"Come my Elisabet." He whispered softly. He took her hand in his and pulled her upright. Elisabet felt well and so happy as they moved across the room together. They made no sound descending the stairs and as Elisabet picked up her skirts to follow her Cavalier she saw two perfectly rounded, supple legs ending in two elegant and shapely feet.

Mary came in with the post.

"Two for you," she said handing Elizabeth the envelopes. One had her father's handwriting on it but the other, the other had her brother's writing on it. She opened this first with trembling fingers, clumsily tearing off a corner in her haste. Inside was a sheet or paper with unknown writing on it. She read this first.

'Dear Miss Bateman, you have never met me but your brother and I shared this dug-out for some time and as he left this partly written letter I thought you would want to have it .Please accept my sincere condolences for your great loss. I only wish that his body had been found to be given an honourable burial. Let us pray that this might yet come about.'

He had signed himself illegibly at the bottom. Elizabeth then opened John's letter. There was only one side of paper partially written. He had begun as usual, 'Dear Sis' and had written that he was well and had gratefully received her parcel the day before. His time out of the front line now seemed like a dream once they were back in the mud and shelling. 'We shall have peaches and milk for tea' he wrote ' if the Germans let us as some terrific shelling has just started.' Here the letter ended.

Had they enjoyed their peaches Elizabeth wondered. John had been blown up by a shell which had hit part of the trench she knew from her father who had received a short note from the commanding officer. It must have been a direct hit because nothing of him had been recovered when they dug out the wounded. Folding both sheets of paper carefully and putting them to one side Elizabeth picked up her father's letter. She skimmed through it quickly and then sat down to read her brother's letter more slowly and the sheet of paper accompanying it. It was then for the first time the delayed shock of her brother's death hit her and she realised that there would never be any more letters and he would never come back....she wept.

Some time later, much later she read what her father had written. 'There has always been a John and an Elizabeth in every generation of our family' he had begun. 'It was a family tradition just as it was passed down that we had aristocratic blood. I didn't know about the monk. My father always believed that there was something valuable hidden in the house for there was a piece of paper showing that a John Bayteman had bought the cottage in 1662. How did he get the money to purchase it we wondered, an illegitimate and orphaned boy. But he did and Bateman's coming after him held on to it through good times and bad until I came along. I was newly married to Amy, your mother, at the time and you were a few months old. The little back room which we used as the scullery was dark and damp. I decided to enlarge the window which I did fairly competently using wood and glass begged from the neighbours and then I decided to take up the flagstones which were worn and uneven and relay them.

Imagine my surprise when in one corner my spade hit something and I found a dozen gold coins. They had obviously been hidden there for some time and fearing that I might be cheated out of their true value if I took them to a museum I sold each one privately and secretly. I bought shares in a firm making rifles and in another making army uniforms. I kept enough for us to leave Sparrow Cottage and couldn't wait to shake the dust of it off my shoes. I became a very rich man and by the time that John was born a titled landowner. So you see Elizabeth you never knew of the family stories and traditions. I wish now that you had. If you look carefully in the churchyard you will see where all the Bateman's have been buried and presumably Elisabet and the soldier too.'

Well, thought Elizabeth no wonder I feel that this cottage is my home. I shall see if David Enleigh will sell it back to me so that it can come back into the family again. Taking pen and paper she wrote him a short note and asked Mary to deliver it when she left.

When David Enleigh was admitted to the cottage the following evening he thought that even the soft glow of the lamp and firelight could not hide how ill Elizabeth looked now. He sat by the fire refusing the proffered drink and waited. She obviously was going to say that she did not want to rent the cottage any more. She must have made arrangements to return home when her father visited.

"David, Mr Enleigh," she began hesitantly, "I have loved living here." She paused uncertain how to continue. "I have felt from the first moment that this cottage welcomed me. Now I find out from my father that members of our family lived here until as recently as thirty years ago, when my father left and sold this place to your father." She stopped and cleared her throat. Her chest was heaving as if David thought that even speaking was too arduous for her poor, weak body. Her next words shocked him out of his reverie.

"I wish to purchase the cottage from you."

"You wish to, to buy it?" David was aghast.

"That's what I said." A ghost of a smile played across her thin features. "What would you consider a reasonable sum?"

"Well, I don't know."

"Don't know how much or don't know if you will sell?"

"Surely you will want a professional to look it over and..." His voice trailed away.

"No." Elizabeth's smile was broader now. "I want it now, as it is. Will you sell it to me.?"

"Well put like that I suppose that I can hardly refuse. I have no tenant for it , I don't want to see it standing empty again. It isn't worth much, it needs a lot doing to it."

"Name a sum." Elizabeth urged him.

He did.

"Agreed." She said it so quickly she had hardly had time to think thought David and it crossed his mind that she would have agreed to any amount he put forward so badly did she want it. He wondered why it was so urgent.

"Shall we settle it now?"

"Now!" David thought she really is in a rush but he merely said out loud, "don't we need solicitors and so forth?"

"Not really, look read this and if you agree we can settle it this evening."

David took the sheet of paper. On it Elizabeth had written a short note to the effect that he was willing to sell the cottage to her and left a space for the amount to be entered . All he needed to do was to fill in the agreed sum and sign. She passed him a second sheet. This differed only in that it said that she had requested the purchase.

"To safeguard you," she nodded to the second paper, "so that no one can say that you took advantage of a sick woman."

He signed and so did she.

"Take this to my bank tomorrow, David." She handed him an envelope. "They will pay you the sum we have agreed on, I'll just write it in now." She slipped the paper out, added a figure and a few words and handed it to him.

"If you are sure?"

"Quite sure David and thank you." She rose slowly, "will you accept that drink now to seal our bargain?"

David agreed that he would.

❖

On the following Sunday Elizabeth arranged that Bill would drive her the short distance in the car to the village church for she felt strangely tired. She had rested for the greater part of each day but just getting dressed brought a hopeless wave of fatigue over her. She took time to dress and rest well before he arrived. She was just skewering her hat into position with a large pearl ornate hat pin when she heard the car pull up outside.

"This will be the last time that I shall sit in it." She remarked as Bill helped her in.

"How did you know?" Bill's face looked surprised.

"Know what?" asked Elizabeth.

"That I am going to sell it to Amos. I can't afford to keep it running on my wages. Not that I'm not very honoured and pleased that the Captain was so generous to leave it to me but Amos wants it so that he can run his market day service to Newark. He has declared that he will never have another horse. I'm to drive for him. It will make me a bit of extra money and he says he don't want to see another horse in his stables again."

"Why's that?"

"He says that young Jonah would never have gone and joined up if they hadn't taken the horses, doted on them horses that lad did. Amos is that upset by the lad's death he's got to have some one to blame and I suppose blaming the horses is harmless enough."

"It's a good idea," replied Elizabeth harking back to the market day taxi idea. She looked sadly thoughtful, "I suppose that he really does miss Jonah dreadfully."

"That he does Miss but Mrs Amos she's worse, she cries for him she do." He gave the starting handle a quick turn, the engine sprang to life and Elizabeth sat back as they moved slowly round the bend and down the church drive. Bill pulled on the break and came round to help her out.

"Will you be all right now Miss?" He asked as they reached the top of the stone steps to the churchyard.

"Yes, quite, thank you, Bill." Elizabeth smiled at him and watched as he descended and turned the car round on the slope and returned through the village. The few minutes watching Bill had enabled her to regain her breath after the exertion of mounting the steps. Then she went along the path but not to the church door but began to pick her way between the long grass and the crooked headstones. She stopped and where it was possible she read the names carved there before moving on. At the very edge of the graveyard and above the high wall which held back the earth on this side she saw a collection of stones, some quite unworn, others mossy and weathered. All of them she saw had the name Bateman in one spelling or another.

Amidst them was a grassy mound covered with the leaves of bluebells and beside it a newly dug hole. She turned, hearing footsteps behind her. Two men carrying a shrouded form on a kind of wooden stretcher were coming towards the grave, preceded by the vicar holding a book and intoning the words of the burial service. They seemed to be completely unaware of Elizabeth's presence there as they carefully lowered the still lifeless body of Elisabet Bayteman into the hole and back filled it. When the vicar had gone the two gravediggers stood leaning on their shovels.

"Sad her babe gone and then 'er." Remarked the younger of the two.

"Still they be together now," added his companion. "Tis the other poor motherless babe I do feel sorry for."

"Aye, poor babe, mother dead and father unknown, tis well that 'e 'as Mistress Petters to care for 'im"

Giving the newly filled grave a final pat they walked away.

Bill found Elizabeth lying on the damp grass two hours later when he had come to find her after Mary had realised that she had not returned to the cottage. Of the bluebell mound and the fresh grave there was no sign.

❖

Elizabeth knew that she was very ill by the number of people around her bed, the doctor, Mary and also now her parents..... when she woke again only Mary remained sitting quietly knitting. She stopped and put down the little bootee which she had almost finished when she saw that Elizabeth's eyes were open. She gently took hold of Elizabeth's cold hand which was lying on the coverlet.

"Miss Bateman shall I call your parents?"

"No, Mary..." Elizabeth found speech difficult. Her chest felt tight, breathing painful.

"In my box, my jewellery box.. For you..."

Mary rose and fetched the box, putting it on the side of the bed.

"Open it." Elizabeth instructed.

Inside Mary saw a letter and a package wrapped in brown paper with her name on it.

"Take them home, open them later."

Mary nodded, returned the box to its place and put the two items in her bag. They sat there silently, Mary holding Elizabeth's hand as the light faded in the sky. Seeing that Elizabeth had at last fallen asleep again Mary lit the night light for her and taking a candle for herself, tiptoed downstairs to tell Elizabeth's mother to come up.

CHAPTER TWENTY-TWO

Bill and Mary lay together in their big, feather bed. A scant moonlight shone through the casement and silvered the thin, flowered curtains.

"You asleep, Bill?" Mary whispered, reaching out to find her husband's hand beneath the bed clothes.

Bill's reply was to clasp her hand gently in his big, calloused one.

"I've got something to tell you." Mary rolled over and whispered in his ear. She could not see the expression on his face but she knew that he was smiling by the timbre of his voice when he replied,

"Well, I never, well I don't know if that don't beat all. Do you think that we might have a little lass this time ?"

"Would you like that?" Mary asked.

"I would too," Bill murmured happily, "a little lass to sit on my knee. Not that I don't love our Ben, mind, but well a little lass. That would be grand."

Elizabeth woke with the birds. The room was suffused with soft, yellow rays of sunlight. She rose eager to begin the day. Her hands felt deft and supple as she buttoned her blouse. She brushed her hair vigorously and knotted it at the nape of her neck. She turned her head this way and that the better to admire her glowing locks in the little mirror. She turned and gazed with pity at the still, grey figure stretched out on the bed. Leaping down the stairs, she spun into the living room and was surprised to see her brother, John, standing there by the small front door as if he had just entered the room.

"Good morning John," she said with surprise, "I didn't know you were coming home on leave, have you let mother and father know?"

When he did not reply she continued, "Come and take off that muddy great coat....." her voice faltered and died . Another man stood partly behind her brother, a shadowy and indistinct figure, Elizabeth sat down in the nearest chair.

❖

Bill Peters was singing as he stropped his razor, slightly out of tune as always. Mary smiled as she poured boiling water into the teapot. Once Ben was off to school she would go and tell Elizabeth their good news , it would cheer her no end thought Mary especially as she and Bill had already agreed that if it were a girl one of the child's manes would be Elizabeth and if another boy then they would call him John after their two new but good friends. Bill lathered his chin and scraped, still singing. Washing off the tiny globules of lather still remaining and wiping himself on the towel he came to sit at the table.

"We shall be all right Mary," he said, spooning porridge up and blowing on it. "I shall sell Captain John's car to Amos and we shall have money in the bank."

"I know," Mary sighed, "but what if they call you up to go over there to fight?"

"Not me love, I'm not volunteering, the Captain told me enough to stop any silly ideas like that. Its not glorious over there he said its not like they say in the papers, its mud and pain and noise. I don't suppose that they will make me go they seem to have enough volunteers, not with me working on the land like." He scraped his bowl, carefully chasing every last morsel and rose to don his cap and coat.

Mary gave Ben his breakfast next and saw him off to school. She watched with pride as his sturdy, little legs carried him down the road to where his friend Jimmy waited at his cottage gate. For another hour she tidied, cleaned, prepared vegetables and then made dough and put it to rise by the fire. All done, she thought surveying her comfortable and cosy nest with pride. She was just putting on her coat when there was a sharp rapping on the door. Now who can that be she thought as she went to open it. David Enleigh stood on the step. She could tell that something was wrong and so she backed inside and motioned to him to follow. He did so and asked her to sit down on one of the kitchen chairs while he pulled out a second.

"Bill?" She gasped, "has something happened to my Bill?"

"No, not Bill, Mary," he took both her hands in his large ones, "it's Miss Bateman."

"Have you sent for the doctor...." Mary began to get up.

"No Mary, there is no need."

"No need?" Mary stared at him. Surely he did not mean...

"She's dead Mary, I'm so sorry. I know that you have become great friends." He did not know how to continue when he looked into her stricken face. She made again to rise from the chair.

"No Mary, stay here a while, or rather come home with me."

"No, thank you very much Mr Enleigh. I feel I should go across to Miss Bateman."

"As you wish." David Enleigh watched her rise stiffly like an old woman and then taking her arm he accompanied her across the road to Sparrow Cottage.

Much later Mary sat at her kitchen table again and with shaking fingers unwrapped the brown paper parcel which Elizabeth had given her. It contained a note pad closely written in Elizabeth's flowing hand and a small box. Inside the box, wrapped in cotton wool she discovered a small, silver owl with garnet eyes. It was a brooch and under it, wrapped in tissue was another brooch. It was Elizabeth's suffragette badge in purple, green and white. Mary remembered that first day she had met Elizabeth and she had seen it when she had unpacked her cases. Slitting open the letter with a knife Mary read Elizabeth's letter.

'My dear friend' it began, 'I'm sure I can call you that Mary after all the months of loving care and company you have given me. I say given for although you were paid by me to clean and cook your loving kindness was freely given. I have been so happy here, it has truly become my home and so I have bought Sparrow Cottage from Mr Enleigh and I leave it to you and Bill. When my will is read all will become clear. Yes, I know that I am very ill and if you are reading this do not mourn for me too much Mary for I am happy and I shall ever be when I go to join my brother. It is strange that he has always been so much more than a brother to me and I suspect but I do not know as he never said, that I have always been more than just his elder sister. I have written out Elisabet Bayteman's diary, journal, call it what you will, for you. As you will see by the family tree which I unearthed in the parish registers she is your ancestor as well as mine and I suspect

Bill comes into it somewhere as well. You might like to follow that line yourself one day when you find the time. The original I have packed up and addressed to Mr Enleigh and the book of hours for the cottage was his property when I found them. I believe that the ring I found is also his for the same reason and you will find it in my jewellery box, so please offer it to him. Talk to him about them Mary . You may be able if you want to keep them in the family to buy them from him. The brooch from my suffragette days is for you for I know from Miss Mason that you are a secret sympathiser and yours too is the little owl which I bought in Newark when we went there, keep it as a reminder of a lovely day. Think kindly of me Mary, I always meant well even if it did not always happen as I wished it to.' She had ended with a big, bold 'E'. The pictures and newspaper cuttings that Mary had seen that first day were folded inside the envelope.

❖

The church was cold and damp on this February Sunday of 1649. Six year old John Bayteman fidgeted. The service had been long and boring. His aunt Petters touched his arm and shook her head.

"Nearly over now," she whispered.

The vicar came to stand in front of his parishioners, but instead of intoning the blessing he said, "I have news that last sennight Charles Stuart was beheaded...." He did not finish. His voice was drowned by angry murmurs above which could be heard quite clearly a woman's shrill tones,

"Shame, shame I say on those who have done this vile deed!"

He held up his hand for silence. "Let us pray," he intoned quietly. Heads bowed the villagers waited but no words were spoken. In the silence some said their own prayer for their murdered King, others prayed for themselves, fearful of this new, uncharted, uncertain future without a monarch.

On leaving the church the vicar touched Widow Petters' arm ."Have a care," he said in an undertone, "Parliament's men are everywhere and what you have said could be called treason now."

"Treason, is it?" The lady replied with venom, "then this is also treason," and raising her voice so that all might hear she shouted,

"God save His Majesty. God save our new young King Charles!" And marched off, head held high, down the path.

Mary Peters pulled the coverlet of her daughter's bed straight and looked around the room. This old room with its low, wavy beams and small window was flooded with early morning light. Bill had stripped off all the old, faded wallpaper and she had painted the walls. The doors of the little, hidden cupboard that Elizabeth had discovered shone with bees wax polish. Inside on the shelves were folded her daughter's clothes and spare bedding. When they had first received the keys of Sparrow Cottage from Elizabeth's solicitor Mary had wanted to put her daughter into one of the other bedrooms for some inexplicable reason, but as small as she had been then Elizabeth Peters had insisted that she wanted this room for it was Elisabet's room. Although she had pointed a fat baby finger at her own chest as she had said it Mary was not really sure it was that simple. Too many Elizabeths had been associated with this room in the past. Bill had taken the matter entirely out of her hands by agreeing smilingly that it would indeed be his daughter's bedroom.

Descending the stairs Mary consulted the clock in the living room over the fireplace. She must hurry; Bill would be back soon with the car to take her to Southwell to register her vote. She. Mary Peters, to vote at the very first general election where women were allowed to vote. A great day this, December 11th 1919. But not as great and glorious as it should have been. The victory was tarnished and the women saddened by the staggering casualties of what they were now calling The Great War. Exactly year and one month since the guns had fallen silent. Would the rest of them ever recover from the war's tragic blot? She knew Amos wouldn't. Four years now since word had come of Jonah's death, such a long time and yet so short, cruel, deep wounds like those inflicted over the last four years did not easily heal. Mary shook herself mentally. This would not do. She must go and register her vote, for herself and for her lost friend Elizabeth Bateman who had believed, campaigned and in the end died for it.

Mary Peters carefully arranged her best hat on her freshly washed hair. She brushed invisible specks from her coat and pulled on her gloves. You'll do, she thought. She owed it to Elizabeth and all those other women that today she should be smartly turned out when she went to vote. Pinning the oval purple, green and white badge prominently on her coat lapel she pulled the door of Sparrow cottage shut and joined the rest of her family in Amos' car. Bill had been busy all day taking people into Southwell and now he was to drive them. Little Elizabeth Peters sat quiet and demure at the side of her older brother Ben. Now three years old she was still chubby and dimpled whereas Ben, though still sturdy, had grown tall in the intervening years.

They drove up the hill and then down into the town, they could see the pepper-pot towers of the Minster for most of the downward run and then they were driving slowly past where workmen were busy clearing the ground for a stone memorial of some kind to be erected at the top of Burgage. Money was already being collected and donations counted to build it. What it would be like Bill and Mary could not imagine. It was said that all the names of the men who had died would be etched on it. Mary hoped that this would include the men lost in the surrounding villages as well for a small place like Hockerton could not afford such an expense and she did not want young Jonah to be forgotten.

"Is that for Captain John?" Ben asked.

"Yes, and all the other soldiers who did not come home as well." His mother replied thinking of Mr Peasebody and young Jonah.

"I think that I might be a soldier like Captain John when I grow up," Ben stated.

"It will be a bit boring," his father remarked , pulling the car up outside the polling station to the stares of another couple about to enter.

"Why?" Demanded Ben as he alighted from the car.

"Well," Bill helped his wife down and then picked up Elizabeth, "there aren't going to be any more wars, that's why." came the assured reply.

"Oh right then, said Ben nonchalantly, "then I suppose I shall have to be an engine driver." He thought of the little train that they had had to wait to pass before they could cross the railway line, "It was my second choice anyway."

Outside the polling station a policeman stood guard .

"Or I might just be a policeman " Ben said taking his sister's hand and waiting outside as His parents went in. Mary followed Bill proudly. She stood in the little, wooden, makeshift booth, pencil in hand. Was this what it had all been about then; this bit of paper with its three printed names , this stub of pencil fastened down on a length of string? Was this why Elizabeth had been imprisoned, force-fed, her health ruined, just so that she, Mary Peters could put a black cross on a ballot paper?

Mary, coming out saw the man sitting at the table glance at the badge on her costume jacket but all he said was, "Thank you madam." As she dropped her folded paper in the battered box's slit.

In Flanders fields rain splashed into pools in abandoned trenches, plopped into shell holes greening over and dripped down white crosses like tears.... But the desolate pockmarked land was not entirely abandoned, it was peopled by the bodies of men never to be laid to rest beneath one of the endlessly repeated headstones. Men blown to pieces by shellfire like fragments, beyond recognition or entombed in collapsed trenches decomposing in this broken land. One of these was the earthly remains of Captain John Bateman.

John Bayteman stood in the park waiting as he had each day for many days now. Today would be the last day he would be able to wait for his money was all gone and he was needed back home, if he did not come today.... In the distance there came on the slight breeze the excited barking of dogs and then a man's voice quietening them. As he gazed John saw two tall men saunter into the park, dogs swirling around them. His heart thumped for surely the dark-haired, swarthy-skinned man on the right was the king and so the other equally tall but fairer-skinned man whose hair bore touches of grey must be the man he had come so far and waited so long to speak to. As they approached he doffed his hat and made a deep bow, murmuring, "Your Majesty's humble servant..."

The king stopped and raised his eyebrows quizzically, an amused smile playing on his large and rather ugly features, lighting up his face.

"Another threadbare Cavalier?" he asked, the gentle tone taking any sting out of his choice of words.

"No, sire, if it please your Majesty ...." John's voice stuttered to a halt.

The other man watched, his eyes narrowed, brow furrowed. He tapped his silver-knobbed stick on the ground.

"If it please Your Majesty I would like to speak to his Highness."

Charles Stuart turned and grinned at his cousin, before waving his glove airily and moving away slightly. John bowed again but before he could speak the king's cousin asked, "Don't I know you, sir?"

"No, Your Highness, but you may have known my father. I believe he rode with your cavalry at the beginning of the war."

The prince looked searchingly at John's face. He did remember. This young man looked exactly the same as a young man he had known twenty years ago. But who was he? There had been so many young men he had fought with, ridden beside, sailed with, but he remembered that face. He remembered the young man with the same green eyes the same smile..... .but time had erased from his memory the name.

"And what is your name?" Rupert thought that the name would jog his memory.

"John Bayteman Your Highness."

Rupert's frown deepened, the name was no help at all, it meant nothing to him. He was sure though that the man he had known was not called Bayteman.

"I do remember some one who looked just like you do now but I am distressed that I do not remember his name. My brother, Prince Maurice would have done for the two of them were great friends but.... my brother was drowned at sea ten years ago...."

The prince looked so distressed that John merely thanked him and bidding him good day bowed and left. Sadly he realised that now he would never know who his father was.

The following morning a messenger brought a note to his lodgings just as he was leaving. It was short and expressed the writer's unhappiness at being unable to help him. All he could remember was that the man in question had been wounded in a skirmish to the north of Newark and that he had never been seen again. It was signed Rupert. The messenger also handed over a small leather pouch. Inside were a dozen gold coins.

"From his Highness Prince Rupert." The messenger explained, seeing John's puzzled look. "Your father's uncollected pay."

It is cool in the forests that have overgrown the battle field, the trees hold back the sunlight. It is dark and silent. The once flat fields are still a cratered wasteland, an unhappy, shadowed land where shell cases rotting slowly poison the ground. Beyond the forests the silent crosses stand sentinel for the men who have no grave. Long lists of neatly carved names bear witness on sad stones of men lost in the mud and shelling. One of these unknown warriors is Captain J. C. M. Bateman.

It is cool under the two great yew trees which stand sentinel in the little village churchyard. Many of the ancient stones have now been laid flat to facilitate the mowing of the grass. The wind and rain of the years has eroded the writing on them until it is now all but indecipherable. Further away from the grey, worn stones of the church are the unmarked mounds of even older burials which only ever had a wooden cross but the names of those who rest beneath them are written for all to see in the book , once inside the church, now protected from damp and dirt in the white wrapped rolls and boxes of the air conditioned archives. All except one. One mound has no name in the burial register . The mound under which rests the decayed bones of John, the soldger.

Little Elizabeth Peters trudged up the garden path with her doll.

"You mustn't get your new clothes dirty," she admonished the doll, "Mummy said to be very careful of the mud and not to fall in the pond."

The doll stared back with its uncomprehending button eyes. Elizabeth loved the pond halfway up their long, narrow garden, it was cool and mysterious. But today she had come to pick the bluebells which grew in a large patch between the edge of the pond and the gnarled, old apple tree at the beginning of the orchard. She put her doll carefully in the crook of the apple tree's bent trunk and bent to her task. She picked each stem carefully and as near the base as possible. When she had as many blooms as her chubby hand could comfortably hold she added a few leaves around the edge. She held the flowers at arm's length and tilted her head this way and that surveying them as she had seen her mother do in the mirror when she had just put new trimming on an old hat.

"Yes. Very elegant," she said, "don't you think so Betsy?" She turned to consult the doll.

"Oh...." Another girl stood beside the tree.

"Who are you, what are you doing in my garden?"

The girl made no reply. Her curly hair was dishevelled and her hands and her face none too clean. Elizabeth looked at the girl's long, dark dress with its grubby white collar and cuffs.

"I've seen you before. Who are you?" Elizabeth asked again a little crossly this time. She noticed that the strange girl had a basket of mushrooms on her arm.

"Where did you pick those?" Still no answer.

"You don't live in our village, so where have you come from?" No reply. Elizabeth stamped her foot in anger.

"Why are you so rude? Why don't you answer? Are you deaf or stupid?"

The girl smiled, lifted the hem of her skirt and turned to walk down the path. Elizabeth noticed one of the girl's legs was twisted and that she walked with a hippity hop like a rabbit. Her figure wavered for a minute in the Spring sunshine, shimmered as if passing through invisible heat and then disappeared.

Elizabeth was astonished but not in the least bit afraid. As she picked up her doll and also prepared to go down the path Elizabeth considered telling her mother about the strange girl and just as quickly decided against it. She wouldn't understand, after all Elizabeth knew that her mother's name was Mary and you had to be an 'Elizabeth' to see the 'other time people' who inhabited Sparrow Cottage.

NOTE

The entry in the burial register for 1643 is there for all to see and while the market town of Newark stood out bravely through three sieges for King Charles from 1642 to 1646 there were Parliamentary troops in Hockerton, a mention is made of them in the Upton churchwarden's records..

The layout of the village in 1642 is based on the earliest estate map of 1733 which shows the tree fields of Netherfield, Southwell Field and Sparrowthorn Field beginning to be enclosed. The village in 1914 is based on the Victorian Ordinance survey and the Tithe Commutation maps.

The first siege of Newark did occur over two days in February 1643 and there was fighting around Beaumond Cross and along Northgate. Parliament's men were repulsed.

However all the characters who people this story in both 1642-3 and 1914-15 are imaginary and based on no person in the village past or present. Who was John the souldger? No one knows and the events described are merely my fictitious imaginings.